From Highbury with Love

Book 1 of the Highbury Variation

Corrie Garrett

Kindle Direct Publishing
LOS ANGELES, CALIFORNIA

Copyright © 2021 by Corrie Garrett.

All rights reserved. No part of this publication may be reproduced, distributed or transmitted in any form or by any means, including photocopying, recording, or other electronic or mechanical methods, without the prior written permission of the publisher, except in the case of brief quotations embodied in critical reviews and certain other noncommercial uses permitted by copyright law.

Corrie Garrett
10424 Clybourn Ave.
Los Angeles, CA 91040
www.corriegarrett.com

Publisher's Note: This is a work of fiction. Names, characters, places, and incidents are a product of the author's imagination. Locales and public names are sometimes used for atmospheric purposes. Any resemblance to actual people, living or dead, or to businesses, companies, events, institutions, or locales is completely coincidental.

Book Layout ©2017 BookDesignTemplates.com

From Highbury with Love/ Corrie Garrett. -- 1st ed.
ISBN 9798739900043

"Seldom, very seldom, does complete truth belong to any human disclosure; seldom can it happen that something is not a little disguised or a little mistaken."
—JANE AUSTEN, EMMA

{ 1 }

LIZZY BENNET WATCHED TWO ROBINS, one a red-breasted mister and the other his plain brown missus, fluffing their feathers in the cold puddle left by the rain.

She shivered a little in spite of her warm pelisse, as they tucked their tiny bodies into the water and fluffed their wings, flicking the freezing droplets up and around themselves.

"I believe there are as many types of friendships as there are birds in the world," Lizzy said to Harriet Smith, a plump, pretty schoolgirl whom she'd come to know in Highbury. "Some tiny and flickering green, some bright red and beautiful like that little robin, some weighty and intelligent. And some ungainly and awkward." She thought darkly of the inexplicable friendship of Mr. Darcy and Mr. Bingley.

"I like birds," said Harriet. "Pheasants are so funny!"

They walked across the green swale toward Donwell Abbey. The morning mist was clinging low to the fields to her west, though the sun was well above the Surrey hills. A light wind blew, and the clouds were high and thin; the wind was invigorating rather than sharp. Her boots sank satisfyingly in the damp grass, and she breathed in the smell of freshly scythed field—she could see a servant in the distance cutting the yellow stalks—and sharp, damp air.

Lizzy was part of a small procession heading back to Donwell, and though the December trees were rather bare, it was still such a quintessentially English, agrarian scene. Several fields lay fallow until spring. A few tidy fields of turnips and other winter crops.

White and pink winter flowers bloomed in the beds by the house, adding a splash of color—hellebores, Mr. Knightley called them, though Lizzy had always heard them called wedding bells or Lenten roses. The trees by the river off on their right had not yet quite given up their greenness.

Lizzy very much looked forward to visiting the Lake District with her aunt, but in the meantime, Surrey was very beautiful as well.

A sparrow hawk winged its way from those trees near the river. His blue-gray wings were spread wide and his orange underbelly was visible from where they walked. Sharp beak, sharp talons.

"Some so-called friendships are downright ill-tempered," she added, thinking of her sweet sister Jane and scheming Caroline Bingley. "They are swift in flight and quick to the kill, even of other birds."

Mr. Knightley, the good-natured, dutiful gentleman who owned Donwell Abbey, was just behind them, walking with Emma Woodhouse.

"I like that analogy, Miss Bennet," he said. "We might even say that some friendships are like the cuckoo, the bird which hatches in a foreign nest and pushes out the rightful members."

Emma smiled. "Would we say that? If we continued the analogy, we might rather say that some friendships that grow slowly die in the nest, and some that grow fast are the most beautiful."

"I fear this has taken on more meaning than I meant," Lizzy said. "What do you say, Miss Smith?"

Harriet giggled as she lifted her skirts. They were making their way over a slightly thicker patch of the lawn. "I am sure I cannot make such grand metaphors as all of you do! Or is it similes? I can never recall. I suppose if I were a bird, I would be a dove."

"Yes, you would," Emma agreed. "A sweet, gentle turtle dove."

Mr. Knightley gestured to the outbuildings of his estate, which they were now approaching. There was a sturdy English stable, a cow barn, a long, low building that was probably groom and coachman housing, and a kennel. All looked well-kept. Cheerful smoke rose from several chimneys. A groom could be seen currying a glossy black horse with two white socks, and another was leaving the kennels, rubbing his hands clean on a brown apron.

"Mind if I let the dogs accompany us?" Mr. Knightley asked. "They love a good run after breakfast."

Emma and Mr. Knightley fell back as he shouted for his keeper to bring around several of his dogs. Miss Bennet walked on ahead of them with Harriet. They made a charming picture of contrasts, Harriet, blonde and rounded, and Lizzy so slender and lively and dark. Though both were very pretty girls, Emma personally admired Harriet's style.

"You haven't been to Donwell in some time," Mr. Knightley said, as his three dogs came bounding towards him at his whistle.

Emma's favorite was the black and white Dalmatian he'd recently purchased, so graceful and dainty.

"No, and I have not seen this beautiful lady for a month; she is so much bigger. Here, Betsy," she called. The dog's short fur was damp with dew, and Emma knew it would stick to the fingers of her walking gloves, yet she enjoyed rubbing her arched neck.

"You'll spoil her. And her name is Bea," Mr. Knightley said, though he also gave a brief rub to his larger two dogs. He said they were crossed between Great Danes and Mastiffs, and Emma only knew that they seemed to weigh more than her. They were perfectly trained, however, being Mr. Knightley's dogs. They would have no more dreamed of putting paws on a lady or barking in her face than of biting their master.

Emma said. "No, she is Betsy, remember? I have declared it; look at those eyelashes! Thank you for inviting us all this morning. Lizzy has not seen much more than Highbury proper as yet."

"Happy to have her. For once, I can heartily approve the new friendship you've made. I still wish you could find it in yourself to cultivate a friendship with Miss Fairfax, but in the meantime, I think Elizabeth Bennet will be good for you. You may even be helpful to her."

Emma stroked Betsy, who was ever so slightly whimpering for attention as they walked up the long gravel path that led to a loop in front of the house.

"I suppose I ought to thank you," Emma said, "but we have lately had such opposite minds on the matter of my friends, that your compliment instead fills me with disquiet."

Mr. Knightley stooped to grab a stray stick with a few crusty brown leaves still attached, thrown down by the storm three days ago, and tossed it, causing the dogs to rush away with an excited yelp.

"Miss Bennet is obviously a very good sort of girl," he said, "cheering and helping her cousins during their bereavement. But more to the point, she is intelligent. I am happy for you to have a friend who is your equal in keenness and liveliness. You do not complain, but I know that you miss Mrs. Weston, and whatever you may say," he spoke quietly, "Harriet can't truly enter into your deeper thoughts and feelings."

Emma wiped her hand on her striped spencer. There was too much truth in what he said for her to deny it, though the impulse to rise to Harriet's defense was strong. "I admit that Lizzy is a welcome addition to Highbury, and that she is excellent at raising my father's spirits. She seems to know just how to joke with him. Although I've told her that if I made her long, solitary walks known, she'll never hear the end of it from him."

"And I am sure she merely laughed at you. It is good for you to have a friend who is in no way afraid of you. Who is, in some ways, probably your superior."

Emma fought back an ungenerous impulse to point out that Mr. Knightley had long reproached her for lack of diligence and occupation, and yet Lizzy was far less accomplished at playing and drawing and those ladylike things that marked a diligent young woman!

But Emma knew that criticizing her new friend was unworthy of her, and, of lesser but still material importance, that she would be diminished in Mr. Knightley's eyes by doing so. "Lizzy is certainly better read than I am; I suppose that is what you mean. I heard you speaking to her of philosophy."

Mr. Knightley smiled. "I see your forehead furrow and I will apologize. Superior was too strong a word. I will instead repeat that I am happy for Miss Bates and Miss Fairfax to have her, and for you to have a true friend your age."

He tossed the stick for the dogs again, the wind slightly lifting the straight black hair on his forehead. "By the by, I have a friend from Derbyshire visiting me next week. I shall bring him to call on your father directly."

The conversation continued on to the other notable events of Highbury, namely the sad, though not entirely unexpected, passing of old Mrs. Bates, Jane Fairfax's subsequent return and unfortunate collapse of health, and Miss Bates's own cheerful nature for once cracking into something like melancholy. This last was so unprecedented as to have prompted Mr. Knightley to write a letter to Miss Bates's second cousin, Mr. Bennet.

Miss Bates had long maintained a correspondence with this gentleman that consisted of long letters to him, and a yearly Christmas ham from him.

Miss Elizabeth Bennet's arrival, to offer encouragement, help, and good cheer to her cousins, was widely applauded as a mark of great gentility and goodness on the part of the unknown Mr. and Mrs. Bennet. Any addition to Highbury high society was notable, and Miss Bates was so well-liked, that any relation of hers was doubly welcome.

Emma herself had been rather surprised to take such a liking to Lizzy. Judging only by Miss Bates's tedious description of Mr. Bennet and his five "delightful" daughters, Emma had expected the worst.

She was not sorry to be proved wrong.

In this instance, anyway.

{ 2 }

WHEN THE LADIES HAD RETURNED from their walk with Mr. Knightley, and Harriet was headed back to Mrs. Goddard's school, Lizzy was invited to take tea with Emma and her father.

This was in a very warm, small room that he had deemed partially safe from drafts and so had chosen as his usual haunt. It was so oddly sized and out of the way that Lizzy wondered if it had once been a servant's room, but the fittings were so fine that seemed unlikely.

There were old family tapestries on the walls, which he liked to describe, with many asides to Emma to remind him which ancestor was depicted in the hunt or which in the garden scene.

There were no books at all, for "mustiness and dust you know, very bad for the lungs," Mr. Woodhouse often said. "I have strongly urged Mr. Knightley not to spend so much time in his library, but he will not change his ways!"

Above the fireplace was a large carved mantlepiece, the wood of which gleamed like a rich, dark mirror. It almost shone as bright as Mr. Woodhouse's pale, shiny forehead.

The fire was always roaring, but she'd noticed that Emma always seated guests as far from it as possible. From Lizzy's own experience with a mother whose nerves were never good, she credited Emma for the graceful way she handled her father's ill health and crotchets.

Lizzy felt there was no harm in the old man, other than perhaps a rather fixed determination to have his own way, and that way was for everyone to be excessively careful of their health.

Lizzy was able to deliver the news that there was "no significant change with the two ladies" of the Bates household. Miss Jane Fairfax was no worse, but not yet ready to rise from her bed. Miss Bates had cried over her toast in the morning, but with many expressions of thankfulness, and had sat in the sun of the front window for half an hour, before lying down again.

It was actually indifferent news at best, but Lizzy tried to make it such that Mr. Woodhouse was no more fretful than he had been before.

He sipped his cup of weak tea, tugged his lap-blanket a tad higher, and wagged his head solemnly. "The loss of Mrs. Bates is grievous, I don't deny. She has been my friend these forty years; forty years, bless my soul! But I don't know when Miss Bates has had a day of melancholy. Her spirits are generally far higher than mine; not but what high spirits can lead one to over-exertion, but still I would think high spirits better than low."

He sipped his very pale tea. "You must do what you can to cheer her, my dear Miss Bennet. Sunlight, yes, and please tell her she must call on me at her soonest availability. That exertion cannot be considered too much, since it is just what she usually enjoys, and I should never excite anyone. I do think Perry would agree that I am not one to overexcite a nervous woman."

"I am sure you couldn't—wouldn't." Lizzy finished the last crumb of her scone with appreciation. "Perhaps I may be able to coax Miss Bates to call tomorrow. I quite agree with you, sir, that seeing her particular friends would be as good as a tonic."

"As good as a tonic! I do not think we can say that; no, one *can* go too far. But it was prettily said, and I do see the compliment you intended, and thank you for it."

He paused, remembering the original recommendation but not who had made it. "A visit from Miss Bates would be excellent, but really she cannot be too careful. It is when one is pulled and gloomy that infection sets into the chest. I have said it many times; she cannot be too careful." He noticed Lizzy's empty plate and his generosity prompted him to add, "Do take another scone, Miss Bennet; you must if you want. Though I myself find these lemony ones too rich, too sweet. Do you find it so? Perhaps half would be best."

Emma served Lizzy another scone. "She will be fine, Papa. Can you not see the color in her cheeks? Miss Bennet has been walking around Donwell Abbey with me this morning and will be the better for a little indulgence. Lizzy, I will package the rest for you to take back to Miss Fairfax and Miss Bates."

It was decided, and as Mr. Woodhouse inevitably dozed in the mid-afternoon, Emma walked Lizzy back to Miss Bates's small set of rooms on Highbury's main street.

Lizzy swung the basket of scones through a riff of wheat along the roadside, scanty golden stalks that grew like weeds, and must have fallen from the seeds caught in a farmer's hat or trouser leg. They would have been long since harvested if properly sown in a field but were instead standing stubborn into December.

Lizzy clasped her bonnet against the breeze that kicked up, blowing tendrils of hair free, and tugging on her skirt. "Do you know Jane Fairfax very well?"

"No, not well. We have hardly seen each other since early childhood. And those few times she was…" Emma trailed off, possibly recollecting that Lizzy was Jane's third cousin. "She is unexceptionable, but we have never had much conversation."

Lizzy swung the basket again, knocking the heads off the dry stalks. "I see. She is so worn, poor girl, I do feel for her. But… I cannot draw her out at all! I have been wondering if it was her circumstances or nature. I thought perhaps she would want to speak of her grandmother, but no. Even when I am trying to confirm whether she feels sick or feverish for the doctor…she says she is fine even when flushed quite red. It is so strange. My sister Kitty is often unwell, but she will tell us all about it if we ask! Even if we do not! Then there is Lydia, my youngest sister—you have never heard a young woman speak as fast as Lydia when she is in a fever! And my mother—well, she suffers from nerves and *never* silently. A patient, selfless sufferer? I do not know what to say to poor Jane! A trifle more selfishness, and I should be far more comfortable."

It was this sort of frank conversation that had both surprised and pleased Emma upon becoming acquainted with Lizzy. It was exactly the sort of thing she thought about people but rarely told anyone except Mrs. Weston… and Lizzy was more irreverent than Mrs. Weston.

"I know exactly what you mean," Emma exclaimed. "Jane Fairfax is everything womanly, reserved, well-bred, well-taught… she is nigh on a saint! But does one truly *want* to be friends with a saint?"

Lizzy laughed. "You have just reminded me of a conversation I had with a most pompous gentleman a few months past. He *would* go on about his ideal woman, listing a veritable paragon. I denied any knowledge of such a woman, but now, if you are right, I have found her."

"A pompous gentleman? Why was he describing such a list to you?"

Lizzy sighed gustily. "It is a convoluted story, full of silly sisters and motherly machinations and sickly colds. I was able to laugh at him at first, but his pride has been at the expense of mine, or perhaps I should say, *my family's*. Suffice it to say that if I ever see Mr. Darcy again, I shall thank him for making the intervening months pleasanter with his *absence*."

"Mr. Darcy? Why, Mr. Knightley has a friend of that name who shall be visiting next week."

"How odd. Is he a gentleman of these parts?"

"No, I believe Mr. Knightley said his seat is Pemberley, in Derbyshire."

Lizzy nearly dropped the basket of scones. "Good heavens. The very same! And Mr. Knightley is so clearly the gentleman. I cannot understand how Mr. Darcy collects such excellent friends!"

With this elliptical statement, Emma could in nowise be satisfied, and their brief walk down the main street became a much longer, dawdling walk, including many particulars, while shopkeepers, farmers, and village lads streamed by them.

"And that was the same ball at which Mr. Darcy asked me to dance; though he looked as though he regretted it every moment. And I—well, I was so ill-tempered at the disappearance of my friend that I was in a teasing mood, which is a great punishment to men with overlarge egos. I only hope Mr. Darcy will quit Highbury on finding me present. I don't think it impossible!"

Other details were included, but only those that Lizzy thought it prudent to share. As much as she liked Emma, she did not know her well enough to trust her with the intimate details of Mr. Bingley's abandonment of her sister, and all the emotions, recriminations, and speculations upon that sad event.

It was, as a matter of fact, almost entirely on Jane's behalf that Lizzy was here in Highbury. Lizzy had thought, all things being equal, that it would be much better for Jane to be settled in London this winter, as soon as possible. Then she might be where plan or chance could bring her into Mr. Bingley's presence.

Lizzy was certain that that gentleman was every bit as in love with her sister Jane as Jane was with him. It was only the prejudiced influence of his friend and sister who had taken him away.

Lizzy had no doubt that half an hour spent under Jane's natural sweetness would undo all the damage. Lizzy had planned to suggest a London visit when her Aunt and Uncle Gardiner came for Christmas. But when her father had shared the letter about Mrs. Bates's death and Miss Bates's collapse, Lizzy had seen an earlier opportunity. She would go on a visit of mercy, which would take her right through London, and Jane would accompany her there.

{ 3 }

LIZZY OPENED THE SMALL BLUE DOOR between two of the shops on Highbury's main street, which led to the stairway to Miss Bates's rooms. Her rooms were above one of those shops, and the steep stairs led to a rather small apartment, which at least had the benefit of a windows in the front and rear.

The front room, the parlor, was old-fashioned and worn, with threadbare spots in the floral carpet and sun-bleached curtains which were once a deep red and now an uncertain orange. The overall impression was of cleanliness and neatness, however, for which Lizzy gave the credit to Miss Bates.

Lizzy set the scones by the fire on a wooden table with delicately carved, carefully repaired legs—a relic of finer times.

The fire was nearly out, but as the day was warming to one of those fine, hazy December days, Lizzy thought they would rather not waste more firewood until evening.

There was no hallway in the house, merely the rooms which opened into one another, and Jane Fairfax appeared unsteadily in the doorway of the bedroom. Her dark hair looked newly combed and pulled severely back. Her clothes were straight. Only the flush in one cheek showed that she must have just risen from her bed. Her face was composed, but she staggered with weak knees when she stepped forward.

"Good afternoon." Lizzy moved and took Jane's elbow, helping her to one of the chairs by the table. "I would recommend you rest some more, but we have a lovely treat from Hartfield today."

Jane nodded and swallowed weakly. "Thank you, Miss Bennet, for your help. I am feeling quite well today."

"You really must call me Lizzy sooner or later. But just try this scone, I think it could rouse any appetite. Shall I go tell Patty to ready a pot of tea? I think it would do you good."

"Yes, please." Jane swallowed with a wince.

Her throat must still be quite sore, but Lizzy would not know anything about how Jane felt from the woman herself. Jane said every day that she felt "quite well." Every day, until she all but collapsed back into her narrow bed. Lizzy was sharing the front bedroom with her, and Jane slept fitfully, sometimes with panting breaths, sometimes with terrible congestion.

Lizzy went down the stairs to the kitchen which was behind the shop. Their home did not have bell pulls or other such niceties. Nor could Miss Bates afford many servants, but she had Patty, a girl of all-work she paid out of her meager finances.

Lizzy did not at all mind the lack or judge Miss Bates for her plain manner of living, but it could not be denied that it was a bit chilling to see how an unmarried lady of uncertain and shrinking fortune spent her years.

The lack of a bell pull was nothing. The lack of fire in the bedrooms, the careful way in which tea leaves were hoarded and larder scraps saved… it was all good thrift and Lizzy had to admit that she hated it.

Her mother had never studied economy, nor had her father enforced it. Lizzy had long thought that Kitty and Lydia were sadly shatter-brained about money, but she'd realized lately that she herself was rather nice in her expectations.

At any rate, how sad that Miss Bates should have only this to look forward to, and probably even less as she grew older! Jane Fairfax's situation was not any better. She was intended to be a governess by her "kind" relations, and any *less* kind fate Lizzy could not imagine.

But Lizzy returned to Jane Fairfax with a cheerful smile.

"Mr. Woodhouse renewed his invitation to you and Miss Bates, whenever you should feel able to go out. He is such a funny one." Lizzy placed one of the scones on a rose-pattern plate for Jane. "He cannot help offering any guest the best treats available, only to succumb to pangs of guilt immediately. Perhaps if their cook were to pre-slice the tea things in halves, he would be pleased. Though perhaps that would drive him into fourths. The fractions might become complex."

Jane only said, "He is a kind man; my aunt often says so."

Lizzy nodded, temporarily defeated. Jane was no doubt an excellent person, beautiful and elegant, but she seemed to have no discernible sense of humor.

But then, of course, Jane was feeling low, and Lizzy shouldn't judge her on that. Lizzy truly tried not to push conversation on Jane and Miss Bates. She did try to suit herself to their preferences, but it was not in her nature to sit silently for hours on end.

How Lizzy missed Jane, her own sister Jane! Her Jane was quite as sweet as this one, but she did appreciate laughter, even in the midst of affliction. Or Charlotte! Lizzy looked forward to seeing her friend soon, time having palled the ridiculousness of Charlotte's husband, Mr. Collins, and Lizzy's own mortification at his proposal.

The plan was for Lizzy to continue to Hunsford to visit Charlotte after she'd spent several months here in Highbury. Thankfully the two towns were not far apart.

But in the meantime, Lizzy was not one to repine. Highbury was quite an interesting place to spend the winter, even if she and Jane Fairfax seemed to have no spark of connection at all.

The tea revived Jane a trifle. She always had excellent posture, but it looked slightly less pained after a cup of tea. Lizzy poured out another for her, before Jane noticed that Lizzy wasn't drinking.

"Do take a cup for yourself, Miss Bennet, I insist."

Lizzy waved her hand, knowing it would be better to save the rest of the small pot for Miss Bates. "I drank so much at Hartfield; I am sated. Emma did give me some of the village news, if you would care to hear it?"

"Certainly, but perhaps we had better wait for my aunt."

"Of course."

Jane savored her second cup slowly. For a woman of Jane's temperament, Lizzy suspected it was rather a punishment than a help to have a stranger present while she recovered from a collapse of health.

Lizzy was still trying to make out the facets of Jane Fairfax's character, but it was clear that she was either the reserved, loyal type, someone who would be a true friend but allowed almost no one close enough to find out, or else was a proper, cold woman of little emotion. Lizzy couldn't think the worst of her, so she hoped Jane Fairfax was the former. Jane seemed intelligent and sincere, but either unwilling or incapable of accepting Lizzy's overtures of friendship.

Lizzy picked up a book she had left on the tiny, narrow mantle above the nearly-spent fire. "I know it is hard to have a stranger to stay with you just now, while you and Miss Bates are grieving and unwell. I hope that perhaps you will consider me a friend before I go."

Jane inclined her head. "Of course. We very much appreciate you, Miss Bennet."

Lizzy sighed. That was an excessively polite way of holding Lizzy completely at arm's length. She opened her book.

It was two days later, when Lizzy was executing several small errands for Miss Bates, that she met a far more friendly face: she stumbled upon Harriet Smith in a most excited state.

The day was less windy than before, but damper and colder; each cobblestone in town seemed to harbor its own tiny heart of ice, freezing the toes within boots and stockings. The sky was overcast and ruffled gray. One of the small errands—which Miss Bates repeatedly urged Lizzy to ignore if she did not feel like it— was to return a book that Mrs. Goddard had loaned her some weeks ago. Lizzy was happy for the short walk to the school where Mrs. Goddard and Harriet lived, and had all but wrested the book out of Miss Bates's apologetic hands.

The day may have been cold and dim, but Miss Smith alone seemed to bring the sunshine.

She stumbled out of the front door as Lizzy was coming up the road. Her shawl was askew and she was hastily adjusting it, while keeping firm fingers on her reticule, as if it held something precious. The school was a modern, tan sandstone affair, looking rather worn with cloudy windowpanes, and iron loops pounded into the lawn where the female students played Pall Mall. The wooden ball and mallets were gathered tidily on the steps to the front door.

Lizzy had made Harriet's acquaintance nearly immediately upon arrival, as Harriet was often with Emma at Hartfield. And since Mr. Woodhouse's gloomy nature demanded daily updates on Miss Bates's health, Lizzy also found herself often at Hartfield on Emma's invitation.

While Jane Fairfax might never consider Lizzy a friend, Lizzy felt that Harriet already did.

Harriet's cheeks were glowing and her mouth wanting to curve up. "Oh, Miss Bennet! I am just off to Hartfield. I must see Emma. The most amazing thing!"

"Is the good news such that you can share it with me? I should much like a reason to smile as you are doing."

Harriet pressed small hands to her round pink cheeks. "Oh, I am distracted. I must gain composure before I see Miss Woodhouse. She is always teaching me how to be ladylike."

Lizzy smoothed the rumpled shawl over Harriet's shoulder. "I daresay she will not mind." She was still quite curious what had occurred, but if it involved a man, which seemed possible, perhaps it would be best if Harriet were discreet.

On the other hand, Lizzy had spent two very dull days in quietness with Jane and Miss Bates. "Perhaps if you tell me it will settle your nerves."

"I think it might only make it more real to me, and thus more agitating." Harriet ducked her head shyly. "Mr. Martin—of the Martin family I was speaking to you about, the ones I spent the summer with?—he has written to me. He has written me a proposal." Harriet raised her reticule, in which the tip of a white letter protruded.

"I must say," Lizzy said, rather struck. "I think writing a letter a very good way to go about it, if the gentleman is uncertain. It avoids so much potential unpleasantness or awkwardness." She laughed grimly in remembrance of Mr. Collins. His letter would have been interminable, but at least she would have been spared the most ignoble interview of her life.

Harriet stilled a little. "Unpleasantness? You mean if I should refuse him?"

Lizzy shook herself out of recollection. "I was thinking of another situation entirely, forgive me. I am not acquainted with Mr. Martin, but your very joy speaks well of him. He is a farmer, yes? And you are friends with his mother and sisters?"

"Oh yes, they are the sweetest girls and made me feel such a part of the family. I was so sorry when Beth graduated and no longer came to school. Indeed…" she paused as if she was saying something she should not, "if I married him, I think I should feel myself to be going *home*. Mrs. Goddard is everything amiable and upright, but a school is… is just not the same as a home, is it?"

"Unarguably. And is he, forgive me for asking, but is he a prosperous farmer? You think he could support a wife? Tell me if I go too far!"

"No, it is good for me to think through these questions. You and Miss Woodhouse are so clever! I do not know precisely how he stands, though he told me Mrs. Goddard could apply to Mr. Knightley for further particulars. But I was always most comfortable there!"

Lizzy saw that Mrs. Goddard was looking out of her sitting-room window. "Well, you look quite composed now, so I shan't keep you. I'm sure Miss Woodhouse will be agog to hear the news, knowing you so much better than I! But I shall take liberty to hope that all will turn out as you wish."

"Oh, thank you. I do quite feel—That is, I should dearly hope—But I cannot think until I have seen Miss Woodhouse. Farewell, Miss Bennet!"

Lizzy finished her errands, rather wishing she had instead accompanied Harriet to Hartfield. It was the most exciting thing to happen since Lizzy's arrival. She found Harriet a sweet, persuadable girl, with no great abilities of mind, but also no great follies.

With such a mother and such sisters as Lizzy had, she had no disposition to slight Harriet's character.

It was nice to be involved in a successful romance, even if Lizzy was only at the extreme periphery.

{ 4 }

It wasn't until the next morning, when Lizzy walked over to Hartfield to give her daily update, that she found out the results.

Mr. Knightley had just arrived also, having walked over from Donwell Abbey as he seemed to do quite often.

Emma was in the garden, using a stick to fish leaves out of the small fountain east of the house. It was a cascade feature, somehow ingeniously supplied by the nearby creek, Lizzy supposed, and it rushed prettily over colorful stones to a small, round pool, though now a bit mucked up with debris.

Emma tossed aside her stick. "Mr. Knightley, Lizzy! I am glad you are come. My father heard from Mrs. Cole that Jane Fairfax has developed a cough, and he asked me three times whether I think he ought to send to London for a physician for her. I believe I would have been lost if not for his complete trust in Mr. Perry."

As a group they went indoors so Lizzy could give a better report on Miss Fairfax and Miss Bates's health to Mr. Woodhouse.

Lizzy gave as good a report of the convalescents as she could. "Not quite ready to pay visits yet, but they wish to assure you and Miss Woodhouse that you shall be the first of their calls, the moment they stir out of doors."

It was time for Mr. Woodhouse to take his morning walk, and after some back and forth, Mr. Knightley convinced him not to delay it. "I'm not a stranger, sir. You must not stand on ceremony."

"Then I shall go. I leave an excellent substitute in my daughter and Miss Bennet. She and Emma will be happy to entertain you while I take my three turns—my winter walk."

Emma had not yet mentioned Harriet, but Mr. Knightley immediately asked, "Where is Harriet this morning? Was she not to make a long stay at Hartfield?"

"Yes, to be sure," Emma said. "She is only gone back to Mrs. Goddard's to retrieve her things. I expect her to return at any moment."

"She is a pretty little creature," Mr. Knightley said, "and I am inclined to think very well of her disposition. Her character depends upon those she is with; but in good hands she will turn out a valuable woman. Do you agree, Miss Bennet?"

"I don't pretend to know her well, but...yes. She is sweet and anxious to please; I believe Miss Woodhouse has been a good example."

Mr. Knightley crossed one booted foot over the other and leaned back in the chair. "Ah, your friend gives you the compliment, Emma, and I will agree. You have improved Harriet. You have mostly cured her of her school-girl's giggle, at least. She really does you credit."

"Thank you both, but I distrust your attitude, Mr. Knightley. You usually prefer to censure rather than praise me."

Mr. Knightley smiled. "Then you do not know my news. I am not often before the Highbury gossips! I do not pretend to fix on times or places, but I must tell you that I have good reason to believe your little friend will soon receive an offer."

From Highbury with Love

"Indeed! From whom?" Emma exclaimed.

She seemed completely sincere, and Lizzy looked on in confusion. "He must mean Mr. Martin, no? Did Harriet not tell you yesterday?"

Mr. Knightley nodded at Lizzy. "Yes, Robert Martin came to the Abbey two evenings ago, on purpose to consult me about it. He wanted to make sure it was wise, that she wasn't too young, or he, for that matter. Whether she was above him." He nodded decisively. "He had thought through the whole affair and only needed someone he trusts to concur. His father died some years ago, you know. But I never hear better sense from any one than Martin, and I assured him he could not do better. And since Miss Bennet has heard of this, I assume he proposed?"

"Yes, she had just received a letter when I encountered her yesterday."

Emma folded her hands. "I had hoped you were speaking of an actual *gentleman*. Mr. Martin did speak yesterday—that is, he wrote, and was refused."

This was obliged to be repeated before either could believe it.

Lizzy opened her mouth several times without finding words. The thought of Harriet's glowing face yesterday made her unhappy.

Mr. Knightley was so indignant he couldn't stay seated. "Harriet Smith refused Robert Martin? I hope you are mistaken."

"I saw her answer. Nothing could be clearer."

He'd paced to the grate and poked the fire savagely. He now turned back. "You saw her answer? You *wrote* her answer, I've no doubt! You have been very busy with her since Mrs. Weston's marriage, but to what purpose? She is unlikely to receive another offer like this! You ought to restrain your interference to people whose lives you cannot so easily ruin. I daresay you might introduce Miss Bennet, for instance, to anyone you please, but you ought to have left this alone."

Lizzy couldn't help adding, "And it is not as if she was indifferent to him! She seemed so excited."

"If I did interfere," Emma retorted, standing, probably so as not to have Mr. Knightley towering over her, "it was for Harriet's good. Mr. Martin is a very respectable young man, but I cannot admit him to be Harriet's equal. By your account, he does seem to have had some scruples about reaching above himself. It is a pity he overcame them."

"Not Harriet's equal!"

They argued and Lizzy sat, forgotten. She felt the usual discomfort at being present during another family's argument and didn't feel she had much to add; Mr. Knightley was saying it all.

But then he seemed to recollect Lizzy's presence. "I apologize, Miss Bennet; I have been surprised out of my normal manners."

"Not at all," Lizzy said. "I am a relative stranger here, but even I can't help feeling disappointed for her. However, perhaps it's as well that I should take my leave now."

"By no means," said Emma, who still looked angry. "Perhaps Harriet was excited by the offer—I daresay she was, as it was her first!—but you agree with me about her birth, do you not? As a gentleman's daughter yourself, you must agree that there can scarcely be a doubt that Harriet's father is a gentleman of fortune. Her allowance is very liberal; nothing has ever been grudged for her comfort! The sphere in which she moves is above Mr. Martin's. Besides which, she is my intimate friend. Is she not superior to a mere Robert Martin of Abbey Mill Farm?"

If asked, Lizzy was not averse to giving her opinion, though she knew Emma must dislike it. This conversation would have rendered her sister Jane acutely uncomfortable, if not mute, but

Lizzy was not so eager to please and be pleased by those around her that she could not think her own thoughts.

"Harriet may be anybody in the world, but… I've rarely seen more marked signs of love and affection in a young lady as I saw in her. My young sisters are mad for the officers stationed in Meryton, you know, but they do not talk about men the way Miss Smith spoke of Mr. Martin and his family! I do not know the particulars, but if he is as Mr. Knightley described, I should have thought it a love match completely to be desired. *Perhaps* she might do better, but as a gentleman's daughter myself, I know with certainty that she could do worse."

Mr. Knightley gestured to Lizzy. "Thank you. Would that Emma could see the same! Robert Martin would never have proceeded so far if he had not been certain of Harriet's affection. I know him well. He has too much real feeling to address any woman out of selfish, one-sided passion. Harriet must have encouraged him."

Emma's mouth thinned into a line and she set down her teacup rather forcefully, causing it to tip over, which she angrily righted. "Perhaps Harriet did show him courtesy—she could hardly do otherwise, living in his house, which was a very ill-managed thing if you ask me!—but I will take leave to say that you do not know Harriet or her prospects as I do! Perhaps, if I thought she might never receive another offer, I might allow of her accepting such a lowering proposal, but she *shall* have other offers."

Mr. Knightley looked as if he wanted to shake Emma. "'*Allow* of her accepting it?' Do you hear yourself? She was as happy as possible with the Martins in the summer. She had no sense of superiority then. If she has it now, you have given it. That is not the work of a friend."

Lizzy winced. It was true that she did not know Harriet's exact situation, or what other offers, real or imaginary, Emma knew of, but Lizzy couldn't help fearing Mr. Knightley was correct.

"I must put in," Lizzy used the pause to speak, "that although Harriet is beautiful and sweet… that is often not enough to assure her a gentleman's hand, even if there was great affection involved. In my own case—that of my sister, I mean—I have seen that beauty, sweetness, and even elevation of mind are not enough to overcome the disparities of perceived rank. I hope someone may benefit from our painful experience."

Mr. Knightley looked at her rather keenly, but Emma turned her face away.

"You are both unjust to Harriet. Until men do fall in love with well-informed minds instead of handsome faces, a girl as beautiful as Harriet, is certain to have the power of choosing from among many. She is humble, beautiful, good-tempered, ready to be pleased…I will not believe that all gentlemen are so proud as to overlook these qualities."

Lizzy wished that what Emma said was true. Lizzy was not one to argue further when her point was roundly rejected—her mother had cured her of that silliness—but she sighed inwardly.

Emma's argument that Harriet could and would marry well despite her tenuous position was nearly something that Lizzy might have said four months ago, while watching a besotted Charles Bingley dance with Jane!

Humility and sweetness and beauty ought to have carried the day, if truth and goodness were what she'd thought them.

But that idealistic Lizzy had taken a beating nearly as brutal as poor Jane's heart. Lizzy wondered when Emma would be thus disillusioned. Or perhaps she would not be, and her sanguine hopes for Harriet would be answered.

Lizzy rose and pulled on her gloves, nodding goodbye to Mr. Knightley and Emma. "I hope you may be correct, Miss Woodhouse, but I really must be going. May I call as usual tomorrow?"

"Of course, you must visit, my father will expect your update on Miss Bates." Emma looked faintly self-conscious. "I am used to arguing with Mr. Knightley, but you must not think I am angry. Not with you." She glanced meaningfully at Mr. Knightley.

"Yes, I know, your anger is reserved for me," he retorted, "which is just as well, for I am fully exasperated with you."

Emma ignored him. "I would walk you back, but I do expect Harriet at any moment, and it would be unkind to make her wait and wonder."

Lizzy tied the ribbons of her bonnet. "No matter at all."

Emma detained her another moment. "I just recollected that Papa wanted to send some of his own tea to Miss Bates; he finds this blend quite restorative." She rang for the servant to bring the spare tea caddy they sometimes used for that purpose.

Mr. Knightley also took his leave, offering to walk Lizzy back to Miss Bates's rooms since it was on his way.

He carried the little wooden chest of tea for her but was largely silent. Lizzy assumed he was still mulling over his sharp disagreement with Emma. She did not interrupt his reverie.

They had just turned onto the main street that ran through Highbury, when he asked, "Have you been to London?"

"I have been there, yes, my aunt and uncle live on Gracechurch Street. I have never gone about much. My sister Jane spends the winter there."

"Emma has never been."

Lizzy puzzled over the meaning of this cryptic utterance. "I suppose she does not care to leave her father."

"No. He could little spare her and would be extremely nervous if she left... could very easily make himself ill. But I wish, for her sake, that she could. She has gone so little out of Highbury. She sees the world..." He struggled for the right words.

"As she finds it in books?" Lizzy offered, having been accused of that once or twice in her life.

He laughed. "No, even that would be better. She sees the world as an extension of Highbury, where she has reigned supreme since childhood. She sees the world as something that will conform to her will, and she has been too little challenged in her ideas."

"I gather *you* challenge her, sir."

"Yes. But I am only an old brother-in-law, she does not greatly attend to me." He nodded to several men they passed on the street. Lizzy had been slightly surprised that he offered to walk her back alone, but supposed he was held in such high esteem here that no one thought it untoward. Besides which, she was generally known to be Miss Bates's cousin, and so probably anyone watching them assumed he'd fallen in with Lizzy on his own visit to his old friend.

The truth was that Knightley was accustomed not to stand on much ceremony with Emma, and in the frustration of the morning, had forgotten that Miss Bennet stood in rather different circumstances. He accompanied Lizzy all the way to Miss Bates's rooms before passing off the chest of tea, leaving his respects for the ladies of the house.

He made a mental note to send Larkins here with more wood and probably some of the winter apples. He thought little more of that part of the morning, though Mr. Martin's disappointment at Harriet's refusal continued to haunt him.

He would have been surprised to learn that that one walk animated more than a few tongues, a walk taken as it was just before midday—when he was generally to be found busy about his own estate—and a walk taken with the pretty Miss Bennet who was known to come from a good family of large property in Hertfordshire.

In fact, Mrs. Cole, who had it from Mrs. Perry, told Mrs. Weston that it was strangely particular for Mr. Knightley, who was so long a bachelor.

"Perhaps he is finally ready to bring a mistress to Donwell Abbey!"

{ 5 }

LIZZY BOUGHT A ROLL FOR HERSELF for a penny and ate it slowly while she and Emma waited for Harriet to buy honey buns for her friends. The smell of yeasted bread and sour dough loaves and warm ovens seemed to billow out the open front door in an almost visible butter-yellow cloud.

After nearly a weeklong visit with Emma, Harriet had expressed a wish to bring some treats to the older girls at Mrs. Goddard's school, a few of which were her particular friends, and so Emma had invited Lizzy to accompany them to Mrs. Wallis's bakery and then to the school.

The last time they'd spoken privately, nearly a week ago now, still hung in the air. Emma spoke in a determined and cheerful way of the weather, of the coming visit of her sister and nieces and nephews from London, and other unimpeachable topics.

Perhaps Emma thought Lizzy would bring up the same arguments about Harriet's marriage, and that was why she talked to insistently, but she was mistaken. There didn't seem to be any point to it. Most likely the unknown Mr. Martin, rejected definitively, was not just waiting around for Harriet to change her mind.

Across the street at the post office, a porter was attempting to load crates of chickens onto the back of a coach, which noise was rather overpowering. Emma broke off, grimacing at the noise drowning her out.

Lizzy was just about certain the leftmost crate was going to fall the moment they drove off. If Lydia were here, she would take odds on it.

That was when Mr. Knightley and Mr. Darcy rode past them on two fine horses.

It was only a moment, then the gentlemen turned into the Crown Inn, which was only a stone's throw past the bakery, but it gave Lizzy a slight sinking in her stomach. The chicken coach finally got on its way, but Lizzy forgot to watch if the chickens capsized.

Emma looked to her. "Would that be Mr. Darcy? He is a very tall man, is he not? Very gentlemanly."

"Yes, very tall, at least." Even those few seconds had reminded Lizzy what a proud, disagreeable expression Mr. Darcy usually bore. She did not precisely *mind* his coming; like Wickham, she felt that if Darcy wished to avoid her, *he* ought to leave, not she. But all the same, she wished he had not come.

Her poor sister Jane had been settled in London for weeks now and had not *once* seen Charles Bingley, though she'd written to his sister, Caroline. Lizzy was not sure whom to be angrier with: Bingley for forgetting Jane, or Darcy and Caroline for convincing him to do so. Getting Jane to London was more than half Lizzy's reason for coming at all, and it was frustrating to have it all be for nothing.

"I wonder where they go next? Probably the Coles," Emma said.

Only a few moments later the two gentlemen came striding back out to the road, having apparently stabled their horses at the inn. Mr. Knightley turned directly toward the bakery.

"Emma," he said, "I thought I saw you. Allow me to make introductions. We have just been visiting your father." His voice was rather grave for the occasion, and Lizzy could only assume he was still upset about the business with Harriet. But he continued, "Here is my friend, Mr. Fitzwilliam Darcy. Mr. Darcy, this is Miss Emma Woodhouse and Miss Elizabeth Bennet."

Mr. Darcy's face had grown a trifle pale, Lizzy thought, and perhaps a little more wooden and inflexible than general, but that was the extent of his reaction to the surprise of seeing her.

"Miss Woodhouse, Miss Bennet." He bowed to them both, then addressed Lizzy, "It's been some months since I saw you in Hertfordshire. I hope you and your family are well."

"Thank you, we are as well as can be expected. Sadly, the neighborhood is quite broken up since you departed. My friend Charlotte is now married and living in Kent, my sister is in London, and, of course, one or two other friends also departed."

If this made him at all self-conscious, he did not show it. "And you yourself are here in Highbury, I see."

"Yes. I am the bad penny which will keep turning up."

Darcy smiled slightly but made no answer. He was startled, but by no means displeased to see Elizabeth. So much the opposite, that he rather questioned his delight at this unexpected second meeting. It was still ridiculous to think of this girl—her family were in no way more eligible than they had been two months ago!—but his eyes did not seem to care.

Emma and Mr. Knightley finished the introductions, and Emma asked, "How did you become acquainted with Mr. Knightley, sir? For I know you have not visited Highbury, and Mr. Knightley rarely leaves except to visit his brother."

"Yes, but I am a long-time friend of Mr. John Knightley," Darcy explained. "We were at school together."

"Then you know Isabella?" Emma asked. She explained to Lizzy, "Mr. Knightley's brother is married to my older sister, Isabella. Thus Mr. Knightley and I are brother- and sister-in-law, which is just a close enough relation as to create occasional vexing questions of seating arrangements and dancing!"

Mr. Darcy bowed again. "I have had the privilege of meeting your sister. I have also met the children. Er, some of them."

Emma laughed. "I do hope not all at once. When all five are together, they are a precious, but tumultuous maelstrom. Isabella is not usually so relaxed as to bring them out to guests."

Mr. Darcy felt himself calming, and something like a natural smile escaped. "As it happens, I brought my younger sister with me, who quite adores infants. She spent a very happy afternoon with your nephews and nieces, for which Isabella had my sincere thanks."

Lizzy could not picture Mr. Darcy and his tall, arrogant sister—from Mr. Wickham's pithy description, Lizzy could entirely picture her!—spending more than an hour with several small children.

Mr. Darcy continued, "You have quite a look of your sister. I can see the resemblance well."

Emma smiled upon him. "Any friend of John and Isabella's must be a friend of mine."

Mr. Knightley looked from them to the bakery. "Do you wait for someone? I wanted to introduce Darcy to Mr. Cole."

Emma looked back. "Yes, for Harriet. I think she has been drawn into conversation with Mrs. Wallis."

Lizzy, who was observing Mr. Darcy, indulged in a slight bit of ironic interference. She stepped back. "The Coles are always so happy to see you, Emma. You should go along, if you wish. I'd be pleased to accompany Harriet to Mrs. Goddard's."

It was not that Lizzy suddenly saw Mr. Darcy and Emma as a match. Not at all. She did not entirely know what caused her to push them together, except that there was a slight vindictiveness to her thoughts, a feeling that in Mr. Darcy, Emma would realize what Mr. Knightley had been trying to say about gentlemen. They were not all interested in charm and beauty, but could be, sadly, as proud and prejudiced as you would never wish to meet.

Or perhaps it was that she didn't want Mr. Darcy spending time with Harriet. Harriet was not an idiot, but she was not a *clever* girl, and would not recognize subtle signs of disdain and condescension from Mr. Darcy. Most likely he would simply ignore Harriet, but either way, Lizzy felt protective.

Emma was not unhappy to go along with Mr. Darcy and Mr. Knightley up the street to visit the Coles, but she went into the bakery to apprise Harriet of the change herself.

Lizzy acquitted her of being a careless or unkind friend, but as Lizzy was learning, an attentive but misguided friend could do far more damage.

Emma went on, taking Mr. Knightley's arm and inquiring after his business in Highbury, but Lizzy and Harriet followed not long after. Mrs. Goddard's school lay in the same direction.

The street was moderately filled, but Harriet, by wont of stretching up on her toes, was able to see Emma and the two gentlemen.

"He is very fine and tall, is he not?" Harriet said. "I do wonder that Miss Woodhouse has never married. Perhaps Mr. Darcy may capture her attention! He is quite as handsome a man as Mr. Elton."

"I suppose he is." This artless speech rather perplexed Lizzy. The parson, Mr. Elton, was a handsome enough man, rather dramatic in his sermons, almost like a thespian, and somewhat languishing in his manner. But he was certainly not someone Lizzy would consider a standard of male beauty. Before she could decide what else to say, Harriet clutched her arm.

"Oh, Miss Bennet. It is Beth and Mary; Mr. Martin's two sisters." Harriet's fingers were quivering with distress.

The two young ladies whom her gaze was fixed upon were on their side of the street, perhaps coming to the bakery or post office themselves. They were plain country girls, one rather pretty and both with round, red cheeks and high foreheads. Their clothes were not dissimilar from Lizzy's plainer day-dresses, though compared to Emma's London-made wardrobe, were definitely lesser.

"It will be alright," Lizzy said. "Merely bow and smile as you would normally do, to show that there are no ill feelings on *your* side and that will go far to put them at ease."

"Oh yes, I would not for the world make them think I no longer desired to be—Beth was my best friend at school! But then, I suppose I cannot truly be her friend when I have—when Mr. Martin no doubt thinks me—"

Lizzy pressed her hand. "I understand you, but here they are."

The two young ladies had spied Harriet with a flash of uncertainty, two ducked heads, and a flurry of whispered words.

Harriet smiled and half-curtseyed as they came abreast of them, a smile that in Lizzy's eyes conveyed nothing so much as miserable uncertainty. Lizzy was relieved for Harriet's sake when they both responded to her smile with brief nods and flashes of lips. It was quick and Lizzy would have gone on, but then the older Miss Martin showed some slight hesitation, as if unsure whether to stop, and Harriet also hesitated.

"Good morning," Miss Martin said, bobbing a curtsey.

Harriet managed to speak with a dry throat. "I have not seen you in town in s-some weeks. How is your mother?"

"She is fine, thank you. She had a trifling cold in November." Their eyes turned naturally to Lizzy.

"This is my friend Miss Bennet; she is staying with Miss Bates." Harriet performed the introductions, and the girls gave polite greetings before heading on their way.

"There," said Lizzy, as they went on, "that was very cordial. Everyone behaved just as they ought."

"Yes, I suppose so. I hope Emma will think so, but perhaps I had better not have introduced you! I do apologize if you did not wish it. Emma says the Martins are precisely the sort of people which she does not know socially, for they do not need her help but are not of her world. Which is quite true!"

"I am not so fine as all that." Lizzy felt more and more the justice of Mr. Knightley's criticism. It was one thing for Emma to place herself on such a high form but doing so with Harriet was both ridiculous and unwise. "They seem well-spoken, kind young ladies."

"Yes. But they were very quiet. I can only suppose it is due to Mr. Martin's communications about me. Oh, it is very hard! When last I saw them in town, Beth invited me to accompany them, and we spent the whole morning together. Nothing so comfortable! I wish Mr. Martin had *never* proposed."

"It is the nature of unsuccessful proposals that they should be regretted. Yet I do feel some sympathy for the men. They will not know if they do not ask. That is, assuming they *believe* the answer given. I have no sympathy at all for the vulgarly persistent."

"I cannot imagine that Mr. Martin would ever so act," Harriet said. "He is—he has such delicacy of feeling!" Harriet touched her red cheeks gingerly. "Although he *is* a farmer, and as Emma says, cannot truly be expected to have the feelings of a gentleman. Mr. Elton also has a very delicate sensibility."

Lizzy was certain she had just heard a complete summary of the conversations that must have occurred at Hartfield in the past week. So; Mr. Elton! He must be the "other offer" Emma had in mind for Harriet. How strange!

In general, Lizzy was excellent at taking people's character, and she much thought that Mr. Elton was dangling after Emma. Lizzy wished she knew the gentleman better! Might he have a preference for Harriet? It was true that *he* would be a fine catch for *her*, but—perhaps because of Lizzy's own recent difficulties with the persistent Mr. Collins—she felt an instinctive prejudice against the man.

He had recently executed a favor for Emma, getting Harriet's portrait framed in London. That act of service *might* be construed as a compliment to Harriet, but the picture hung at Highbury, and had repeatedly been described to Lizzy—both by old Mr. Woodhouse and young Mr. Elton—as a product of Emma's talent. Not much was said about Harriet except by Emma.

No, Lizzy had not yet learned to doubt herself, and she was certain that there was some serious misunderstanding here. And not even a very intricate one. Mr. Elton hoped to get Emma, and Emma—with a lack of vanity, to give credit where it was due, and excess of innocence—did not realize that her beauty and her *fortune* made her by far the more likely target.

But the immediate problem was that Harriet was in a fair way to being persuaded into a *tendre* for Mr. Elton.

Lizzy disliked the whole affair excessively. Only pain for Harriet lay in that direction, and having seen Jane recently impaled on the sharp spike of unfulfilled hope, Lizzy felt absolutely no compunction in undermining Emma's efforts.

Wisely, she also knew that disparaging Emma's opinions or advice would be less than useless.

"Mr. Elton is very gentlemanly. He visits Hartfield quite often?"

"Oh yes," said Harriet. "He is most considerate. Emma says he is very properly respectful of Mr. Woodhouse and takes care not to ruffle him."

"Yes, I'm sure." Lizzy lowered her voice slightly, though they were out of the busy part of town now, past the Kingston road and on the lane that led to Randalls. "It seems to me that he looks rather often at Emma during his sermons. Have you ever wondered if Emma is the star that brings him to Hartfield?"

Harriet's brow furrowed. Lizzy hoped very much that she wasn't dealing a serious wound. But surely, if Harriet was delighted to receive a proposal from Mr. Martin only a week ago, she could not yet be *in love* with another man.

Lizzy had also noted that when there was only a growing admiration or new inclination in the case, the next most satisfying thing for a young woman was to have him for her closest friend. Even Lydia, who was none so selfless, had been happy for Lizzy when Wickham sought her ought. Lydia had been quite miffed on her behalf when he began to dangle after Miss King, far more miffed than Lizzy, who took it prosaically.

As Lizzy expected, after a moment of confusion, a slow smile dawned on Harriet's face.

"Mr. Elton and Miss Woodhouse! Why—I wonder that she has never—But you may be right! She is the most wonderful young lady in the world, and I cannot imagine him *not* admiring her. Have you really seen him do so?"

"Yes, I have." Lizzy saw no reason to beat about the bush. "I cannot say if Miss Woodhouse favors him, but I think it would be a very respectable match. Him being settled in the neighborhood, after all, is a great advantage. And he is already such a favorite with her father. Then too, her fortune would make him entirely comfortable."

This last made Lizzy feel a little horrible, but as a young lady who herself knew the pain of having no great fortune to speak of—certainly not enough to allow a gentleman of lesser means to prefer her—she supposed she had the right to say it. Better to disillusion Harriet now than when she truly fancied herself in love with Mr. Elton.

Harriet nodded slowly. "I think he has some means himself, but I quite see what you mean. And he *is* a favorite with Mr. Woodhouse."

Lizzy braced herself for one last bit of meddling. "I do not think it has even occurred to Emma that he might come to Hartfield for her. In fact, she is so generous that I daresay she might try to gift him to someone else, if she could! She is forever sending me home with gifts for Miss Bates and Miss Fairfax."

"Yes," Harriet agreed wholeheartedly, "Miss Woodhouse is excessively generous and kind! Yet she seldom receives anything—a real, true gift, I mean—yet she deserves all the nice things in the world!"

"Very true."

Lizzy felt she had done quite enough, and her conscience did not trouble her as she left Harriet with a wave at Mrs. Goddard's tidy school.

Lizzy could probably not get Mr. Martin back for Harriet—no more than Lizzy could bring back Bingley for poor Jane!—but she could at least prevent wound upon wound.

Lizzy returned to Miss Bates's home, feeling ruefully that she had probably been of more use today than the rest of her visit put together.

{ 6 }

MISS BATES, MIDDLE-AGED, PLAIN, AND POOR, considered herself a fortunate woman.

She was certainly known everywhere as a happy woman. Happy disposition, happy manners, happy countenance.

But as she rose from her bed that evening, after resting most of the afternoon, she still felt slightly feverish. Her skin was warm but her body cold.

Miss Bates hadn't been able to eat much for dinner. Now her mouth was quite dry, and a dreadful taste lay on her tongue. Some good hot tea would be delightful, once she was fit to be seen. She heard low voices in the parlor; Lizzy and Jane must be there.

She blew her nose firmly in her handkerchief and forced herself to wash her face in the basin, though the water had been sitting out all day and was cold. It felt even more bitterly cold to her flushed face, but she knew she looked a fright and must make an effort to cleanse herself. She found her spectacles, where she had set them next to her washbasin and perched them on her nose.

The looking glass in her room was yellow and rippled, but that was no matter, for she only needed to make sure her hair was tidy. Nothing like lying down for most of the day to leave oneself sadly crushed and tangled. She'd put the better-looking glass in Jane's room, of course, for Jane was young and beautiful and ought to see herself clearly. That good glass had come from Emma, when she had received a beautiful new one from her father last summer.

The second-best glass was in Miss Bates's mother's room, but that remained empty for now. Miss Bates had not yet rearranged anything from the way it had been before her mother, the elderly Mrs. Bates, had passed away.

She felt tears pricking her eyes. It was most unexpected to lose her mother, even at her age, and it had left Miss Bates feeling quite the orphan. She resolutely wiped her eyes.

How providential that Miss Lizzy Bennet had offered to come for a time! Otherwise Miss Bates would be leaving poor Jane quite alone and untended! And Miss Lizzy was so cheerful, so active, so friendly! She did not stand on ceremony but treated them quite as family, in a most respectful way. Miss Bates was quite pleased with her.

What had she ever done to deserve such kind family connections?

When she came out into the low light of the parlor, lit by two candles and the fireplace, Jane and Lizzy were both present. Jane was near the fire, wrapped in a shawl, and Lizzy sat near the small table with the candles, reading aloud from a book.

"What a picture you two make," Miss Bates said. "Such lovely young ladies; such a warm fire; such a cozy, domestic moment! It could be a painting, do you not think, Jane? It would be a lovely painting."

"How are you feeling this evening, Aunt?" Jane asked. She was looking sadly pale, but always so brave!

"Quite well. In fact, I think I must be on the mend. Dear Jane, how do *you* find yourself? If Miss Lizzy were not here, I should always reproach myself for failing you when you are unwell!"

"No, no. I, too, am feeling perfectly fine. Miss Bennet and I were on the brink of having tea. She has been so kind as to read aloud, but I am sure she is feeling dry."

"I will just go down now," Lizzy said. "I spoke with Patty and she is also going to send up some light toast and two boiled eggs. I think both of you ought to try to eat a little, if you are feeling so well. You both ate nothing earlier."

"Lovely, lovely." Miss Bates sank into the chair across from Jane. "Thank you, my dear. We should be so dull if you were not here."

Lizzy's footsteps disappeared down the stairs, and Miss Bates again felt tears welling up in her eyes. "Oh, goodness me. I do not know what is the matter. I am perfectly fine." She was compelled to search for the hidden pocket in her waistband in which she tucked her extra handkerchief.

Jane leaned forward to squeeze her forearm gently. "I think perhaps you and I are getting out a lifetime of tears in just a few weeks."

"I don't know what I should have to cry about in my life." Miss Bates sniffed and wiped her cheeks, though tears still ran. "I have so many friends. It is such comfort to live in a town where one knows everybody! It is few who are fortunate to have such a community. Though you, Jane, yes. Your poor mother and father! And I do not like the idea of you becoming a governess. Excessively kind of the Campbells to help you on in that way, but… Oh no, please do not cry."

For Jane was also beginning to weep. Her cheeks and nose wrinkled as she fought it back. "I do not know why I cry either. I have every reason to look forward to my future, if only I could tell you—but then, it is better not to count on what may not happen."

She fetched her own handkerchief. "What a pair we are. How I have missed you."

"And I have missed you, my dearest Jane."

Lizzy returned just then and looked at them with comical dismay. "When I left, you were both assuring each other of your perfect wellness. Yet I come back to this?"

Jane gave a watery chuckle. "We are a sight, no doubt, Miss Bennet. But not everyone can laugh as you do, and when we cannot laugh, sometimes we must cry."

"I did not mean to belittle your feelings," Lizzy said. "In fact, if you desire me to, I will skip ahead several chapters in our book to the baby's funeral. Lydia and Kitty always cry buckets over it, and my own eyes do not stay precisely dry. Then we may all weep copiously and sleep the better for it."

Miss Bates laughed and shook her head. "You are so witty! Is she not witty, Jane? But no, no baby's funeral if you please. I am sure I am already a watering pot enough without it. I do say, isn't it funny that a crying woman should be called a watering pot, when watering pots are such useful things? But no, please, no funerals."

"Very well, but only if you will both promise to at least *attempt* a boiled egg and a piece of toast."

{ 7 }

LIZZY DID NOT HAVE OPPORTUNITY to observe the effects of her small foray into deviousness with Harriet until the following day, and even then, she didn't dare hope for much.

Thankfully Miss Bates *was* feeling better and was determined to call on Mr. Woodhouse.

She wore a warm brown pelisse, but as Mr. Woodhouse had got word that Miss Bates was ready to sally forth, he sent his carriage for them. This quite overpowered Miss Bates.

"Always such a thoughtful friend, he is. And what a friend he was to my dear mother! Mr. Woodhouse is quite the richest gentleman in the neighborhood, and of the oldest family, and yet he sat with Mamma twice a week for nigh on twenty years. Such good manners! Such a conscientious spirit!"

Emma and Harriet were at Hartfield, and they greeted Miss Bates with many words of pleasure. Most of the talk centered on Miss Bates and Miss Fairfax, and Lizzy knew that was only right and fair, but she couldn't help feeling a little selfish. She wanted to know if her seeds had born fruit.

At any rate, Mr. Woodhouse's warnings about overconsumption were for once unnecessary, for Miss Bates could eat very little. But between urging her to eat more and recommending any and every remedy for melancholy that came to his mind, he also mentioned that Harriet was collecting riddles.

"I've tried very often to recollect something worth their putting in," he said. "So many clever riddles as there used to be when I was young—but I cannot remember them! Perhaps you, Miss Bates, might recollect a clever riddle or two?"

"Oh, dear. A clever riddle from me? I have heard many, but I was never good at recitation. Or should I say memorization? I am sure if once I *remembered* it, I could *recite* it, but...I shall ask Jane! She shall have several for you, my dear Miss Smith, never doubt it."

Mr. Woodhouse was still sunk in deep thought. "Emma's dear mother was so clever at all those things! But I can remember nothing—not even that particular riddle which you have heard me mention; I can only recollect the first stanza; and there are several. *Kitty, a fair but frozen maid, Kindled a flame I yet deplore...* And that is all that I can recollect of it, but it is very clever all the way through."

Emma was gentle. "Yes, Papa, it is written out on our second page. We copied it from the Elegant Extracts."

"Aye, very true. I wish I could recollect more of it. *Kitty, a fair but frozen maid...*"

Lizzy was enjoying Mr. Woodhouse's eccentricity but despairing of any other conversation, when Mr. Elton was announced.

He seemed rather taken aback at the relative crowd in the drawing room.

"Oh, Mr. Woodhouse, Miss Woodhouse! Your most obedient servant. Miss Bennet, Miss Smith, how do you do?" There was a small, folded paper in his hand, and he attempted to put it surreptitiously in his inner pocket. "Miss Bates, I am happy to see you out and about—"

Emma was too fast for him. "Oh, Mr. Elton, what is that paper? Have you brought a riddle for Harriet? Pray do not put it away. Miss Bates will not mind if you pass it along, for we were just speaking of our collection."

His startled look, imperfectly hiding either dismay or consternation, made Lizzy cover a laugh with a slight cough. Emma was ruthless!

"Well, ah, yes, it is. Belongs to a friend of mine. I… I do not offer it for Harriet's collection, precisely, but I daresay you will not dislike looking at it."

"Thank you!" Emma was all smiles and politeness, and she would probably have put it aside for her and Harriet to peruse later, but she had reckoned without her father.

"Another riddle, excellent! Do read it my dear, slowly and clearly so that we might all guess. I like to hear a thing read slow and clear. No one reads like my Emma."

Miss Bates beamed. "Yes, please. I like a riddle of all things, although I am much too silly to discover the key. You will please explain it to me when you have figured it out."

Emma's hesitation and Mr. Elton's redness were roughly equal, but Emma recovered first. She smoothed the paper on her knee.

Lizzy thought Mr. Elton's looks and words rather confirmed that it was *Emma* whose opinion was wanted. She stole a glance at Harriet and was beyond pleased to see her with a happy, knowing smile. Harriet even winked at Lizzy with a secretive twinkle in her eye.

Success! Lizzy winked in return and Harriet bit her lips to suppress a most inappropriate grin.

Emma knew better than anyone that her father would not relinquish something his mind had taken hold of, and he wanted to hear the riddle. To deny him would be to make a strange fuss that would occasion more remark than it was worth. No matter. Delaying or dissembling would only make it more awkward for poor Mr. Elton.

How foolish she had been! She had been greedy on Harriet's behalf, and now was paid back for her impatience.

She read, slowly and clearly,

"My first displays the wealth and pomp of kings,

Lords of the earth! their luxury and ease.

Another view of man, my second brings.

Behold him there, the monarch of the seas!

But ah! united, what reverse we have!

Man's boasted power and freedom, all are flown;

Lord of the earth and sea, he bends a slave,

And woman, lovely woman, reigns alone."

There were two further lines, but Emma, reading quickly ahead, did not read them aloud. "What a pretty verse," she said instead. Having pity on Mr. Elton and Miss Smith, she did not look at either of them.

"Aye, but what does it mean?" asked Mr. Woodhouse. "I do not know; I never heard this one before. I much prefer riddles I have heard before."

"Yes, Papa. But I shall read it again and explain and then you will like it quite well..." She cast a quick eye over the lines, and soon discerned the meaning. "Yes, it is very pretty! Let me explain it to you." She reread the first two lines.

Harriet offered, "'Luxury and kings'—perhaps crown? Or throne?"

Emma was impressed at the disinterested tone Harriet had managed, as if the riddle had nothing to do with her! Her guesses were wrong, of course, but metaphor and allusion were not Harriet's forte.

Miss Bates leaned forward. "What a lovely phrase. Perhaps palace? King? Court?"

Emma bestowed a smile of surprise on her, "Why, yes, Miss Bates, you have nicked it! It must be *court*. The next syllable will be, 'the monarch of the seas.'"

"Mermaid!" exclaimed Harriet.

"Rainbow?" said Miss Bates.

Lizzy put in after a moment, "*Ship*, do you think?"

This was exclaimed over and as Emma read the last stanza, putting the syllables together, the meaning of the whole, *courtship*, was widely applauded.

Her father was much struck by the last line, "*Woman, lovely woman*. That is right, that is very true. How your mother would like it. Do read it again, Emma."

Emma chanced a glance at Mr. Elton, and he was looking, though rather flushed, not unhappy. She offered him an apologetic smile and though appropriately hesitant, he nodded his forgiveness and understanding. She did appreciate a man who could communicate with his eyes; he would do excellently for Harriet!

Emma read it once more for her father, again suppressing the last two lines. Those must be for Harriet's eyes alone.

When she was finally allowed to pass the paper to Harriet—"It must be copied down," Mr. Woodhouse declared, "an excellent conundrum!"—she squeezed Harriet's hand.

Harriet squeezed hers back, and Emma was again impressed that Harriet's face showed no self-consciousness, but rather an uncomplicated happiness.

Emma had not been sure until this moment that she had *actually* accomplished anything much in the improvement of Harriet's manners, but this moment made her as proud as any mentor could be.

Lizzy accompanied Miss Bates home again—in the carriage—as the sky began a sputtering drizzle. But she was quite satisfied.

Lizzy had seen; she had felt; she had much to congratulate herself on. Harriet's heart had accepted the probability that Mr. Elton cared for Emma, and none too soon!

It also proved that Lizzy's guess was *correct*. If there had been no audience, Mr. Elton might have proposed to Emma that day!

But no, probably the riddle was an attempt to feel his way. He wanted to make certain Emma was receptive to his suit before he spoke of it to her. She was unquestionably a young lady of beauty and fortune, and he, though handsome and comfortable, was reaching above himself.

Back at Miss Bates's, out of the rain, up the stairs, and through the parlor, Lizzy helped that lady to her room. She even offered to help her change into a dressing gown, as Miss Bates found herself rather exhausted by the outing.

Miss Bates was surprised—"So humble! So kind! But my dear Miss Bennet ought not to lower herself in such a way!"

"It is not lowering if I do not think it so, and your cheeks have gone rather white after coming up the stairs. Do treat me as if you were my own dear aunt and allow me to help you to bed."

After this was done, presently Jane Fairfax came out to ask how the visit had gone. They had not sat together above five minutes, however, when Patty ran up to tell them that Mr. Knightley had come to call on Miss Bates and the other ladies of the house.

"He said, 'If you was at home to visitors,' mum."

Lizzy looked to Jane, who began to shake her head, and then seemed to stiffen her spine. "I really must begin again," she said, as if to herself. "Yes, Patty, please show him up."

Mr. Knightley wore the subdued brown breeches and riding boots of an impeccable country gentleman, but Lizzy thought he did it rather better than most gentleman she was acquainted with in Hertfordshire. He had hair between brown and black, which he kept rather short, and the brow of a conscientious man.

He bowed to Jane Fairfax and to Lizzy, politely taking a seat on the edge of the extra chair. His voice was pitched low and quiet. "I see Miss Bates must have retired, for I hear she has been out to Hartfield today. I am glad to hear she is in better heart."

"Yes, as was I," Jane said.

He nodded.

Lizzy sighed internally. Jane was elegant and patient, but *not* a conversationalist.

Mr. Knightley persisted. "And how do you find yourself, Miss Fairfax? Better, I hope?"

"Yes, much."

If Lizzy had not gotten such short answers herself every day for the last two weeks, she would have thought there was something wrong.

Mr. Knightley did not seem to mind, however. "Mrs. Weston was telling me that they shall hold a small Christmas party, and inquiring of you. If you and your aunt are well enough, I will send my carriage to carry you all there." He encompassed Lizzy in his nod. "My friend Darcy shall come as well. And the newest development is that Mr. Weston expects his son, Frank Churchill. They received a letter from him only yesterday."

Jane Fairfax plucked a dainty handkerchief out of her sleeve to cover a sudden cough. "Oh, I see. Is that—Did they expect him?"

"There was some talk of him coming to them just after the wedding, which would have been considerate, but it came to nothing. Perhaps this is his belated attempt to honor his father and new stepmother, but I doubt it shall actually occur. He has often promised and never arrived."

"I hope he will," Jane said.

"Yes, indeed. And I hope a party will lift your aunt's spirits. You and Miss Bates have had a trying autumn and winter, though I am sure having Miss Bennet to stay has been a comfort."

Jane no doubt wished Lizzy at Jericho, but she nodded anyway.

This polite say-nothingism was too much for Lizzy. "I must warn you, sir, that Mr. Darcy does not overly care for balls at which he is not well-acquainted with the whole set. I am afraid he may disappoint you and decline."

Mr. Knightley raised his brows. "Why no, Miss Bennet, you are quite wrong this time. He has already acquiesced. I warned him dancing would be the order of the day—I am not much of a dancer myself—and told him not to feel burdened to come on my account. But I could have saved my breath; he said he wouldn't miss it."

"Really? That does surprise me!" But in remembering the first part of her meddling yesterday—encouraging Emma to accompany Mr. Darcy—Lizzy wondered if *Emma* was the reason for Mr. Darcy's sudden willingness to dance.

If so, wouldn't Caroline Bingley turn green! For Emma was no more his ideal woman than Caroline was, although Lizzy thought Emma—despite her mistakes—was far better than he deserved.

Then, too, Darcy was supposedly meant for his cousin, Anne de Bourgh. Perhaps he was ready to shake off the expectation of family and tradition? If this was for Emma, Lizzy wondered if she would even consider him. Hopefully not!

"What is that you're reading?" Mr. Knightley asked, gesturing to the book which Lizzy had laid aside on the table.

They spent a comfortable quarter hour discussing books and authors and extracts, and even Jane came out of her shell enough to contribute.

Later, when Lizzy had time to consider, she was curious to see how Mr. Darcy behaved at the party. Lizzy was inclined to think Emma would be better off with the languishing parson, Mr. Elton, than proud and vindictive Mr. Darcy. At least Mr. Elton could write an amusing riddle and be polite in conversation. That was more than Lizzy could say for Darcy!

Still...the days would be fraught with interest if Emma *was* his object.

How glad Lizzy was that she'd come to Highbury; what stories she would have to tell her sisters! It nearly put her in charity with Mr. Darcy.

{ 8 }

EMMA HAD A CHARITABLE VISIT to pay to a poor sick family who lived a little way out of Highbury, down Vicarage Lane.

Vicarage Lane, of course, was where Mr. Elton lived, and in the course of things, Emma thought it best that Harriet accompany her. She called at Mrs. Goddard's school to collect her little friend. It made her path rather longer, but Emma did not mind a walk when it was in pursuit of a worthy goal. She took one of the footmen and sent him back once she had Harriet.

Emma was always glad to walk with Harriet rather than a servant, it was one of her chief enjoyments of Harriet's friendship. Lizzy, also, was excellent company and always willing to walk... but not quite so comfortable.

About a quarter of a mile down the lane rose the Vicarage, an old and not very good house, almost as close to the road as it could be. It was not ideal but had been very much smartened up by Mr. Elton. Emma naturally slowed as they approached.

"There it is," Emma said. "You and your riddle-book will go there one of these days."

Harriet had the open temperament of the innately honest, and she would normally have hated to have a secret from Emma, but in this case, it felt more like a delightful surprise for her dear friend. Emma's continued belief that Mr. Elton cared for Harriet was just another sign of her extraordinary modesty and goodness!

Harriet could not help protesting, however. "One of us, perhaps. What a sweet house!—How very beautiful! Those yellow curtains!"

The yellow curtains were quite modish but didn't quite match the situation or the house. Emma could only suppose such admiration was proof of Harriet's growing affection for Mr. Elton. The "one of us" comment, Emma labeled under Harriet's modesty and uncertainty.

"I do not often walk this way now," said Emma, as they proceeded, "but I shall gradually get intimately acquainted with all the hedges, gates, pools, and views on this road when I come to visit you."

Harriet smiled. "Do you never—Do you think of marriage, Miss Woodhouse? With such another as Mr. Elton?"

Emma laughed. "I have very little intention of ever marrying at all."

"But I cannot believe it!"

"Well, to be tempted to marry, I must meet a man very superior to those I already know. Mr. Elton—" Emma recollected herself before saying anything disparaging. "Mr. Elton is out of the question."

"Dear me! But if he were not... He is, as you have said, so much the gentleman! Such pleasing manners!"

"But I have none of the usual reasons to marry. If I fell in love, I suppose, I might be motivated! But I do not think I ever shall. Do not look so dismayed, my dear. What has caused that perturbed expression to mar your brow?"

"It is only—in thinking on love and matrimony—how terrible it feels to disappoint a man when his affections are marked! I mean, if a man were in love with you— Oh, perhaps I should tell you? If there should be some mistake..."

"My dear Harriet, if this is about Mr. Martin, I desire you to raise your chin immediately. It is *not* the responsibility of a woman to prevent a gentleman's disappointment. Mr. Martin will be fine, and probably all the better for a slight lesson in how to go on. A woman never *intentionally* wounds, but it is no part of her duty to acquiesce when her heart and circumstance are not favorable."

"No, certainly you are right. It is not on *that* score that I am concerned—"

But they had arrived at the cottage. Emma always entered into the troubles of the poor of Highbury with ready sympathy. She tried to give her assistance with as much intelligence as good-will, not expecting more gentility than she ought, but engaging with frankness and calm.

The smell in the small cottage was not prepossessing, but Emma had a strong stomach and never became faint. She was still listening to old Mrs. Brown, while holding the youngest upon her lap, and occasionally offering another spoonful of broth when the old lady paused, and three more visitors arrived.

Lizzy had again begged Miss Bates for any small task to accomplish, and that lady—having heard from Mr. Woodhouse of the sickness which had struck a local family—had wanted to send some token of care during their trying time.

Miss Bates's resources were slim, but even had she far less, she would still have managed to give some away. So she sent

Lizzy to visit them, bringing a blanket which she had knitted the previous winter, and two loaves of bread.

She decried Lizzy going alone through most of the town, as Lizzy would have to do to get to Vicarage Lane, but Lizzy countered that she would take the road to Randalls and then cut across the Highbury Common to the footpath which led nearly directly to the Vicarage.

Miss Bates's mouth had opened in surprise. "How well you know Highbury already! It is quite astonishing. Is it not astonishing, Jane?"

Lizzy did not allow it to be anything out of the ordinary and escaped with the blanket and the bread before too long.

On the footpath, she was overtaken by Mr. Knightley and Mr. Darcy.

"Good morning, Miss Bennet," said Mr. Knightley. "I believe we are bound for the same errand." He nodded toward the cottages in the distance. "I am taking the opportunity of showing Darcy the area."

Mr. Darcy bowed slightly to her and Lizzy nodded coolly.

Mr. Knightley continued, "To our right, Darcy, you have the parish school, the church, and the vicarage. If you continued past that shrubbery, you'd come up to Hartfield from the side."

"Yes, I see," was his short reply. "And how do you find your vicar?"

"Name of Philip Elton. Good enough. Quite popular with the females, but has no major vices that I've found, which makes him better than many. I expect he will marry soon; he was born with a competence but would much rather have a gentleman's income."

Lizzy may have made a slight noise as she listened to this explanation. Yes, Elton wanted Emma and her thirty thousand pounds.

Mr. Knightley looked to her. "You sniff knowingly, Miss Bennet. Has Emma been filling your head about him? I am half-convinced she's trying to snare him for her pretty little friend, Harriet Smith. A foolish notion. Elton would never be so improvident."

A flash of guilt crossed his face, perhaps a sudden recollection that Lizzy herself was a woman of little means.

Lizzy switched the basket to her other arm. "I daresay. He asked all manner of questions about my father when first I came. A rather transparent gentleman."

"Yes," Mr. Knightley agreed. "Transparent to some, at any rate."

Mr. Darcy reached for Lizzy's basket. "Allow me."

"It is not heavy," Lizzy objected, but he took it anyway.

They arrived at the cottage and Lizzy was relieved to find that the cottage was full enough already—with the presence of Harriet and Emma—to make it foolish for her to remain overly long. She delivered her goods with Miss Bates's kind wishes and quickly took her leave.

Mr. Darcy had waited outside while Mr. Knightley entered, perhaps for the same reason, or perhaps because he did not like poverty.

"How do your cousins go on?" he asked. Lizzy had intended to nod and be on her way, but perforce stopped.

"They are improving daily."

"I see you still appreciate a long walk."

"Yes, very much." Jane Fairfax was not the only one who could play this game.

Mr. Darcy looked toward the small, grimy window, which imperfectly framed Emma and Harriet. "You and Miss Woodhouse have become friends, I believe?"

"Of a sort. How do you get on with Mr. Knightley?"

"Perfectly well. Sensible man."

"He is very different from Mr. Bingley."

Darcy opened his mouth, shut it, and began again. "Yes. Bingley is the best of good friends, but Knightley is a far more experienced man than I. It has been productive to see how he organizes the management of his estate and tenants, how he prioritizes the decisions one must make."

"Whereas Mr. Bingley may benefit from *your* experience? I congratulate him."

Her tone was a little too pointed for him to miss her displeasure. He looked; he frowned; he deliberated.

Lizzy raised her brows. "We were all most saddened by Mr. Bingley's sudden departure in the fall. I gathered that you and Miss Bingley were quite persuasive in detaining him in London."

"Whether he comes or goes is not my doing. He is his own man."

"That is what those with undue influence say to assuage their own consciences."

"My conscience does not need assuaging."

Lizzy smiled with teeth. "Have you happened to meet my sister in town this past month?"

Color came into his ears and forehead and Lizzy was satisfied. How dare he say—to her face!—that he had done nothing wrong in detaching Bingley from Jane?

Of course, *he* did not have regrets, but he should at least be conscious that it wounded Jane, and through Jane, Lizzy. But he did not care. The man was arrogant; he would never question the rightness of his actions.

"I have not had the pleasure of seeing Miss Bennet in London," replied Darcy. "I gather she is fixed there for some time?"

"Yes. I shall go on to visit my friend at Hunsford, and in April or May, return to town and then home with Jane."

"Hunsford? Oh, yes, your friend, Mrs. Collins. I also will be in the neighborhood; I owe Lady Catherine a visit."

"I have a great curiosity to meet her. And her daughter, Miss Anne de Bourgh."

Darcy inclined his head. "Anne is not strong, but I know she enjoys visitors."

Lizzy wondered at his complete *sang-froid*. She had heard from Wickham how Darcy and his proud, sickly cousin were to make a match of it one day, but one wouldn't know it by his tone.

Darcy continued. "Do you enjoy your visit? Do you miss your home?"

Lizzy's defiance rose to answer. "Yes, I do miss home. I cannot be a day from Meryton before I am despondent over my loss. What is home if not a place to negatively compare all other locals against?"

Darcy's brow furrowed quizzically. "You jest. I cannot imagine you want to be always at Longbourn. *You* cannot always live in Meryton."

"Can I not? Please do not tell anyone else for they may believe you, if you say it in that strange tone. I will most likely be the Miss Bates of Meryton when I am older; I can only hope I am so well-liked as she is. Though I daresay it is her kind disposition which engenders the town's affections, so I must not aim too high."

Lizzy should have gone on her way at once, but somehow Mr. Darcy had compelled her to stay and argue. Unfortunately, her delay in talking to him allowed her to be caught by the outflow of the others.

Emma asked whether Lizzy would accompany her back to Hartfield to visit her father; she also called upon Mr. Knightley to do so. "Father loves an impromptu party—that is, as long as no one uses the word *party*. He had an indifferent night with gout, and I know he would be the better for cheer. Do, all of you come back with Harriet and I!"

And as, only a little further down the lane, they came abreast of Mr. Elton—also on a visit to old Mrs. Brown—there soon was a party of three ladies and three gentlemen.

Mr. Elton bowed rather more theatrically than the occasion demanded. "Whither away? I must accompany you. Do you know, Miss Woodhouse, I have just realized that Miss Bennet and I share a common acquaintance. There is a fellow man of the cloth, a Mr. Collins of Hunsford, in Kent, who I believe is her cousin. And his patroness is the esteemed Lady Catherine de Bourgh, who is, I believe, Mr. Darcy's aunt." He bowed to Mr. Darcy.

Lizzy wasn't sure what to say of this, except a simple assent, but he did not seem to need much answer.

"Isn't it diverting how these connections do happen? I have sometimes speculated that good English families can be linked in six persons or less. The Woodhouse, family, for instance, is known to be second cousins with the Cavendish family, headed by the Duke of Devonshire, you know."

If he kept up the bowing, he should look like a jack-in-the-box. He continued in this vein, and would have definitely taken Emma's arm, but she maneuvered adroitly, and Mr. Elton ended up offering an arm to Harriet as they made their way to Hartfield.

Emma struck up a conversation with Mr. Darcy, and Mr. Knightley squired Lizzy at the rear of the small parade.

Lizzy, though still annoyed by Mr. Darcy and his callous manner, couldn't help observing Emma's schemes with an inward chuckle. Emma might arrange as many walks and solo conversations as she wanted, but Harriet was safe from her machinations at present!

Mr. Knightley had gone somewhat grim and dark about the mouth. Did he care so much for Emma's plans for Mr. Elton and Harriet?

"I must tell you," Lizzy spoke softly, "that I have dropped a word or two in Harriet's ear. She is not expecting any proposal from Mr. Elton, whatever Emma may say."

Mr. Knightley turned to her. "Beg your pardon, what's that? Oh. Yes, excellent. I am glad, though how you managed to convince her of anything that did not come from her goddess Emma's mouth is a miracle."

Lizzy laughed. "Too true. I was somewhat unscrupulous, but I did it out of concern for Harriet."

He nodded, but still appeared distracted. If anything, his dark look seemed directed at Mr. Darcy and Emma. Mr. Elton, too, darted occasional glances at them, looking particularly pained when Emma laughed at something Mr. Darcy said. Lizzy could not quite believe he'd said anything humorous; perhaps Emma *would* be a good match for him.

Mr. Knightley all but glowered.

"Do they trouble you?" Lizzy asked. Was it possible that finally another man was seeing Mr. Darcy for the unpleasant person she knew him to be?"

"No, not at all. Forgive me." Mr. Knightley turned the conversation to other channels, asking Lizzy to tell him about her home in Hertfordshire.

It was not until later—when they had accomplished their purpose in cheering Mr. Woodhouse—that Emma's day, which had begun so happily and continued so hopefully, came crashing to a humiliating anti-climax.

Mr. Elton had outlasted everyone else, even Harriet. He lingered by the front door, all the while leave-taking, yet never taking leave.

Finally, he came to the point. "I have a matter of some... delicacy to discuss. Would you do me the honor of stepping into the study for a moment?"

Emma, realizing he must wish to ask her something about Harriet, or perhaps something about the Westons' party—though why on earth that would be delicate there was no knowing—opened the door at once and led him in.

Her father's study, being on the ground floor, far from his room and near the front door—treacherous draughts!—was not often used.

The grate was cold, as Emma did not think it necessary to waste a fire in an unused room. If her father wished for a book, she often found it for him herself. It was not dusty, however. The wooden shelves and desk shined as if freshly oiled. It was a trifle dim, without any candles, and musty, perhaps because of the thick green carpet her mother had had laid down. The north-facing windows were overshadowed by the wall that protected the vegetable garden and did not let in much light.

Mr. Elton paced in the dark room for a moment, and then took one of her hands. "My dear Miss Woodhouse, my affection can no longer remain unstated. I have these past months received your smile, your friendship, your approbation—I do so hope!—but I must ask for more. I must ask for words. Will you do me the honor of accepting my humble hand in marriage? The hand of one who adores you, who—"

Emma tugged her hand free. "Accepting your hand...? What are you doing?"

Mr. Elton sank to one knee on the carpet. "The happiest moment in my life was when you looked upon my poor poem and gave me such a smile and such a nod of your beautiful head, as made it clear that you understood and welcomed my attentions! Please do not draw back in alarm. I would never have spoken if not for that. Perhaps I have been too soon—if so, I apologize from the bottom of my poor heart which is so entirely yours. But please say I have not been too forward. Please say that you will consider accompanying me on that great journey of life as my companion and better self."

Emma stared at him, his flushed cheeks and quivering lips. "You wrote that poem for *me*? But it was Harriet's book! I only nodded to you, smiled at you, to apologize for reading it aloud to my father!"

"I clearly addressed it to you. To you, Emma, my goddess, my—"

She squeezed her eyes shut for a moment. "Oh, stop. I can't stand that sort of talk. I never dreamed of this conclusion."

He rose back to his feet. She noticed in passing that the knee of his breeches had gained significant dust and that she must ask the housekeeper to have the carpet taken up and beaten well.

"This conclusion? How could it be otherwise? My heart is drawn to you as a lodestone to a magnet." He kissed her hands fervently and Emma, disgusted, drew back again.

"Stop. I apologize for the pain it may cause you, but I was under the misapprehension that *Harriet* was your love."

"Harriet? Harriet Smith?" He scoffed. "I do not think so little of myself to make *that* a necessity. Even Miss Bennet would be unthinkable, though she is the daughter of a gentleman. If I were in other circumstances, I daresay Miss Bennet would—" He bit his lip. "You have distracted me from my purpose. I care only for you. Please tell me it is not in vain."

"It is wholly and completely in vain." Emma put her hand behind her back as he made some small motion as if to capture them again.

"Then... have you been flirting with me?" he asked. "You cannot have misunderstood our many interludes."

"Our *interludes*? You forget yourself, Mr. Elton! All I can say is that there has been a great misunderstanding. Good day, sir."

Emma jerked the door open and strode to the wide front door. It was heavy but the hinges were regularly greased, and she opened it without difficulty. She was resolutely thankful that no servants were present to witness her humiliation.

Mr. Elton looked torn between confusion and anger. "I cannot believe you have been indifferent these past months. Has the coming of Mr. Darcy altered your intentions? He has £20,000 a year, they say, but I thought you surely would not wish to live so far from Hartfield and your father!"

Emma crossed her arms against the cold wind and a few drips from the eaves blowing in the open door. "My intentions are none of your concern, sir. I will not answer impertinent questions."

Mr. Elton doffed his hat and swept out of the house with an air of injured dignity.

Emma closed the door, feeling nearly faint for the first time that she could recall. She went back into the dark study and shut the door, sinking weakly down onto the great chair by the empty fireplace. Good Lord. How blind she'd been!

What an insufferable interview. She had never encouraged Mr. Elton in *that* way; how dare he accuse her of it?

But even as she thought the words, she realized they were untrue. Every nod and smile and invitation—for Harriet!—he had interpreted wrongly. And she had no one to blame but herself.

And it might have continued on even longer; horror! He probably only spoke today because he was rendered uneasy by Mr. Darcy's presence. As if Emma had any intentions in *that* direction! She, who had made no secret of the fact that she did not intend to marry.

She clenched a fist. If only people in general did not *disbelieve* a woman's rational words, this might have been avoided.

But what a muddle! Emma pinched the bridge of her nose to ease a growing headache. Poor Harriet. It would be painful; it would be humbling.

When the door suddenly swung open, her butler drew back in surprise, and Emma swept to her feet. "It's fine, Benton, I was just going."

He held the door for her. "Your father requested another search be made for the Children's Lullabies. He wishes to find *Kitty, a fair but frozen maid.*"

Emma sighed. "And we have already copied it out. I will talk to Papa. In the meantime, please desire Mrs. Trisby to have the carpet in here taken up and beaten. It's gained a shocking layer of dust."

{ 9 }

MR. DARCY, COMPLETELY UNAWARE that he had been the catalyst for more than one noteworthy conversation, walked back to Donwell Abbey with Mr. Knightley.

They used the footpath again. A light, but chill wind was blowing in clouds from the east. The fine morning was turning into a gray afternoon, and it was one of those December days which would probably end in a cold, drenching rain. The men made good time and conversation was sparse, both being wrapped in their thoughts.

As friendships went, theirs was on the trajectory to be one of the solid, quiet sorts. They would probably not see each other above once a year, probably less, but would spend that occasional visit in serious, open, and useful dialogue about their respective duties. If circumstances allowed for more frequency, they might someday describe the other as one of their closest friends.

In intelligence, they were matched; in background, similar. Both men had come into their estates at a young age with a younger sibling to look after. Mr. Knightley was nearly ten years older than Mr. Darcy, but in maturity they were not dissimilar. The main difference was their upbringing and personality.

"I've known Miss Woodhouse since she was born," Mr. Knightley said presently. "And we've become quite good friends since John and Isabella married."

"Helpful that your estates are close," Mr. Darcy agreed. "John mentioned last month that he was thankful for it."

"Yes. Emma bears it well, but Mr. Woodhouse is a most fearful, anxious sort. His own health is poor. He also lost his wife untimely and has never felt sanguine since, though I think he was always nervous."

"Unsurprising."

Mr. Knightley did not know quite why he continued. "On the one hand, as she is like a sister to me, I hope that Emma marries eventually and moves away, to experience a freer kind of life; but on the other hand, I do not know how Mr. Woodhouse would bear it."

"No doubt he would, if required to."

"Yes." Mr. Knightley could say no more. He could not help seeing that in many respects Mr. Darcy would be an excellent match for Emma. Darcy was of similar rank and fortune, and more importantly, a conscientious and thoughtful man. He was also the sort of tall, handsome fellow that women admired, and just the right age for Emma.

He would not treat Emma lightly, or cause her to experience the kind of betrayal in marriage that too many women (in Knightley's opinion) were forced to ignore.

Darcy was also intelligent, which Emma needed. Being so bright and headstrong herself, she would march right over a stupid man.

Mr. Knightley did not like it, exactly, but it was not for him to dislike.

From Highbury with Love

Mr. Darcy, perceptive in some ways but not in others, which is a maxim true of nearly everyone, yet more so of gentlemen, was not aware of the subtext.

"A woman may be settled too near her family. Too near for the general comfort or benefit of either," he said, thinking of an entirely different scenario, and yet entirely confirming Mr. Knightley's half-held suspicion.

Mr. Darcy, to do him justice, was wondering why Elizabeth remained the undisputed queen of his heart, while Emma did not so much as cause him to blink. Emma had the better figure, by regular standards, and was by far better in situation. Her father's estates were extensive, and her inheritance would be near to Georgiana's if he had to guess. She would be a perfectly acceptable choice. She also was clever, free from vanity, and far more natural than Miss Caroline Bingley could dream of being.

And yet, he felt nothing. Whereas Lizzy—whom he'd heard describing Hertfordshire to Knightley, along with its citizens and dramas and personalities—captured his attention immediately. Why should one face and voice and mind so captivate him when no others did? Darcy was not a romantic; he had never planned to marry purely for love. He had not given it great thought, but he'd always expected that where his mind led his heart would follow.

He still thought a match with Elizabeth would be imprudent in the extreme... but he was also beginning to think of it with a certain amount of guilty resignation. If Providence did not want him to fall under her spell, why had she turned up under his nose here in Highbury? Why were they scheduled to travel to Hunsford at the same time?

He could withstand a few days or weeks; he had done so and left her in Hertfordshire.

But this was worse, and he had not even her family to remind him of the drawbacks. If he was not engaged to her by the end of his visit in the south, it would be a miracle of self-control.

{ 10 }

AFTER HER HORRIBLE INTERVIEW with Mr. Elton, Emma sent a note to Harriet that very afternoon, inviting her back to Hartfield the following day. She offered, as an excuse, and also to salve her own feeling of guilt, that Harriet could collect several bouquets from the hothouse to decorate the dining room at Mrs. Goddard's school for Advent.

Emma received Harriet in the garden the next morning, reluctantly receiving her thanks for the generosity.

"Such beautiful flowers!" Harriet said. "Amazing that any can grow this late in the year."

"Yes, it is the least I can do," Emma said, handing Harriet the small knife she kept nearby for pruning and cutting.

Harriet held it in surprise. "You wish me to choose? I am sure I do not know—I do not know which would look best or which you might wish to save for Hartfield."

Emma shook her head. "Choosing and arranging flowers is a lady's province, one of the few concrete things she can do with her own hands for the beautification of her home. I have been so little benefit to you Harriet, let me at least instruct you in this. Do your hands not ache with enforced stillness at times?"

"I cannot recall feeling so." Harriet moved uncertainly to a white rose. "I often help with the sewing and mending for the girls—Mrs. Goddard says I am excellent at the invisible stitch!—but I am sure you are right."

"But it is when I have been embroidering that the ache attacks the worst!" Emma pointed to several stems while Harriet snipped. "But I am afraid I must broach a much more painful topic. I—oh, dear—I believe myself to have been completely mistaken in Mr. Elton. I have encouraged you to think of him, to honor him, to meditate on his perfections...and to believe he requites your feelings! Oh, Harriet, I have been the worst of friends, for my own desire for your happy settlement blinded me. He has no such intention towards you, but instead has shown himself to be conceited and arrogant. It pains me to the heart to share this, but you must know the truth."

Harriet snipped another flower and put it in the rush basket provided for them. Her sweet lower lip was caught between her teeth and she turned uncertainly to Emma.

The look was too much for Emma, who had been lashing her conscience for nearly a day. She gently seized Harriet's hands. "Please do not hide your grief from me. Who should bear you up in this terrible disappointment if not me? I was mistaken in him, grossly mistaken."

"But I am not disappointed," Harriet said. "That is—I *am*. Has he truly shown himself conceited and arrogant? His manners were always so agreeable! We were both cognizant of it. I thought—Miss Bennet and I were convinced that it was *you* he loved. I *am* disappointed, but only for you, my dear Mis Woodhouse!"

Emma was not immediately able to reply to this. She recalled; she doubted; she hesitated. Did Harriet truly understand what she said?

Harriet now squeezed *her* hands. "Perhaps there is some mistake, and if so, it must lie with me! I ought to have told you sooner that I did not mind his preference for you. Mind it? I have been so happy for you! How could anyone think of Miss Smith when Miss Woodhouse was near? But perhaps even now the difficulty might be overcome. You are the sweetest and best of friends; so modest! So selfless! Please do not deny Mr. Elton on my poor account! I could not be happier than for you to have the felicity of being his wife."

"The *felicity* of being—I am sorry, Harriet, my mind has begun to froth. Do you mean to say that you and Miss Bennet... spoke of this? I thought—I knew, rather—that you were thinking of becoming Mrs. Elton. The vicarage! The horrible yellow curtains!"

Harriet smiled uncertainly. "Only the kindest of friends could have believed it possible he would prefer me. I have realized this fortnight at least that it was you who excited his admiration and affection."

"Well—I did not want his admiration and affection. I have told him so. But I am excessively thankful that you were not injured as I thought."

Emma's relief was nearly balanced by a sense of *ill-usage*. "I am sorry to harp on one point, but I cannot believe that you and Miss Bennet *discussed* me. That you gossiped—yes, I must say gossiped—about a connection between me and that man!"

"No, no! I am sure—I am *almost* sure we were not gossiping. We only just touched on his preference for you. Quite natural!"

"His preference? And the possibility of Mr. Elton and myself? I am sorry to say, but the vulgarity of the idea—"

Harriet's eyes filled with ready tears. "Vulgarity? I am so sorry! You spoke so highly of him, of his sermons, his gallantry, his—Oh, it is *I* who have been a terrible friend. Do forgive me, Miss Woodhouse! And please do not allow my lack of understanding—my *in*elegance—to color your opinion of Miss Bennet. I know that she thought of nothing but your happiness; the mistake must have been mine. Such an inferior education I have had! You have said it, and I see that you are perfectly right."

This contrite speech pulled Emma back from a truly immature and sulky response, and she soothed her friend as best she could. As her attempt united both truth and genuine goodwill, she was more successful than she deserved.

"I have been the fool," Emma told herself sternly, "and I am benefitting from a *very lucky* circumstance. I must not allow my pique to blind me to the very real folly of what I attempted."

This attitude of self-censure could not but leave a lasting impression. An entire night and day were spent in this unusual state of self-recrimination; it was a penitence both necessary and painful; it gave her greater respect for the heroes of the church.

It also left her decidedly cool toward Miss Bennet.

{ 11 }

EMMA WAS NOT REQUIRED to see Lizzy Bennet for nearly a week. As Miss Bates was now really improving, Emma's poor father was feeling less troubled over her, and did not require daily updates. Lizzy would still have visited if invited, of course, but Emma did not invite her.

Thus they did not meet until Miss Bates managed to repeat her visit to Hartfield, again in the Woodhouse carriage, again with Lizzy rather than Jane Fairfax.

To think Emma should come to prefer Jane Fairfax over Lizzy!

Emma almost allowed the visit to pass with addressing the matter, but Emma hated unfinished business. Particularly when she felt a niggling sense of guilt about it.

After their visit, she asked Lizzy whether she would like to walk with her, rather than returning directly in the carriage.

The sky had cleared and a wintry sunshine bathed both girls, warming their backs and bonnets as they went down the lane.

"It is only a few days until your sister comes from London, yes?" Lizzy asked. "Do you have many preparations to make?"

Emma knew that it was unlikely Lizzy knew what had occurred last week, for Harriet was a dear girl and actually *not* given to gossip. She had probably told Lizzy nothing. But Emma still felt a bit of annoyance at Lizzy's confident and oblivious air.

"Yes, the preparations have kept me quite busy." These time-consuming duties included agreeing with her housekeeper that the usual arrangements should be made for Isabella's five children, selecting fresh flowers to cut the day before they came, and reassuring her father that the coming snow would not strand Isabella and her family, helpless and ill, on the pernicious London road. This last was truly a task of some hours and repeated daily application, but Emma did not begrudge it.

Emma took a deep breath. "I must ask... No, I must thank you, I suppose, for disabusing Harriet's mind of Mr. Elton's preference for her. I was mistaken in him. You were quite wrong about any possible alliance between myself and that gentleman, but I am sure it was kindly meant."

Lizzy only looked fixedly at the road and the blue sky beyond. "Ah, did he finally propose? I am glad to have prevented Harriet suffering any further pangs this year. If I have done so, I am quite glad."

Emma was not satisfied. Her better angel urged her to drop the issue, but she spied a smirk on Lizzy's face, and prudence fled.

"His behavior was not what it ought to be. However, I must ask you to refrain from speculating on my eventual marriage. I allow that we have not been acquainted long, but I must inform you I have no intention of marrying, and certainly not to such a puffed up, empty-headed, toadying man as Mr. Elton."

Lizzy huffed an almost laugh as they turned right onto Highbury's main street. "And yet you would have foisted that man on your dear friend?"

"I was mistaken in his character. I already admitted it."

"Yes, he has revealed his arrogance and bad judgement to you, but you did not think highly of him before, did you? I can't believe you ever thought him a particularly intelligent or refined man—he is always so languishing."

"I don't know what manner of vicar you are accustomed to, but I assure you he is above the average in my experience! He is temperate, polite, gives a good, short homily, and has nice manners. There was a littleness to him I did not until now discover, but he is far from objectionable for such a one as..."

"Such a one as Harriet?" They were now abreast of the bakery where they had recently stood with Harriet while she bought buns for her friends.

"Yes, to put it plainly. She is not nice in her requirements, and I do long to see her settled well."

Lizzy shook her head. "You already know my sentiments. You simply do not realize how few gentlemen are ready to make a disinterested choice in a bride. Without any fortune or portion... I fear she will long regret Mr. Martin and his family."

Emma unclenched her teeth enough to talk. "In at least one way, you have hit the nail on the head. Her affection is more for his family, for the sisters and the mother, than for the son."

They came to a stop on the pavement outside the blue door of Miss Bates's home. "No wonder, since she has had neither."

"One does not marry for sisters!"

"Why not? Many women must lower themselves to marry for much less! My own dear friend—" Lizzy broke off in frustration. "Harriet would have had a family who loved her, whom she loved! And I think you fool yourself that she did not care for Mr. Martin. Do what you will, but do not deceive *yourself*."

There was just a hint of contempt in Lizzy's retort, or Emma imagined there was, and her nostrils flared as she glared. "Good day, Miss Bennet."

Emma turned away angrily. By previous arrangement, the carriage which had brought Miss Bates home had waited for her. She strode over and the groom opened the door with alacrity. Usually Emma had a word of thanks for John, but she entered the carriage with flaming cheeks and gloved hands flexing into unladylike fists.

From Mr. Knightley she might take such censure, but from a simple country girl with no family or status of note...!

Over the following week Emma did not remain heated in her anger, but she had even less desire to see Lizzy Bennet.

Harriet was less necessary also, and even less so when Emma's sister Isabella finally arrived. Of course, Emma introduced them, and invited Harriet to Hartfield several times, but a friend, however dear, could not quite compete with the presence of a sister, a brother-in-law, and five nieces and nephews.

Emma refused to think through Lizzy's words about sisters and family.

Mr. Knightley was there every day, often with Mr. Darcy, to visit with John and the others. Between the family and the two extra gentlemen, the house was livelier than it had been in years.

Mr. Elton had temporarily left Highbury—Emma could only be thankful—so he did not intrude his offended pride or unwanted gallantry to her happy family circle.

Mr. Knightley only tasked her with Mr. Elton's name once. He came up to her after dinner, as she was sorting the music on the pianoforte. Isabella had rifled through the pages that afternoon, struck with a wave of nostalgia, and played through a few tunes, weeping happily.

Emma reordered the loose pages, and Mr. Knightley leaned against the instrument. "Mr. Elton has gone to Bath."

"Yes, I heard."

"He has many acquaintances there. Particularly a family of young ladies."

"I wish them joy of him."

"Highbury gossip says he did not take leave of you, and only sent a note to your father."

"Since when, Mr. Knightley, do you participate in gossip? Who would dare to do so with you, expecting only a set-down?"

He raised a hand. "*Touché*. It was Mrs. Weston; she worries about you."

"Such gossip from me would earn your censure, yet Mrs. Weston is only being considerate? I knew she was always your favorite."

He ignored this sally. "I am not always so severe, am I? I offered you the tidbit on Mr. Elton with the greatest goodwill."

"Well then, prove your good offices. I have not seen Mrs. Weston much of late, with Isabella and the children here, so tell me the latest. Namely, is Frank Churchill truly coming to their party? He has only two more days to arrive."

"I can offer even better coin in this matter. I saw him arrive not two hours ago. I passed his carriage on the Randall's Road as I was leaving her."

"What?" Emma exclaimed. "He has finally come and nobody knows of it?"

"I daresay many people do by now, but you have been here. And Darcy..." Mr. Knightley waved his friend over to them, who had just come in with John. "Darcy, you are acquainted with the Churchills, are you not?"

"Yes. I have some acquaintance with the family. Mrs. Churchill is friends with my aunt, Lady Catherine de Bourgh."

"And Frank Churchill?"

"I only know him in passing. A popular young man, I believe, several years my junior."

Emma clapped her hands. "Mr. Frank Churchill! Finally here! Mrs. Weston was my governess, almost a mother to me for so many years, and she is now *his* stepmother. I feel a familial claim upon him. He shall be delightful and we shall all dote upon him."

Mr. Knightley looked faintly ill. "I shall not."

"I do wonder..." Emma broke off. The arrival of Mr. Churchill inspired all her (chastened, but not dead) matchmaking desires. He would be quite a prize for some worthy young woman. He did not have much individual fortune, but his aunt was known to be quite wealthy, and Frank would inherit.

Emma first thought, of course, or poor Harriet, but then another thought obtruded.

She was still upset with Elizabeth Bennet; it stung to know that that young lady had both noted and corrected Emma's bad reading of Elton's character and affections. (No correction is pleasant but being found deficient in intelligence was infuriating.)

Emma was not a vindictive or even a sore loser, but she felt that the most satisfying conclusion in the world would be to match Lizzy with a fine gentleman. It was a solution both magnanimous and ever so slightly savage. How those both should be true, Emma did not care to examine.

Instead, she asked, "Do you know if Miss Bennet will come to the Westons' party? Is she invited?"

Mr. Darcy looked up from the carpet, and Mr. Knightley glanced keenly at Emma.

"I know," she answered with a laugh, "you are shocked that I am so cut off from my friends. I can only say that I have been very busy about domestic matters, and that is a statement a man dare not condemn a woman for making."

Mr. Knightley shook his head. "I know you have been busy, but have you not visited Miss Bates and Miss Fairfax once in the past fortnight? You set the tone for many in Highbury, Emma, could you but see it. You must not neglect them."

Emma's heart twinged with discomfort. It was true that she often let too much time lag between her visits to Miss Bates. Such a silly, prosy, repetitive woman! But still, Emma ought to have visited. Her lapse this time was less to do with homely duties and more to do with avoiding Lizzy. "I will not neglect them; I do not neglect them. I gather they *are* coming?"

"Yes. I will send a carriage for all three of them."

"Excellent!" said Emma. "Now, if only you kept your own carriage and carriage horses, how much easier your charity would be!"

Mr. Knightley took the music from her and tapped it efficiently into place on the pianoforte. "To use once a quarter? My income does not extend quite as far as yours."

"It does; merely, you choose to be oddly frugal. But I will not tease you about it tonight. I will only look forward to the party. If only Harriet could come, it would be perfect! But she wrote today that she is getting a dreadful sore throat."

{ 12 }

LIZZY, AFTER A TIRESOME WEEK capped with an awful letter from her sister Jane, was also eager to be distracted by a Christmas party.

Every line of Jane's letter conveyed both continued grief and a fixed determination to be content. It was disheartening in the extreme. Lizzy was nearly counting the days until she would continue on to visit Charlotte and Mr. Collins. To think she should be so thankful to see that man again!

There could be no doubt too, that it was continually depressing to see how Miss Bates contrived to live on such paltry means. Every week seemed to reveal another layer of the degradation of living in cheap rooms, dependent on the largesse of others for any treat or luxury. And with nothing more to look forward to!

Miss Bates grew ever more cheerful as the days passed and her health improved, while Lizzy, now acquainted with her situation, wondered why it had taken her so long to break down in the first place.

A lifetime of Lizzy's mother's prophecies about their eventual poverty and the necessity of good marriages had not had an *ounce* the impact of one month in the life of Miss Bates.

Lizzy, for the first time, wondered if she was too nice in her requirements for a husband. She could not marry without respect;

Mr. Collins was still unthinkable. But if there should come another opportunity her way—less objectionable but still leaving her heart untouched—she felt a growing uncertainty as to her answer.

Not that Miss Bates was unhappy with her lot. She was not! But Lizzy was not Miss Bates. Her heart craved interaction and enlargement and the company of superior minds. It was not so much the meanness of Miss Bates's life that disturbed Lizzy, but the smallness of it. The sameness.

Then, too, there was Jane Fairfax to consider. She was beautiful—her dark hair was always in plain bands but it did nothing to hide her classically beautiful profile—and she was wonderfully accomplished. And yet... she was doomed to slave away as a governess and give up all polite society!

Lizzy felt her sanguine, willful carelessness about the future begin to slip away.

On the evening of the 25th, Lizzy, Jane Fairfax, and Miss Bates put on their fine clothes and readied for the party at the Westons'. Miss Bates wore black, still in deep mourning for her mother, and Jane wore half-mourning because her darkest gown was gray, she could not go darker without a new dress. Lizzy wore a gown of palest green.

She felt odd wearing color, but then, she liked color, and to be in mourning for a distant cousin of her father would be a stretch. Miss Bates could not stop telling the two young ladies how well they looked, though her warmest effusions must be for her dear niece.

Truly, Jane Fairfax *was* looking better. However, if Lizzy had thought that a return of health might help that young lady warm up to her, she'd been wrong.

When Mr. Knightley's carriage came—Lizzy had been posted by the front window to offer fastest intelligence—the ladies put on final wraps and descended the stairs.

The clouds were in thick bars, but a little moonlight shone through the thin patches. The backlit clouds offered a strange glow.

And snow was falling in luscious, fat flakes.

"How beautiful," Lizzy said. "Snow for Christmas. And such a sky!"

"Oh, my dear Jane," said Miss Bates. "Ought we to go out in the snow when you are just recovered? If it should turn to rain or slush! Or if the drifts become high! I am persuaded we ought to be prudent. But then poor Mr. Knightley has been so kind to arrange for a carriage. One should not like to be *un*thankful!"

Jane Fairfax was already taking the footman's hand and climbing into the carriage. "I feel quite well. We are barely a mile from Randalls; all shall be well."

And so they were bundled into the carriage. It *was* a cold night, but the drive was not far, and Mr. Knightley had caused several blankets to be left on the seats for them, and a hot brick rested on the floorboards.

"Mr. Knightley is the best of men and neighbors," Miss Bates said. "I do wonder that he has not married, for he is the perfect gentleman! I am sure he has not gone above two days without sending us some gift in the last month. Apples, firewood, newspapers... such a perfect gentleman!"

"He does seem to be a superior man," Lizzy agreed. "None of that arrogance that so often leads prosperous men into poor behavior."

"Superior! Yes, that is the word for Mr. Knightley."

Jane Fairfax only looked out the window.

When their carriage arrived at the Westons' comfortable house, Randalls, it was portly, affable Mr. Weston and an unknown young gentleman who strode out the front door to hand them down.

They offered their hands to the ladies to prevent their slipping on the crushed snow and handed them carefully up the few steps to the front door.

Mr. Weston was an older man, distinguished and friendly. "We are delighted you are joining us, Miss Bates, Miss Fairfax, Miss Bennet! Here is my son, Frank, home at last!"

Frank Churchill's hair was between fair and ginger, and he looked quite the London gentleman—significantly more modish than any other gentlemen in Highbury. Indeed, his style was more that of a Bond Street beau than a country gentleman like Mr. Knightley or Mr. Darcy. He bowed over each of their hands, and when his father took Miss Bates in on his arm, he squired both Lizzy and Jane.

"Miss Bennet, how do you do? And Miss Fairfax, it has been some months since we spoke at Weymouth; I understand you have been ill? I hope you are fully recovered."

"It has been a very long autumn."

This, Lizzy reflected, did not quite answer the question.

"Indeed, it has." He led them into the warm drawing room, which sparkled with candles and cut glass. The lights reflected off the tie pins in the pure whiteness of the men's cravats. It sparkled against the jewels on the ladies. It was almost shockingly warm after the biting cold outdoors.

Lizzy blinked her eyes to adjust. The room smelled of delicious orange pomander balls—she spotted them on the mantle—as well as a spicy Christmas punch. The many lamps that were lit, polished and shining, lent a glow and a warm-oil scent to the room.

It was not a large party, not a crush, by any means, and as Lizzy had become acquainted with nearly everyone present in the last several weeks, she did not feel at all out of place.

While Jane Fairfax was drawn into conversation with Mrs. Weston and Mr. Knightley, Lizzy went to greet old Mr. Woodhouse. She knew Emma, who stood beside his chair, was probably still angry with her, but he was making signs to her and she must obey.

"I must introduce you to my poor, dear daughter Isabella," he told Lizzy. "She has sadly moved to London, which is very bad, but she is home now."

Isabelle greeted her in a friendly way, though her attention was scattered. "Oh, yes, Miss Bennet? Oh! There are the Coxes, I must say hello, for they have not heard about little Emma's birth!"

Emma curtseyed a little stiffly. "Miss Bennet."

Lizzy moved on to Mr. Weston, thanking him for the festivities and congratulating him on his son's visit.

Although some members of the party were not known to each other, everyone seemed to be in high spirits. Even anxious Mr. Woodhouse seemed in good cheer despite the snow.

The only exception was Mr. Darcy. He was just outside the loose ring of candelabras, in the dimness on the far edge of the room. He faced the French doors that led from the drawing room out toward a dark terrace. He was just as tall and nearly as forbidding as he'd looked in Hertfordshire when they'd first met. Prideful man! Here there could be nothing to offend his dignity or rank, and yet he still didn't trouble himself to be agreeable.

She felt vindicated in her original judgement. Perhaps the society of Meryton was inclined to be a little lax, her sisters a little silly, her mother a little loud—but here was perfectly unobjectionable company, and he was the same.

Lizzy observed him for barely a moment, not at all inclined to break his solitude, but he seemed to feel her eyes upon him. He turned and caught her eye. Bowed.

Ugh, she'd been spotted.

"A snowy night, Miss Bennet. Do admire the view."

She took a few steps nearer and saw, past the glare of the lamps, that he was watching the snow fall upon the stones of the terrace. It was filling in the cracks first, creating a spiderwork of snow lines. The half-pillars were topped with it, like the purest white sugar, and the moon came out for a moment, shining between billowy night-gray clouds.

"It is quite beautiful," she admitted. "If someone painted it, I daresay you would say it looked contrived, yet here it is."

Even as they watched, the clouds obscured the moon again, and the terrace became quite dim.

He sighed and turned half-back to face the room. "Do you paint?"

"No, not at all. Nor sketch. Miss Fairfax, however, quite enjoys art. Her portfolio is full of beautifully executed pieces."

"And do you—"

"Oh, Miss Woodhouse also paints. She did a lovely watercolor of Harriet Smith only a few months ago."

"Yes, Mr. Woodhouse showed me."

"Ah, good. Do excuse me, I wish to acquire a glass of negus; I see Mrs. Weston is offering it." Lizzy began to move away, but Mr. Darcy unexpectedly followed her. He began with inconsequentials—the duration of her stay, her relationship with Miss Bates, and her occupation while she was here.

"I have done very little, I'm afraid." Lizzy sipped the glass he handed her. "I fetch and run errands for Miss Bates when she will let me. I read aloud, I take walks, I read silently. I am afraid I am not the sort of woman to perfect a new stitch or fill a composition book while I am idle. I do not apply myself where I do not like."

"What have you been reading?"

"No, I will not be drawn into books. I only brought my favorites, and if you disparage them, I will not be answerable for the consequences."

"I doubt I would. Will you never discuss books with me? This is the second time you have refused."

"I only discuss books with those I know will agree with me on every point. I cannot bear to be crossed and only enjoy the sort of discussions that turn on complete similarity of viewpoint."

"Yet Mr. Knightley says you disagreed vehemently on Coleridge."

"Ah, but *I* disagreed with *him*, not he with me."

"Is that not the same?"

"No, not at all. The person who gives their opinion first takes all the risk; Mr. Knightley was gallant enough to do so, leaving the field open for me."

"So if I venture to tell you *my* opinion of Coleridge..."

"No, thank you, I am too distracted." Lizzy sipped again and moved toward the pianoforte, whose white and black keys gleamed like shiny dice in the lamplight.

"Do you like the pianoforte?" he asked, following beside her.

"What sort of inquiry is this, Mr. Darcy? Have I not said enough to convince you of my inferior skills?"

His brow furrowed a little. "You once said to me that you were trying to make out my character. I suppose I would like to make out yours."

"Ah, you are using my words against me. Unchivalrous. I do enjoy the pianoforte, but my fingering is quite bad for I never practiced as I ought. Mary much preferred it, so she generally commandeered our instrument after she turned eleven or thereabouts. Miss Woodhouse, however," Lizzy continued relentlessly, "plays charmingly. And Miss Bates says Jane Fairfax plays divinely, though I have never heard her. Let us ask Mrs. Weston if there shall be music."

"Only if you also will play," he said. "That is what I want to hear."

Lizzy had a fixed idea in her head of Mr. Darcy, and it included his near complete disapproval of her. Yet, his tone of voice, his eye, his look... was it *possible* that he was trying to ingratiate himself with *her?*

"Then you have very strange taste."

Lizzy abandoned him at the first pretext. She did not wish to be admired by a man she despised, though she still doubted she had understood him aright.

Mr. Knightley did not enjoy the sight of Emma going into dinner on Frank Churchill's arm and subsequently spending most of the evening with him. They spent nearly a quarter of an hour in a tête-à-tête in the east corner, which was *not* well lit.

Knightley knew Frank Churchill only by reputation, and it was not ideal. He was not a cad, but he was considered self-centered and a spendthrift. He apparently spent many a free fortnight at the watering places like Weymouth and Brighton, where he might be amused, but had not, until now, ever found a fortnight to visit his father.

Knightley had no good opinion of such selfishness and carelessness of others' feelings.

Knightley was also aware that Mr. and Mrs. Weston would like nothing better than for Frank to marry Emma. It would settle him nearby, more than comfortably, and unite into one family the two young people they loved so much.

This idea did not sit well with Mr. Knightley. Not for some years. He had even indulged the thought that perhaps Mr. Darcy would preempt such an attachment—the silver lining on an inexplicably dark cloud—but then, Knightley had reckoned without Frank Churchill's ways.

Frank was half the man Darcy was, but he was also witty, talkative, and irreverent. He was a great favorite with the ladies and full of skillful fun and flattery.

Of course, Frank also spent quite a bit of time chatting with Miss Bennet and Miss Fairfax... but he always returned to Emma.

Mr. Knightley split his time between his other friends, also taking a moment to check in with Miss Bennet. "I hope you are finding the society of Highbury to your liking. Miss Bates has a wide circle of friends, though I know you have been largely confined by her illness."

"Not at all. It has been a most interesting visit. Any new set of people have their foibles and prejudices, their heroes and myths. It is most interesting."

"I see that you are a budding anthropologist. A studier of man."

"And woman."

"And what myths do you find current in our small civilization?"

Lizzy smiled. "Well. There seems to be some great mythos over that young man." She nodded at Frank Churchill. "His return is a veritable second-coming; how lucky we are to witness it! Then Mr. Woodhouse; he is the benevolent patron-saint of good digestion. A lesser god in the pantheon, but nonetheless loved for the humility of his aims."

Mr. Knightley laughed. "Pretty well for only a few weeks' time."

"And there is Emma, or Miss Woodhouse, as I should probably say."

Mr. Knightley sobered. "Yes, what of Emma? The princess in the tower?"

"Hm. She *could* be the princess locked up in the tower, if that princess had complete run of the tower, managed the entire village down below, a continual stream of visitors, and no great desire to leave the tower. But no, that does not quite fit."

Mr. Knightley looked again at Miss Bennet. "You do see things rather clearly. I might be afraid to have your eye turned on me."

Lizzy dropped a playful curtsey. "If I discover your part in the pantheon, you shall be the first to know."

Miss Bennet was distracting, but soon Mr. Knightley could no longer bear the sight of Emma in the corner, whispering with Mr. Churchill along with covert looks at various members of the party.

He went to Mrs. Weston and requested music. "I am sure Mr. Woodhouse would enjoy hearing Emma, and there are several young ladies who might play."

"Of course! What could be more delightful?"

This brought about a change, though it was Mr. Churchill who handed Emma to the bench before the pianoforte.

When Emma began to play, Lizzy took a seat on a settee beside Miss Bates, but that good lady, finding herself rather chilled, with much whispering and apologizing, moved nearer the fire. Mr. Darcy took her place.

He crossed one booted foot over the other, and his pointer finger twitched in time with the music. She had now seen him admire snow and music in one night. What next? Poetry?

Emma played well and before long, Frank Churchill joined her to sing a duet. When he escorted her to her seat, Lizzy felt a little discomfort. She was not exactly ashamed of her playing, but in Meryton—with Mary so eager to play—Lizzy never had to.

She thought she was safe when Mr. Churchill's gaze turned to Jane Fairfax, but then Emma leaned over and whisper in Frank Churchill's ear.

A flash of something, maybe annoyance, but then he smiled and came to Lizzy.

"I am instructed by Miss Woodhouse to escort you to the instrument. She says I must not take no for an answer."

Lizzy mentally saluted Emma for this small retaliation, as Emma knew how little Lizzy played. Lizzy only said, "Better ask Miss Fairfax, sir. I am not a performer."

He turned to Mr. Darcy. "Won't you help me, sir? How shall we persuade her?"

"She must do as she likes."

"Well—" This ungallant speech seemed to throw Frank Churchill slightly off. "I suppose I must acquiesce. Miss Fairfax?" He bowed to Jane, who was pressured by the repeated exclamations of her aunt and the goodwill of the party. She had too much good taste to draw it out.

Jane Fairfax, Lizzy found, did not play well. She played magnificently.

Even Mr. Darcy sat up a little straighter.

"I suspected as much," Lizzy whispered. "Emma told me that she was most accomplished, but Miss Bates does not have a pianoforte, so I have not heard Jane play. How lucky that you supported me in declining. Otherwise I should have gone directly before her; the horror! Poor Emma."

Emma looked a little miffed, even as Mr. Knightley leaned over to tell her something.

"Miss Fairfax plays excellently," Darcy agreed.

"In point of fact, she may be the *ideal* woman you once described. She knows languages, art, and music. She has excellent style, and she reads extensively. I told you I had never met such a woman, but I now stand corrected."

Lizzy felt Mr. Darcy's eyes on her profile. "I believe the list was more Miss Bingley's than my own. Nor was it my *ideal* woman, it was merely an accomplished one."

"Is that so different? I am sure an ideal man deserves an ideal woman. Do you not consider yourself ideal?"

"No, far from it." He had taken a more relaxed posture, one foot still crossed over the other and his arm stretched along the back of the settee, nearly to her shoulder.

He seemed to hold his breath for a second. "If I were to make a list, it would include a woman with very beautiful eyes, a lively tongue, and a playful nature, who often supports opinions that aren't truly hers. That is my ideal woman."

Lizzy drew away from him, feeling she had stepped upon ice and found it breaking. "I know you disapprove of me and my family, and that is no matter, for we are not friends. But do have the good breeding not to belittle my intelligence by pretending you feel otherwise."

He colored and straightened. "Excuse me?"

Lizzy faced resolutely forward, though her eyes flashed to his. "False flattery of that sort... For what purpose do you make fun of me? Do you seek to draw me in that you might revel in my naiveté or ill-breeding? Never mind; please do not trouble yourself to answer. Perhaps you are merely intoxicated by too much wine or punch. I don't want to know, but I *do* want to listen."

Mr. Darcy leaned forward, drew back, leaned forward again. He spoke softly. "I do not understand you. I have no desire to make sport of you, and I am certainly not *drunk*."

Lizzy did not answer and when Miss Fairfax pleaded tired fingers, Lizzy seized the moment to join the group around Mr. Woodhouse, who had just realized the dreadful fact that the snow was four inches deep outside.

Mr. Darcy watched her with some attention for the rest of the evening, while carriages were called and people took their leave. Lizzy raised her chin and engaged with others with as little self-consciousness as possible.

When Mr. Darcy took her hand in farewell as she left, looking rather searchingly into her eyes, Lizzy smiled sharply, falsely. "I hope you feel more the thing tomorrow. You are clearly not yourself tonight."

{ 13 }

Mrs. Weston felt herself to be a singularly blessed woman, and she felt every bit of her good fortune during her first holiday party.

When she became, at a young age, the governess to Isabella and Emma Woodhouse, she had already been thankful. They were sweet girls, without a mamma, and with a caring, indulgent, but anxious father. They had needed not just a governess, but a preceptress, a companion, and a mother-figure.

With very little to interfere with their relationship, it was a position to gladden her heart. Mr. Woodhouse came to treat her as a young niece or cousin, and she really believed he would have let her live with them—Emma and himself, that is—until she died. That was a level of security *unheard of* in her profession.

But to add miracle to miracle, she had become acquainted with Mr. Weston—a kind, hard-working, faithful man—who had eventually proposed. She had begun to suspect he might have a preference for her—even a governess is allowed to have a little vanity, a little self-awareness!—but that she should live to be his wife, settled within half a mile of her dear Emma, was a miracle. It was a felicity too incredible to be believed.

Mrs. Weston visited Hartfield the morning following her first real holiday party—to think that she was able to have her own home and servants and parties!—to discuss all the particulars with Emma.

Mr. Woodhouse was keeping his room that day to recover. The snow on the way home had made him quite anxious and his pulse was tumultuous enough to send an urgent call for Mr. Perry, the apothecary.

Emma brought Mrs. Weston not into the formal drawing room, where she usually received guests, but into her own withdrawing room, just off her bedroom. Emma and Mrs. Weston had sat many a cheerful winter morning there in years past.

The walls were decorated with the fruits of Emma's sporadic artistic binges: oil paintings, chalk, chiaroscuro, watercolor, pencil sketches, and more.

Perhaps Mrs. Weston should have been firmer with her, to enable Emma to pursue one vocation long enough for true mastery... but, ah, well. Emma was talented enough to produce, with sporadic effort, what other young ladies would take years to achieve.

If Emma had ever applied to one thing for years, she might have been truly superior, but Mrs. Weston had never been one to fling her hat after the moon. Emma was well enough, brilliant in some ways, and Mrs. Weston never would have been able to channel her energies into one outlet for long.

The sun shone brightly on the snow, which would no doubt melt before evening, but just now made a multicolored sparkle on the windowpanes, almost as a prism.

"Beautiful, my dear Emma," said Mrs. Weston kissing her cheek in greeting. "The morning is beautiful, and you were beyond beautiful last night. I was not the only one who noticed."

She sat across from Emma, who immediately set aside the embroidery frame she'd held on her lap. It held an outline of two symmetrical trees, with a symmetrical bird on each low branch, and a verse in the middle about sparrows.

"Good gracious, Emma. When did you start that? It's lovely and so... worthy."

"Yes, well, I was feeling a great surge of piety last week. I hope the surge shall last a bit longer, for that embroidery is not near finished. But tell me—the party! Did you have a wonderful time inviting people to your own home?"

Emma fished out a box of tiny chocolates that Isabella had brought her as a gift from London. They were bittersweet little tabs, coated in nonpareil sprinkles.

"Oh, Emma! It was beyond anything. Being allowed to order things just as I like, the dinner, the decorations, the arrangements..." she sighed happily, taking one of the chocolates. "Would that I could see you so happy."

Emma laughed. "You already see me so! You know my thoughts. I have all that and more here at Hartfield. What husband could allow me more exactly my own way than my dear father?"

"Yes. I know, my dear, only I cannot help thinking that it is different. It is not just the freedom of arrangements I enjoy. It is the pleasure of pleasing Mr. Weston, of seeing him proud and satisfied. Oh, I cannot describe it."

"Well, you need not. You are in love and many writers have scaled that descriptive precipice before you."

"I hope you will go there someday."

"I do not know. *You* seem to have maintained your elegance and good sense throughout the ordeal of love, but not everyone is so lucky. I do not know that I wish to make a trial of myself by falling in love."

"I hinted at it, but you have not asked me *who* admired you so particularly at the party!"

"Very well, who? I like praise as much as the next young woman, if not rather more."

"Why, Frank, of course! This morning he said, joking with his father, that if he had known there were so many pretty girls here in Highbury he would have come sooner. Miss Bennet, Miss Fairfax, yourself... he praised you all highly. And when we ventured to ask which he found most pleasing, he said, "Oh, your Miss Woodhouse shines them all down. I feel I have known her all my life.""

Emma licked a tiny bit of chocolate off her finger. "I was glad, for your sake, to find him a well-mannered, good-humored young man, and... yes, I also felt that we had been acquainted far longer than one evening. I accept his compliment."

"I cannot tell you how happy we are that he has come. And that you should finally be friends!"

"Yes." Emma still had an idea of pairing Mr. Frank Churchill with Lizzy...if they seemed at all compatible. But there was no denying that this amiable plan of retribution had taken a hit in the face of Mr. Churchill's attentive behavior. The sheer appropriateness of his falling in love with *herself* was hard to argue. She had long felt it so; she felt a proprietary interest in the young man.

Still, she had no *true* desire to avoid becoming an old maid, for unlike Miss Bates or even Lizzy, Emma's singleness would never be rendered hateful by genteel poverty. It would no doubt be better, more magnanimous, to set him aside for Lizzy.

But what if Emma found herself in love with Frank?

Hm. It bore thinking on, though she could not at this moment picture herself deeply in love with him.

"Miss Bennet and Miss Fairfax were also in good spirits," Emma commented, by way of shifting the conversation. "At least,

I *think* Miss Fairfax was in spirits. She said nothing to prove she wasn't, but she is so reserved there is no telling."

"You are too hard on her, Emma. She has not your flow and ease; she is shy."

"Is she, though? I do not think it. She seems perfectly self-possessed, merely she hates to commit herself to a fixed opinion."

Mrs. Weston allowed a small smile to become wider. "Do you know what I was thinking last night? She may be in just the right place and time to find a better fate than that of being a governess. I cannot help but feel for her. *My* situation worked out with utmost joy, but very few do, you know. I would be excessively glad to see such a refined, delicate young woman make a good marriage rather than go into service."

Emma, who had absorbed more than a little of her matchmaking tendencies from Mrs. Weston, leaned forward, offering another chocolate. "Whom were you thinking of? I admit, once or twice I have thought William Cox...?"

"William Cox? No! I mean our dear friend, Mr. Knightley! He sent a carriage for them, and even Jane—yes, I admit she is too reserved for my taste!—mentioned several tokens of friendship he'd sent to them in the past weeks. He returned to her continually during the party and even went into dinner with her. Did you not observe?"

"Of course I did, but please do not attempt to matchmake! Your own happiness has blinded you. He has had an avuncular interest in her these ten years, and of course is a constant, dutiful friend to Miss Bates. It was all kindness; you know his way!"

"I do, and there is much in what you say. I *may* be incorrect, but I am not convinced of it. He is not so very much older than her. More unequal matches—unequal in terms of age—are made every day. In elegance, birth, and personality, they are well-matched. She is reserved; he is judicious."

Emma, who found it easy to give Frank Churchill's potential affections to Lizzy, found it impossible to give Knightley's imagined ones to Jane. "I do not think you can be right. There is an openness, a forthrightness in Mr. Knightley which could not bear to be forever rebuffed. He respects Miss Fairfax, certainly, I have had to hear it since I was twelve, but I do not think it more than that."

"Very well argued, and yet I tell you there was a look on his eyes and physiognomy that spoke of love. A certain angst of cheek and brow. How do we explain that? Perhaps Miss Bennet? He did speak to her on more than one occasion. He told me that she is a well-read girl, with easy habits of conversation. Perhaps she would fit the forthright model you have declared to be his match."

"I did not observe any such angst. Besides, you cannot have thought! My sister's dear little boy will inherit Donwell; would you steal it from him? No, no, Mr. Knightley had better remain a bachelor for the good of all and himself. Perhaps he was a little more frowning and less smiling last night, but I am far from thinking it love. Perhaps he had the toothache."

"Emma."

"Perhaps not. But I am far from thinking that he has any intention of marriage. Why, he is nearly forty, is he not? And has never shown the slightest interest in marriage. Surely if he intended it, he would have done so. No, he is like me. Marriage would not add to his fortune, status, or comfort; he will never marry. Little Henry's inheritance is safe."

"Oh, Emma, do not be selfish. Think how lonely Mr. Knightley would be for his remaining years! How lonely he must already be!

How much happier with Miss Fairfax or Miss Bennet to keep him company of an evening."

"Lonely? When he is forever here with Papa and me? No, you must be content to be married and not marry off everyone else. Now, if you wish to pair someone else with Miss Fairfax to save her from servitude—that quiet Mr. Darcy, for instance—I have no objection."

"I have heard that Mr. Darcy walked you back from the Browns' cottage the other day."

"Highbury gossip!"

"Don't you find him handsome? Quiet, yes, but agreeable. He said everything that was proper to me at the party, which was a particular relief as I was somewhat concerned as to how he might feel. He has no doubt heard, from Mr. Knightley, of my former occupation, and he is Mr. Darcy of Pemberley! It is in the guidebooks! But he was perfectly affable. A little distracted, toward the end of the evening—perhaps with watching you, my dear Emma!—but he still thanked me for the excellence of the dinner."

"I have no objection to Mr. Darcy admiring me—though I am not at all convinced that he does—but I hope he will not think of more. He hails from Derbyshire! Papa could not bear it."

Their comfortable coze continued for some time, but it would be too much to say that Mrs. Weston was argued out of any of her perceptions and speculations, or that Emma's embroidery, and the good intentions behind it, were at all closer to completion.

{ 14 }

THE DAY AFTER THE PARTY, Darcy pulled on his gloves and hat and accompanied Knightley down the cold stone steps to their horses, which had been brought around to the front of the house.

It was a still, frosty day, and the sun shone sporadically down through veils of blanketing clouds but did *not* warm Darcy's back through his brown riding coat. It was a wan, pitiless sky, which could be a punishment for a man who didn't take care.

The snow had not yet melted—most unusual in Surrey—and was some three or four inches deep. Some compacted bits of the path were icy, and the drifts were over a foot. The horses were frisky with the cold, and Darcy and Knightley allowed them to gallop once they reached the meadows that led to the river. Their hoofbeats were slightly muffled by the snow, giving an unusual gentleness to the ride, though neither gentleman was indulging feelings of the gentle sort.

Mr. Darcy looked back upon the Westons' party with great dissatisfaction. Had he been at fault? Had she?

His conversation with Elizabeth, in which she had grossly misunderstood him, had demonstrated that he must have been *long* misunderstood, and that left him strangely uncertain.

On the one hand, he had not meant to speak so freely, to directly tell her that she was the woman he found most perfect and most alluring. A part of him (perhaps a cowardly part) was relieved that she had not taken him seriously; that his rash words had not committed him beyond what he had yet decided to do.

But he also felt rather foolish to have ventured so much when she, apparently, had no idea of it. She thought he had been inebriated!

Mr. Darcy had never played the rake; he had no experience sharing his adoration with a woman. To have his first attempt thrown back at him in such a fashion was a blow.

To be accused of drunkenness!

He wanted to feel perfectly superior to the degradation of her response, to let her harsh words slide off him as he generally did any unworthy criticism.

But he thought too highly of Elizabeth to disregard her.

At the river, Knightley turned to the north, their left-hand side, and led him up it. They stayed well away from the bank, however, for the water was rushing with cold fervor.

Darcy could not stop repeating Elizabeth's phrases to himself. That she "knew he disapproved of her and her family," that he might "make fun of her" or "revel in her naiveté"? She had misunderstood his character, but he could not—now that he came to think of it—decide when she would have formed a *better* opinion.

When he was unhappy and reserved at the Meryton assembly? The few times he spoke to her at Netherfield? Those moments had felt significant to him, already fighting an unwise attraction, but obviously not to her.

Should she have been enamored when he was endeavoring to ignore her mother's gauche behavior at Bingley's ball? (And listening to Caroline's animadversions on her family?) When he had lent himself to Caroline's effort to detach Bingley from Jane Bennet?

It was enough to cause him more than a frisson of self-doubt, *not* a mood he often suffered.

They slowed to enter a set of cultivated fields, shorn for the winter, which Knightley informed him were the outlying fields of Abbey Mill Farm, their destination. The horses' hoofs crunched down in the frozen stubble.

"I hope you enjoyed the party yesterday," Mr. Knightley said. "I have a great respect for Mr. and Mrs. Weston, a truly estimable couple. Her background, as I told you, causes him to worry that she may not be accorded a warm reception by *some,* but she is as well-bred as any lady I know, and far more elegant and agreeable than many."

"Yes, quite," Darcy agreed. "There is much to be said for birth and name, but also for a sound mind and good character."

"I wish Emma understood that. Mr. Martin—he who works Abbey Mill here—is an excellent example. He is a tremendous young man and he offered for her little friend, Harriet Smith! But Emma could not abide her friend marrying a farmer—and that was the end of it."

"Such interference is regrettable, though I cannot help sympathizing to some degree, if she was certain the marriage would be a mistake. I recently dissuaded a young friend of mine from a lady with strong familial objections, and I cannot—No, I cannot think I did wrong."

"Probably not, but I cannot think that your relationship with him can be anything like Emma's with Harriet. Harriet is completely guided by Emma's judgements and whims; she has no reliance on her own faculties or finer feelings."

Mr. Darcy felt a little uncomfortable. "It is hard to know in such a case. When one person's experience is greater, it may be that their wisdom should be used for the benefit of their less-experienced friend."

"Would you act so yourself? No, I cannot think that forfeiting one's future to a friend's ruling is right or safe. Theirs is a most dangerous friendship and so I have told Emma! If Harriet ends a poor, unhappy old maid, Emma will rue the day she overbore her. Their friendship does Emma's vanity no good and Harriet's future even less."

Mr. Darcy couldn't help comparing this to himself and Mr. Bingley. "But do you think those in the throes of calf-love ought to be allowed to go blindly down their path? A friend whose eyes are unclouded can be of great service."

Mr. Knightley shook his head. "But whose eyes are truly unclouded? Can Emma be sure, before taking the heavy responsibility of her friend's fate? But do forgive me, visiting Abbey Mill has brought it all up again. I do not usually air neighborhood squabbles with visitors to the area."

"No, of course."

Mr. Knightley could not listen to Darcy defend Emma's conduct much longer. He skirted the home field and brought Darcy around toward Robert Martin's house, where he lived in great comfort with his mother and two sisters.

Could there be further proof of Darcy's preference and probable intentions toward Emma, than to defend her in this way? Particularly when her behavior was so clearly meddling, conceited, and self-serving? No, Mr. Darcy was determined to think well of Emma, and that was a sure sign of love.

Mr. Knightley himself was always aware of Emma's good points. She was clever, kind, bright, and beautiful, but she was also thoughtless, proud, and, at times, selfish. Even if he wanted to forget her faults and think her perfect, he could not.

Her faults would not bother him so much if he did not *love* her so well—as a sister, of course.

Mr. Knightley abruptly brought the horse to a standstill. "Do you hear that? Either a goat or a woman's cry...?"

The noise sounded again.

He led the way into a small copse of trees, evergreens. They were not far from the house; a good shout would probably raise the inhabitants, but he did not care to do so when it might just be an animal.

"The well is back this way," Mr. Knightley explained as they cut through the trees. "It ought to be closer to the farmhouse but was originally built for the old mill... Miss Martin!"

One of Mr. Martin's sisters, Miss Beth Martin, sat hunched on a stump near the well. She'd probably brushed it off as best she could, but it was clear her dress was wet through where she sat and at her ankles. Her apron was balled in her hands and distressingly muddy as well as a little bloody. It became clear she had been using it to clean and press against her ankle, which she covered with her skirts when they came into view.

"Oh, Mr. Knightley," she said, wiping her face which was wet with a few stray tears and painfully red in the cold. "I am so glad you have come. I was trying to call for my sister or mother, but I do not think they can hear me."

"No, this snow muffles everything." He dismounted at once and tossed his reins to Darcy, who caught them in his left hand. "How badly are you hurt, Beth?"

"Not very much, I hope. The scratch is almost nothing, but I think I must have turnt it badly on that patch of ice. I thought perhaps if I wrapped it tightly... but I could not even hobble inside."

"I shall just carry you back to the house, then. No matter, only it may jar your ankle. Brace yourself."

He scooped her up, which, though he would not own it for the world, was a little taxing. She was a well-grown farm girl, but it was within his powers.

"Oh!" She swallowed an exclamation of pain "Thank you, Mr. Knightley. I am sure Mamma would come searching in a moment, but Robert is out helping Mr. Potts clear a fallen tree from his lane and I do not know how I should get back."

"Just as well I came along, then."

It was only the work of a few minutes to bring Beth back to the house and indeed, her sister was just starting out of the side door with a concerned look on her face when she spotted them coming.

There was exclamation and bustle, but Mrs. Martin was not one to make matters worse by evil anticipations or nervous flutters. She had nursed too many sprained ankles, detached collar bones, and broken arms for her son and her neighbors to be terribly alarmed.

Mr. Knightley placed Beth on Mrs. Martin's bed, as requested—"nearest a fire, where she may rest"—and retired to their front room, which was a combination great room and kitchen.

Mr. Darcy, after he'd looked about and spotted a barn in which to stable the horses, came inside and joined him.

"I am afraid something may have broken after all," Mrs. Martin said, when she returned. "It has that feeling. I shall wrap it up tight and send young Tom for the doctor. Thank you for bringing her back to the house, Mr. Knightley, that was providential. I don't like to think how painful it would have been if we'd had to help her hop in."

Mr. Knightley said everything that was proper, and he and Mr. Darcy accepted a hot cup of tea before they left.

"Now we must ride on," Mr. Knightley said. "I wanted to check on everyone out this way, with this unseasonable cold spell. And if Mr. Potts has a tree down, I'll circle around there next."

"Thank you again, Mr. Knightley."

It was only an incident, and it did not overly exercise Mr. Knightley's mind, except that he made a mental note to ask Mr. Martin if his sister cared to read the newspapers. Mr. Knightley could send his over for several weeks, while the young lady was bedridden. Or perhaps Knightley might ask Emma to loan out some of her own reading material—she was always intending to read great books and instead dabbling in Scottish historicals and poetry.

But of course, Emma was prejudiced against the Martins at present.

And that brought Harriet Smith back to his mind.

Mr. Knightley shared, as men of his temperament often did, an abhorrence for meddling in the affairs of others. He had rather be called any number of names than busybody. However, his conversation with Mr. Darcy—putting aside the unpleasant subtext—gave him to think.

Far be it from him to *matchmake* in the way Emma did, but in this case—when he had already been pulled into the midst of the mess by his close friendship with Robert Martin and with Emma—he could not be accused of that, surely?

He did not deliberate overly long, for once Mr. Knightley made a decision, he acted sooner rather than later.

A note was written upon his return to the house.

Miss Smith,

As I was informed by yourself and Mrs. Goddard of your close relationship with one of my tenant families, and particularly Miss Beth Martin, I take leave to inform you that the young lady suffered a broken ankle and will likely be immobile for some time. As Miss Martin no longer attends the school, and you may not hear of this immediately, I take the liberty of offering first news. I am sure she would be much cheered by a visit from you or Mrs. Goddard, and perhaps—knowing her so well—you might bring a few books which you think she would enjoy.

Yours, etc.

George Knightley

{ 15 }

HARRIET WAS THANKFUL FOR the cozy comfort of her private room at Mrs. Goddard's school, as opposed to the larger dormer rooms the female students shared. Emma had once exclaimed about the smallness of the room, but Harriet did not find it so.

And she was particularly thankful for its warm coziness when she was ill.

Her fireplace was burning, the ashes freshly scraped out. The bed was neatly made up, and her riddle book lay open on the small table beside the fire. The walls were a soft blue, only a trifle water-stained in places, and she had two wall-hangings.

One was a large cloth embroidered by a school friend with a verse: "If your right eye causes you to sin, pluck it out and cast it from you; for it is more profitable for you that one of your members perish, than for your whole body to be cast into hell."

Emma had said it was a somewhat incongruous and morbid verse for the flowers and flourishes which her friend had surrounded it with, but Harriet was uncritical and thought it quite pretty, as well as being far larger a project than she would care to undertake. Harriet, without much in the way of discerning taste, was most impressed by the size of an accomplishment.

The other piece on her wall was valued even more highly—a sketch by Emma of the two of them in a mirror, which Emma had done one rainy afternoon. Emma had declared it to be the roughest thing, unfinished and with all the wrong angles—but Harriet thought it quite amazing, one of the best sketches Emma had ever done.

(In this she was quite right, as Emma's natural eye for detail and symmetry were best suited to sketch work, not the oils, watercolors, and chalks she felt were necessary for a "finished" work.)

Harriet, finally recovering from quite a bad sore throat, had spent many hours lying in her bed gazing at these two pieces.

She had missed the Westons' party, which was sad. She liked Mrs. Weston, and she would have given much to see Emma dressed in her finery. Then there was Miss Bates, always so affable and interested in everyone!

Mr. Knightley she found rather intimidating—to think she should be on nodding terms with the magistrate of Donwell Parish!—but of late he had been quite kind. No doubt that was due to Emma's influence.

Emma's friendship was quite the most amazing thing that had ever happened to Harriet in her life. The teachers at the school told her often how lucky she was. They—and the older students—had always been aware of Miss Woodhouse. Any gossip surrounding her or the other members of Highbury society were avidly discussed at school. But never had any of Mrs. Goddard's students been on terms of intimacy with one so highly placed in their world.

In fact, Emma came that morning to inquire after Harriet's cold and brought one of her own warm shawls to give to her.

"No, do not try to deny me!" Emma said. "For I do not use this shawl any longer. Isabella has just given me a new one she brought down with her from London, and I thought this pink one would suit you perfectly. You are looking better; I am so happy! There is color in your cheeks again."

It was while they were sitting together by the fire, the new pink shawl carefully placed around Harriet's plump shoulders, that Mr. Knightley's note was brought around.

Harriet took it uncertainly from the maid. "A letter for me?"

"From Mr. Knightley?" Emma cried, spying the name. "What on earth can he have to say to you? Do open it!"

The note was read, and Harriet's soft eyes filled with ready tears. "Poor Beth! I am sure my sore throat was most fatiguing, but a broken ankle is far worse. And she does so like to stay busy with her mother, and to visit town of a Tuesday! I must ask Mrs. Goddard when I may visit her; I daresay she will let me use the cart."

Emma's first thoughts were far different. *Well played, Mr. Knightley!* It was done as adeptly as a woman would do it, and she did not give that compliment lightly.

She could not but marvel, for Mr. Knightley rarely pushed in where advice or counsel was not sought. Well, with the exception of herself. He could not seem to forbear correcting *her*.

The letter was so unobjectionable as to *almost* make Emma think that he had done it with no ulterior motives, that he had only thought of Harriet as Miss Martin's close friend. But he was not an idiot; there was no way the rejected proposal could be so quickly forgotten.

No, this was strategy, and Emma thrilled to the challenge.

"Of course you must visit," she said, "but it is barely above freezing today, Harriet! Miss Martin would be horrified if you caused a return of illness by rushing to visit her, when you can do no tangible good by such imprudence."

"No, no, of course you are right. But I must visit her, mustn't I? Despite.... Despite everything that has occurred? She is still my friend. I could take *Romance of the Forest*, for she had not gotten to read it last summer."

Emma was not at all sure of the wisdom of this generosity, but she saw at once that it could not be stopped. "An excellent notion. Oh, and I have one better. You cannot go in the cart to Abbey Mill Farm until the weather warms—I forbid it! But I could take you in our carriage only tomorrow or the next day. Then you should be warm and protected and that will set Miss Martin's mind at ease."

It would also ensure that Emma herself was at hand to observe and gently guide the conversation, should guidance be necessary. Emma had planned in weeks past, if occasion demanded a visit and it probably would, that she would take Harriet and drop her off for a very short visit. No more than a quarter of an hour. That would tactfully let the Martin family know the degree of closeness of future relationships. But now—!

She could not quite depend on Harriet staying so short a time, nor could Emma feel it safe to leave her there alone.

If Mr. Martin were there, Emma hoped that her own presence would effectually put a damper on any recrudescence of affection on either side. It was painful, but it must be done. The friendship between Harriet and this family had sprung up unnaturally, like a cuckoo bird that laid its egg in another's nest. If it was allowed to remain, it should push all the natural eggs and hatchlings to their doom. As one of those others, Emma was determined instead to smother the cuckoo.

Unfortunate, but necessary for Harriet's health and happiness. The alien must be ousted.

"Yes, I will take you tomorrow," Emma reiterated.

"Ah." Harriet did not sound as enthusiastic as Emma expected. "That is most kind of you."

Emma knew when to be straightforward. "You must not be thinking, my dear, that I have any dislike for the Martins! Yes, I agreed with your decision to decline Mr. Martin's proposal of marriage, but that was only as your devoted friend, and in no way a judgement of the Martins' worthiness! I have always heard of them as good, clean, hardworking people, and as I have told you—they are as much above my notice as below it; they do not need my charity."

Emma really believed she was doing her best for her friend, and if she should be crossing swords with Mr. Knightley, that was only a bonus.

"Beth truly was the best of friends when she was here at school," Harriet tried to explain, as she fiddled with the letter from Mr. Knightley. "My summer with them was delightful, completely apart from... Mr. Martin. I hope he will not be at the house."

"I daresay if we went midafternoon, he would be out. What business has a farmer at home during the day? But if he is there, you have no reason to feel badly. He proposed, in a direct, respectful way; you gently declined. There is no blame or censure on either side, and no need to avoid all meetings."

"Yes, I feel sure you are right." Harriet squirmed uncomfortably at the thought. "It is only... There is an awkwardness in the meeting, is there not? I cannot help but feel self-conscious and—and—" *Regretful* was the word she nearly blurted out, but instead colored and put her face in her hands. "I wonder that you can bear with my silliness."

"Not at all, my dear friend. I should like you the less if you had not such tender sensibilities, which indeed, is part of the reason I am convinced you and Mr. Martin would not suit! You, with your gentle nature, fine taste, and elevated susceptibilities, to be a farmer's wife? Well, we need not cover that again. It is no wonder you should feel some reluctance to see him again. In fact, if you should feel unable to make the visit, I would not blame you. You may charge me with your messages and gifts to Miss Martin and I will make your excuses."

But Harriet—while uncertain if she possessed the "fine taste" and "elevated sensibilities" she was supposed to have—did have a lively sense of loyalty. And as she was truly attached to Miss Martin, and felt all the bad luck of her situation, she was determined to renew her friendship as best she could.

"I must go myself. Furthermore," Harriet added timidly, "Mr. Knightley wishes me to do so. He is such a fine landlord; the Martins always said so! He, of course, cannot be expected to know why it is a trifle difficult, but I should not like to ignore what he recommends."

Emma did not quite know how to respond to this. She was not a liar, not even in the service of her charitable aims for her friend, and so she could not agree with this little speech, but nor could she refute it.

"Well, well, the visit shall be made; Mr. Knightley satisfied. I will call for you tomorrow at two. But let me tell you, my dear, of the Westons' party! I have finally met Mr. Churchill and I know you have been as curious about him as I have been!"

{ 16 }

Lizzy looked back on the Westons' party with some tension, but unlike Mr. Darcy or even Emma, she did not have many hours on which to think of it.

Now that Miss Bates and Miss Fairfax were known to be quite well, having gone to the party, it seemed all the town must visit them within the first forty-eight hours. Tripping up the stairs, some came in fine slippers, some in carefully cleaned, worn boots, and some in farmer's brogans which they left at the front door.

Miss Bates was in her element, being overwhelmed by the goodness and graciousness of her friends and neighbors. The tea which had come from Hartfield, rather than being drunk by the ladies of the house, was poured out in copious amounts for her visitors.

The late Mr. Bates, who had been Miss Bates's father, was the much-loved vicar of Highbury for many years. Miss Bates and Miss Fairfax were known to all.

Their position was precisely high and low enough that it seemed everyone in Highbury considered them friends. From shopkeepers and tradespeople to the finest families in the neighborhood—they were accepted and loved.

Lizzy also had Christmas letters from one and all, and spent her extra time replying to each, even Lydia's careless letter which inquired:

How many fine gentlemen do you find in Highbury? Is it quite slow? I saw Wickham and he is still dangling after that nasty Mary King. You say he must have money to live on as well as anybody, but I say it is a great deal too bad he must marry an heiress. However, I suppose if you do not care, I need not either. Oh, you wrote to Mama that that odious Mr. Darcy is there! How unlucky, poor Lizzy! You had better have stayed here to dance with the officers. Our aunt held a small party the day before Christmas Eve, and I danced with every officer present! In fact...

And there was much more in that strain. Lizzy could only assume there had been a spell of terrible weather in Hertfordshire to cause Lydia to sit down and write such a long letter.

Although Lizzy did not dwell overly on Mr. Darcy's strange behavior at the party, she was too female not to give it some thought. There was something bewitching in the idea of attaching a proud man like Mr. Darcy without effort, without intention. But that emotion was gratifying to her vanity, not her heart. She was persuaded that it was very bad for her. It puffed up without any concurrent feeling of love or affection to temper it.

She had gained the (possible) ardor of a man she despised; she ought not to feel anything positive. She knew him to proud and arrogant; if he found her appealing, it should only cause her regret!

She was certainly in no frame of mind to meet with him as she took an afternoon walk several days after the party, but, unfortunately, she did. The cold weather had eased the day before, with the temperatures soaring up until the snow melted and everything turned to drip and sludge.

Lizzy left the main street at Ford's store, turning to her righthand down Randall's Road, a three-quarter mile curve that ran north past the Weston's home.

A gust of wind whipped her skirts about her ankles and legs such that she was momentarily worried about modesty, but thankfully the road turned off at right angles, and although the wind blew, she was not heading into it after a few moments.

The mud was not too much of a problem, for the road was less traveled and not very rutted at all; Lizzy had a good surface to walk on. The cold, crisp air had nearly a smell today—snow on high hills, leaves crumbled to powder, the woodsmoke of many a fireplace.

She passed Randalls, where the strange party had occurred. Three thin columns of smoke showed that several of their fires were burning behind the cheerful, shining windowpanes. The central lawn, which had looked so smooth under the snow and moonlight, was now a brown, leaf-strewn affair.

Soon after Randalls, and its attendant gardens and shrubbery, the lane ended. It poured out onto the Donwell road, which she saw was churned up and quaggy with mud. Lizzy had planned to turn to her left here and towards Mrs. Goddard's school, thinking to visit Harriet and see how she did after her cold.

Lizzy had thought her half-boots would be up to the job since the school was only about a hundred yards down the road, but now she thought not.

The road was very bad, and if her skirt ended six-inches deep in mud, Miss Bates's poor girl-of-all-work, Patty, would be hours getting it clean. Lizzy was still pondering when Mr. Darcy came into sight, from the direction of Donwell Abbey.

He wore his usual trim country gentleman's clothes, and the only nod to the weather were his brogans, the thick, heavy boots often worn by farmers. Lizzy was surprise he even owned them, though perhaps he had borrowed them from Mr. Knightley.

"Hello, Miss Bennet," he said, putting a hand to his hat to keep it from flying off in another burst of wind. "How do you do?"

"Fine, thank you."

"I wouldn't recommend this road. Nearly a foot deep in places."

"Yes. I was just coming to that conclusion; I really must turn back."

"Allow me to accompany you." He turned onto the Randall's Road, easily catching up to her.

The wind blew again, swirling late leaves, dull orange and brown, down from a nearby copse of ash trees. She pulled her skirt firmly around her ankles lest it get ideas.

"There is no need to accompany me," Lizzy protested.

"In fact, there is a need," said Darcy. "I offended you at the Westons' party."

"You would offend me still more by canvassing it again. Let us both forget all that was unpleasant in the evening and remember only the parts we choose."

"An amiable plan, but I feel there has been a misunderstanding that I cannot allow to stand. I do not *dis*approve of you; quite the contrary. I wonder why you have thought so. May I not ask for an explanation?"

Lizzy laughed with discomfort and disbelief. "Why should you need one? You have looked at me with nothing but contempt since our first meeting. At the Meryton assembly you *met my eye* and declared I was tolerable but not good enough to dance with. No, please do not break in. Since then, you have shown disdain for my mother and my sisters. At Netherfield, you seemed to stare at me only to find fault. You looked, frowned, and turned away. How else am I to categorize such a uniformity of behavior?"

There was the slightest hesitation in Mr. Darcy's steady gait; he became even more stiff. "I must apologize strongly for that first slight. It was meant as a punishment to Mr. Bingley for plaguing me to dance, but it was badly done. For some time, I have considered you quite the handsomest woman of my acquaintance. In the intervening weeks, I— I hesitated to speak, for I believe it to be the blackest of acts to raise expectations where none are intended. However, I realize my looks; my silence; and my demeanor would be opaque to one not familiar with me."

Lizzy felt warmth come into her face and could only hope the exercise on a windy day would excuse it; she was not blushing with delight. "I suppose I ought to thank you for clearing up this misunderstanding, but it is irrelevant. You may think well of me, but I cannot return the compliment. As such, it is probably best we avoid solo conversations such as this." Lizzy sidestepped a small patch of ice still lingering in the shade of a tree and took the moment to detach her arm from his.

"But I—forgive me—I cannot leave it at that. I acknowledge my manners have been at fault, but I'm sure you will be able to forgive when you understand the circumstances. I—for weeks now—have wished to ask for your hand in marriage. I have deliberated quite painfully and at length, even more so since we have been here in Highbury. Your misunderstanding of my intentions is all the more understandable."

He came to a stop, framed by the sturdy elegance of Randalls in the distance, the wind blowing a hint of the smoke from their three chimneys past them. "I can no longer fight my inclination. It is absurd, the idea of a union between you and I, you need not tell me. But you... your beauty and liveliness and intelligence have long bewitched me."

He was clearly excited; his face was more agitated than she had ever seen. She felt again that surge of pleasurable vanity at having attached such a man, but it was far tempered by a desire to stop him. He clearly thought only a mistake of manners lay between them, but it was far worse than that.

He took one of her hands. "You must allow me to explain how I ardently I admire and love you."

"You must stop at once," Lizzy said.

She could never say yes—

No, that was untrue. She *could* say yes, but she never *would*, not to this man. And the further he spoke his heart, or whatever passed for his heart, the more humiliated he would be when she refused.

"You have apologized for your manners," Lizzy said, "and that I will endeavor to forgive. My own manners are not so perfect that I can hold a grudge over such a thing—"

"I knew you would not. And I will prove to you in the future that I do love—"

"Please allow me to finish! There is far worse between us than a misunderstanding, and you must be at least partially aware of that. You persuaded Mr. Bingley to leave my dear sister Jane after her hopes were raised... after her heart was *fully* engaged! She may never truly recover from it. I had hoped in London..." All Lizzy's frustrations at this fruitless visit to Highbury and her sister's deep disappointment surged up. To her embarrassment, she felt tears in her throat.

Ruthlessly clearing it, she went on, "And furthermore, less personal to myself, but far more reprehensible, Mr. Wickham shared with us his many trials. Perhaps you were not aware that he had done so, but there can be no excuse for your actions toward that gentleman. It is these things, which speak of character far more than manners, which form the basis of my refusal. I explain only so that there may be no misapprehension and to spare you the mortification of further speech."

Mr. Darcy was so startled as to step back—he had unconsciously come as close as he dared—and his foot landed directly on the strip of ice Lizzy had earlier avoided. His foot slid out and though he did not fall, he stumbled back several steps to regain his balance. His face was red with anger or embarrassment. Perhaps both.

"Mr. Wickham's powers of deceit are great, but surely you—whom I have thought so perceptive—could see him for what he was?"

"A good, kind, much-afflicted young man?"

"Good and kind?" He slashed a hand through the air. "What mark of goodness did he ever display to you? He could not have done so, because he is not. He simpers and smirks and makes himself agreeable, but he has not even a passing acquaintance with honesty. I—I cannot discuss him calmly at this moment. As for Bingley, his situation is more precarious than mine—it would be the height of foolishness to marry for a pretty face when there were such objections as family, connections, and fortune. I highly esteem you, but your family... you cannot think that your mother's comportment, or that of your sister, is right. Even your father at times betrays a reprehensible indifference. I was acting as Bingley's friend."

"I doubt my family would have offended you if their manners were hidden by finer clothes. And you just said that you find it the *blackest of acts* to raise a woman's hopes with no intention to fulfill them—do you feel Mr. Bingley is excused because he did not mean to dash her hopes, but only did it out of carelessness? You are quite a friend. I wonder you do not address Miss Woodhouse! She has a very similar idea of friendship, and woe to any friends of yours, who put their happiness in your hands."

Darcy shook his head, muttering, "This has now become a farce."

A third voice took them both by complete surprise.

"Miss Bennet, Mr. Darcy!" called Mrs. Weston, who had come out into the garden in front of her home, Randalls. She came toward them quickly, though picking her way carefully around soggy drifts of leaves. "Excuse me. I saw you from the window, and I daresay you are heading to town. Miss Bennet, may I charge you with a message?"

Lizzy had whipped around at her greeting; Darcy passed a hand over his forehead.

"Yes... yes, of course," Lizzy managed.

"I must go. Do excuse me, Mrs. Weston, Miss Elizabeth." Darcy executed a jerky bow and turned back up the lane toward the Donwell Road.

Lizzy let out a shuddering breath that was all too close to becoming a sob. "A message, Mrs. Weston? For Miss Bates? I am at your service."

"I only wished to tell Miss Fairfax how much I enjoyed her playing at our party, and to offer that if she, or yourself, would ever like to come play of a morning or afternoon, I would be delighted. We live so near you, and I know the doctor has told Miss Fairfax to walk more. I thought this might be a good destination for her, with the indulgence of music in the middle. Frank also loves music and said I ought to invite you both!"

Her words gave Lizzy time to recover herself and she answered with suitable composure. "Yes, an excellent idea. Jane told her aunt that your instrument is so fine, it was a pleasure to play."

"Wonderful." Mrs. Weston cocked her head. "I don't wish to keep you outdoors in all this wind, but please know that you are as welcome as Miss Fairfax."

She was no doubt rampantly curious about what they had been discussing, particularly if she had heard them nearly shouting at one another. From her expression, Lizzy suspected she'd heard something, perhaps she'd even heard the name *Miss Woodhouse,* which would of course pique her interest.

"Thank you. You are very kind." Lizzy felt that some sort of explanation was due Mrs. Weston for the scene she had interrupted. "I was on my way to visit Harriet, but the mud turned me away. Mr. Darcy was just passing by."

Mrs. Weston again showed her saintly nature in not questioning this. "Oh, you would have missed Harriet anyway. Emma is taking her to visit a friend today."

"Ah, I see. Thank you again then, Mrs. Weston. I will pass on your message to Miss Fairfax."

Lizzy went on, somewhat calmed by the interlude, but soon returning to the anger, dismay, and confusion of her conversation with Mr. Darcy. She was forced to blink heavily once or twice, as angry tears resurfaced. She could blame it on the wind.

Despite desperately wanting privacy, Lizzy dutifully scraped her half-boots before going inside, and even took them off before going upstairs.

Lizzy had never thought of Longbourn as being overrun with servants, but there was no doubt that living with Miss Bates had given her a new appreciation for them. Here, if she left smears of mud or dried dirt on the stairway, there they would remain until

Patty could get to it. *Never* would Miss Bates ask Lizzy to clean, or reproach her for the accident, but she would artlessly comment on the muddiness of the day, apologize for the inconvenience of their rooms, and thank Lizzy again for coming. It was too much to be borne and Lizzy took care not to cause it.

Upstairs, she pled a headache to Miss Fairfax and Miss Bates and cast herself on her bed for a needed cry.

{ 17 }

AROUND THE SAME TIME LIZZY was arguing with Mr. Darcy, Emma called for Harriet, who waited just outside the school with a neat little package of books tied with brown string.

"It is too windy to be standing about," scolded Emma. She took the books as Harriet clasped her bonnet with one hand and took the footman's hand with the other to mount into the carriage.

When Harriet was safely in and the carriage jolted into motion again, Harriet at once began to thank Emma for making the visit possible and for accompanying her. "I know very well you could have sent the carriage for me and *not* come—I would not blame you, for Miss Martin is not your particular friend, as she is mine!—but your generosity in supporting me is beyond anything."

Emma colored a little guiltily at this. Mr. Knightley was sometimes severe with her, but he would be surprised to know how frankly she owned (to herself) that he was (sometimes) correct. He often said, for example, that Emma was lucky everyone already thought so well of her, for they would always take her acts—good, bad, or indifferent—and make them "evidences" of her many perfections.

"If you do not take care, you may start believing them, and then you will be beyond help," he once told her.

He was far from correct in this—Emma was quite aware when she was being painted as more saintly, generous, and selfless than she was. (It was not *quite* as often as Mr. Knightley thought.)

In this case, she had no intention of allowing Harriet to get sucked into the Martin family's orbit once again; she went with the sole purpose of preventing it. This was for Harriet's good, but Harriet's naïve thanks caused a bit of inward cringing.

Harriet added, "I am sure I would have been too frightened to make the trip on my own!"

Emma doubted this was true. Harriet was indeed a good and loyal friend. The power of Mr. Knightley's message, working on a kind heart, was not to be underestimated.

"You would," Emma told her, "for you are too good to allow fear to keep you from doing what you ought. Any lady must be able to overcome mere sentiment, or awkwardness, or what have you, in order to do what is proper. I am proud of you."

"Thank you! Oh, there is Mr. Darcy walking up the road. Should we offer to give him a ride to Donwell Abbey? The road is in horrid condition."

Emma knocked on the top of the carriage and her driver slowed and stopped next to the gentleman. Emma opened the door and leaned out a trifle. "Mr. Darcy, my friend and I are going to Abbey Mill Farm and will pass by Donwell. Can we offer you a ride?"

He doffed his hat. "No, I prefer to walk."

Emma would perhaps have persisted, but she thought it best not to get sidetracked today. She did not want them to arrive late enough that Mr. Martin returned to the house for his dinner while they were still there. Some of the farm families ate as early as four in the afternoon. "Enjoy your exercise then, Mr. Darcy!"

She looked back at him for a moment as they drove on. "He looks unhappy, but he is difficult to read. He has generally that stoicism which one admires in a soldier or general, but it is not quite inviting in company. I prefer to know what a man is thinking."

"Oh, I agree," said Harriet. "I am sure he is a most intimidating man. I do not know what to say to him!"

"I do not find him intimidating, per se, only solemn."

"That is true, but you are *Miss Woodhouse*! Whereas I can count on one hand the number of gentlemen I *am* comfortable with." Harriet began to count on her fingers. "There is your papa; he is so kind! Then Mr. Knightley, though I only venture to say so because I know he is a friend of yours *and* of the Martins; he has so little height to his manners."

"Yes, Mr. Knightley is exactly what a gentleman ought to be. He has not height, but an easy, unaffected manner, for he knows exactly who he is and what is due him." Emma smiled. "Beyond my father and Mr. Knightley, what other gentlemen make your list?" She thought perhaps this would be a sound tactical distraction on the way to the farm. Best to have Harriet's thoughts full of other gentlemen when she saw her friends again. Emma was also curious who might be on her list. William Cox *would* return to mind, and though Emma did not particularly care for him, if Harriet's fancy had alighted...!

But she was immediately disappointed.

"Oh... I don't know. Mr. Darcy is so tall and stern! Mr. Churchill is so witty and quick; I feel he is laughing at me. Mr. Martin—" she broke off. "Then there is kind Mr. Weston. I suppose he makes three gentlemen."

Emma sighed. At least she was spared mention of Mr. Elton, though it was lowering to think that Harriet avoided his name for *Emma's* sake.

Beth Martin was all too aware of her brother's reversals in love. Theirs was a close family, and her brother—although he had not allowed her to *read* the letter he'd written to Harriet—had smiled and given her a quick kiss on the cheek when she asked whether he was writing to her.

He'd first asked advice from Mr. Knightley and come back so cheerful as never was. Then he'd ridden off whistling to deliver the letter to Harriet's school, not trusting young Tom with something so vital. He'd lived in an active, happy dream for the rest of the day. He did not say it aloud, but Beth and her mother and sister could practically hear him making plans for when Harriet should come to them. He eyed the first bedroom, and they saw him measuring it for a new bed. He sat on the stool by the door and noted that it was uneven and rocked alarmingly—one could just picture Harriet over balancing. He thought perhaps they should have new curtains before next spring.

This pleasantness was dashed the following day with Harriet's letter. He did not say anything. He merely read it; folded it; put on his coat and grabbed his hat.

"Why, Robert," their mother had said. "Did you get a response? It is nearly dinner, do you go out now?"

"No, I mean... yes, I must go out to the south field. Don't wait dinner for me."

Robert was not demonstrative, but he felt deeply, and it was some days before he could say that Harriet found she could not marry him.

Robert was resigned; Beth seethed.

She felt some reproach was due to Harriet, but most of the fault must lie with Miss Woodhouse. Thus, Beth was in no very amiable mood when Harriet arrived with Miss Woodhouse, the latter shedding smiles and elegance in a nearly visible aura that surrounded them both.

Mr. Martin, on the other hand, was so happy to see Harriet when she alighted from the Woodhouse carriage, that he quite forgot, for a moment, all that had passed.

In January there was not so much for a farmer to do. He wasn't thrilled about the snow for his winter crops, but he had moderate hopes that they would still germinate, so he wasn't cast down. After caring for his animals, he was free to be about the house more than normal. He had kept Beth company for an hour, playing backgammon on a board that belonged to his father. Then he had fixed that stupid stool that never wanted to sit right, as well as oiling the hinges on the doors, which his mother said were getting stiff.

When he heard the carriage arrive, he went out, wondering if Mr. Knightley had come back. Instead, it was the Woodhouse carriage, and when the footman opened the door, it was Harriet who descended first.

She was so pretty, so sweet, so trusting! He went to her at once and put out his hand. "This is like you to come, Miss Smith. Beth will be ever so happy to see you. Thank you for coming."

Her little hand quivered in his for a moment before it was withdrawn. "Oh, yes. I—I also brought some books for her." She turned in confusion back to the carriage, but Miss Woodhouse was already descending with the package.

"Yes, here they are. How do you do, Mr. Martin?"

He bowed. "Very well, Miss Woodhouse. Honored to have you visit us."

She inclined her head.

He escorted them inside and Harriet introduced Miss Woodhouse to his mother, but his quick joy had dimmed. His mother served the visitors some of her delicious, sweet rosemary cake, which they took in to eat with Beth, where she reclined on his mother's bed, propped up with pillows.

Robert took himself off.

He had been severely disappointed that Harriet declined his proposal. There had been embarrassment and regret—he loved her so well, he had thought she cared for him also!—but a large part of his distress was for her. What sort of scrape might she get into if she got among the wrong set? Miss Woodhouse was unimpeachable, but would their closeness continue indefinitely?

There could be no denying that Harriet was sweet and good, but she was also persuadable. He had thought almost as much of giving her a mother—in the person of his dear mother—as he had of becoming her husband. She needed both. She needed a *family*, and his was—in his admittedly prejudiced opinion—one of the best.

Of course, he also thought her beautiful—far too beautiful for him, if she had not also been so warm and encouraging! Seeing her did not help any of it.

Mr. Martin took a long, hard walk, determined not to return before they left.

Harriet chatted with Beth and Miss Woodhouse and hoped that her cheeks were not flaming with color as she felt they must be. The cake was moist and delicious, but she choked on it not once but twice. Her throat could not coordinate with her mouth.

His voice! His hands! His kind face!

Harriet was very much afraid that she was a silly girl. A silly, underbred, ungrateful girl—for who else would even consider ignoring Miss Woodhouse's advice and settling her life with such a one as Mr. Martin?

He was not a gentleman like Mr. Knightley, it was true, but he was... was so appealing! Harriet felt a tingling in her stomach and forced herself to attend to what Mrs. Martin was saying about the new soap she'd purchased.

Beth seemed colder and quieter. Even Mrs. Martin was stiffer than she had ever been. Harriet had never run out of things to talk about with Beth, or with Miss Woodhouse, but with the two of them together, she was at a loss.

It was Emma and Mrs. Martin who kept the conversation going.

When another lull came, Beth said a little more warmly, "Thank you for coming, Harriet. We had such fun with you this summer, it quite brings back old times."

"Yes. For me also."

Mrs. Martin tilted her head. "I do think you have grown taller, Harriet."

Harriet swallowed another bite of cake, brushing a crumb off her pelisse. "Oh yes! I nearly forgot how Mr. Martin measured us all on the window frame. I daresay I have gained half an inch, though I am still so short."

Emma looked vaguely toward the window. "How delightful. I am so glad Harriet was able to come today, as Mr. Knightley desired her to do."

This caused a query and explanation of Mr. Knightley's note. Mrs. Martin could not praise him enough for another mark of thoughtfulness, but Beth looked carefully at Harriet.

"Would you not have come otherwise?" she asked. "Since Robert is out, I will just speak freely enough to say that we are always happy to have you. In fact, I hope you will come again this summer. I know Mamma would want you as well."

"Of course I would," that lady responded instantly. "Whatever has passed is past, and I should be delighted to have you. Mrs. Goddard said that you had never looked so well as you did after a June and July with us, and if you do not take it amiss, Harriet, you look none too strong! You must come again."

"Your—Your kindness is overwhelming. I do not know—"

"I'm afraid I have to claim Harriet this summer!" Emma cried. "I have always longed to take my father to the seaside, and I simply could not part with her for such an adventure."

Mrs. Martin was too refined to cavil at this, though Mr. Woodhouse was known never to leave Hartfield, but Beth was made of sterner stuff. "Then in the fall, or better yet, spring! You have not seen the lambs with their ewes and the ducklings and goslings... you would be delighted, Harriet. Surely Miss Woodhouse cannot need you forever."

"Oh, I do not know—that does sound delightful." Harriet looked pleadingly at Emma.

Emma's fine mouth was a trifle thin. "You must do just as you like, my dear."

"Well, I would never want to leave you if you wanted me, but perhaps—" Harriet's eyes were becoming shiny with tears.

Emma, realizing the very real distress she was causing her friend by making her deny them to their faces, relented slightly. "I'm sure you can find time to visit your friends. It needn't be decided today."

"True. You are all too kind. I never expected to have so many good friends."

"Oh," Beth exclaimed, in a near-genuine approximation of sudden remembrance, "Robert procured *Romance of the Forest*, on your recommendation. He has been reading it to me, and we both are enjoying it prodigiously."

"Oh—yes?" said poor Harriet. "That is excellent."

"Yes. The descriptions are divine and the hero so noble! And quite moral as well. If only Robert had not gone out, I could have had him read the next chapter and see if you remember how it goes. He does not often go out at this time."

Mrs. Martin shook her head. "Sometimes he does; he always works hard."

Beth lowered her voice. "I daresay Miss Woodhouse is acquainted with the circumstances, so I do not scruple to say that Robert took it very hard."

"Beth!" gasped her mother.

"I do not think," said Miss Woodhouse, "that much good can be done by retreading the past."

Beth moved restlessly in the bed. "No, of course not, I beg your pardon. But that is all the more reason to visit and put this all behind. Besides, Robert is busiest in spring."

"May I slice more cake?" Mrs. Martin said. "You do look so pale, Harriet."

"She has been quite ill, and on that score, I think we must be going," Emma said. "My father does not like us to be out after dark and these winter days are so short! Thank you for your hospitality."

"Oh, I would never inconvenience Mr. Woodhouse." Harriet rose at once. "It was wonderful to see you, Beth, and I hope your ankle will be healed in a trice!"

"Thank you, Harriet. You must come again when it is not so cold; and for a proper visit in the spring."

Back in the carriage, Emma went limp momentarily against the squabs, leaning her head straight back, before squaring her shoulders and giving a little shudder.

"That was far worse than I dreamed. Pretty well for a twenty-minute visit! How dare Beth Martin speak to you of her brother's feelings. It was unfair to *him*, and monstrously unfair to *you*. I know she is your friend, but I am quite at a loss. What an awkward conversation. And the way she pressed you to visit! You could not in civility refuse, with the way she went on and on. There are ways, Harriet, as every lady learns, to politely extricate oneself from obligations of that sort. You may be her friend without committing to a long visit; when the time comes, I will help you get out of it."

Harriet pleated her shawl between her fingers and flicked off another stray crumb of cake which clung to the fringe. "May I not visit, then? I mean, *ought* I not to visit? It sounds childish, but I *do* so enjoy the animals. But I must be guided entirely by you, for I am so ignorant. Would it be improper to visit, considering I declined Mr. Martin's offer? Do be honest; must I be estranged from them?"

"My dear Harriet, do you so earnestly long to stay with them? From Miss Martin's manners, I must confess myself shocked at your intimacy. She is a stranger to the finer feelings and sensibilities that define you."

"Oh no!" Harriet paled as violently as if Emma had insulted her instead. "Miss Martin is not so. I do not know why she was rather different today. I daresay the pain from her ankle—and then she *is* so attached to her brother. I must excuse her. I assure you she is ever so friendly and kind!"

"Friendly and kind, I grant her. A lady, no."

"Mr. Martin must have been *very* upset for her to tell me of it. Do you think—Do you think he suffered for long? Oh, I hate to think of causing him a moment's pain. Do you know, he only lost his father two years ago? Beth says they were so attached. It makes me quite miserable to think of hurting him."

Emma wished with all her might that there was some *other* gentleman for her to turn Harriet's mind to! It was one thing to counter fire with fire, but Emma had no one in her arsenal. It made things a trifle difficult.

"I do not know if he suffered, but he did not seem at all put out to see you today, which speaks of perfect tranquility. You, and I must say he, acted exactly as you ought."

"Yes, I had not thought... But you are exactly right. He was so affable. Therefore—I am sorry to return to this, but I do need your advice!—would it be acceptable to visit them? If he is perfectly recovered?"

Emma clasped Harriet's hands. "There are two dangers in the event. One is that he will once more fancy himself in love with you. The other is that you will fancy yourself in love with him. Do you absolutely think that your heart is under such control, your mind so indifferent, your affections so tranquil, that you can see him daily, in his own home, without succumbing? I say this without the slightest hint of judgement, but only as your dear and loving friend. If you feel yourself out of all danger, by all means, visit! But, if you feel, as I'm sure any female might, that the combined flattery of his sisters, his mother, and himself, might compromise your heart and good sense, you ought not."

It was a good shot, but Emma erred in one point, and like a chink in the armor, Harriet clung to it. "But he does not flatter me, Miss Woodhouse, I should hate for you to think so. None of them do, and Mr. Martin is not at all given to pretty speeches like Mr. Elton."

"You may not have realized—"

"But I should! Such things always put me to the blush. I dislike it above everything, and I'm sure Mr. Martin never did so."

Emma sat back. One could not keep earnestly clutching a friend's hands forever; it was a time-limited maneuver. "Very well, Harriet. You must do as you think best."

"Oh, I did not mean to be ungrateful for your advice! You are perfectly right, I am sure. There is such good sense in what you say; good sense and truth. I will seriously consider what you have said, and I will not make any rash promises to Beth if I think myself in danger. You are so wise, Miss Woodhouse! What would I do without you?"

You would marry Mr. Martin, Emma thought dryly. And you may yet, for I have been thoroughly rolled up!

{ 18 }

WHEN MR. KNIGHTLEY NEXT WALKED over to Hartfield to visit Emma and Mr. Woodhouse, he was not in a position to know whether his letter to Harriet had born fruit.

Emma did not leave him in suspense, though she already had a visitor in Mrs. Weston, who sat with her in the drawing room, on the point of taking tea.

"How dare you send Harriet to visit the Martins?" Emma poured him a cup of tea also, and though it steamed, it looked no hotter than the gleam in her blue eyes. "They all but browbeat her into visiting again this summer, and if she does, Beth Martin will have Harriet recanting her refusal before a week is done."

Though she was angry, Emma's hands never wavered as she gracefully added the cream he liked in his tea and handed him the saucer and cup. "Well, sir?"

She only spoke like this because her father was absent, otherwise she would be more elliptical. He preferred the straight-forward attack.

"Well, nothing, Emma. You have always known my views on the matter. Good day, Mrs. Weston."

"Good day, Mr. Knightley."

"I trust you already know the particulars," he said, "otherwise Emma would not scold me so freely."

"No more freely than you generally scold me," Emma cut in. "You! Who have so often preached to me of minding my own business."

He sipped his tea and set it on the gold and green lacquered side table. "I admit, I feel invested in the matter, on behalf of Robert Martin. And since I hold to my belief that Harriet Smith could do no better, my other opinions are unchanged. Unless," he looked speculatively at Emma, "you dream of someone else in particular for her. Who is the man? Perhaps my friend Darcy?"

Emma scoffed. "*That* is ridiculous, and not because of Harriet's situation, but because of her personality. Mr. Darcy likes to be challenged, and Harriet abhors conflict. No, she would make almost any gentleman an excellent wife, but Mr. Darcy is something out of the usual way."

Emma was thinking more of Harriet, and wondering whether, after all, Mr. Frank Churchill would do for her. If only there were two such gentleman!

But Mr. Knightley heard only an unusual compliment for Mr. Darcy and surprised himself with a burst of annoyance with Emma. He spoke with unwonted harshness. "I wonder you do not leave that girl alone. Matchmake for Miss Bennet if you must—she will land on her feet regardless—but leave off Harriet."

Mrs. Weston and Emma's eyes both flew to him in surprise.

"Excuse my tone; I suppose I am a little out of sorts this morning." He took up his cup again.

Emma took her own. "Well, as before, we must agree to disagree, but I will not poke you about it. I know—more than most—that an elderly gentleman's moods can be testy and must be indulged."

She said this with a smile, and Mr. Knightley knew she was only teasing him, but he struggled to respond with lightness.

Mrs. Weston shook her head. "My dear, Mr. Knightley is in the prime of life, as you well know."

"It is fine," Knightley said. "I suppose thirty-seven does seem infirm to twenty. But take care what you say before Mrs. Weston, Emma, we are much of an age and it will not do to be insulting your friend."

Mrs. Weston laughed. "For me, this decade has been a surprise of delights, so I am immune. A good marriage is of all things the preserver of happiness. I do wish everyone could be as happily settled as I am. Even you, Emma."

Mr. Knightley returned his empty cup to the tray, getting to his feet. "No, Emma swears she is happier by far as a free daughter than an entrammeled wife. How often have we heard her say so?"

"As to that," Emma replied saucily, "there's no saying."

Mrs. Weston gave Mr. Knightley an expressive glance. "Indeed. I have wondered if our many visitors to Highbury this winter might change Emma's mind on that score. Perhaps your own as well."

"I cannot pretend to know either of your minds, and as I must continue about my duties, I'll instead bid you both a good day."

He went down to the hall, where the Hartfield butler helped him into his great coat and handed him his hat and umbrella. "Thank you, Mr. Benton."

The butler opened the door for Mr. Knightley, but both were surprised to see Frank Churchill in the act of raising his hand to the knocker.

"Oh, there's a trick," Churchill said, "opening the door before I've knocked. Capital service." He came in and put his hat and cane on the table, removing his gloves one at a time. "I hear my mother is here, Benton, and I've come to join her."

His entire lack of formality spoke of great familiarity with the place.

"How do you do, Knightley?" Churchill went on. "Just on your way? Sorry to miss you. No need to announce me, Benton, I know my way."

"Yes, sir."

Mr. Churchill ran lightly up the stairs and Mr. Knightley went on *his* way somewhat grimly. He could not misunderstand Mrs. Weston's arch attitude with Emma, though whether she was referring to Mr. Churchill or Mr. Darcy, he wasn't certain.

Either way, Emma would probably marry in the next year or two, which is what anyone who loved her would want. Mr. Darcy had ridden off to London rather suddenly this morning, but he promised to be back in a night or two. What errand had he in London? Was it related to Emma?

She might now, at twenty, think life as mistress of Hartfield was the best life had to offer, but she had never been to London. She had never been to the seaside. She had never seen the Lake District or the white Dover cliffs, let alone the beauties of Paris or Madrid. There were a thousand and one things she might do and see in her life, and as Mrs. Weston said, a good marriage was a great preserver of happiness.

If not one of those two gentlemen, it would eventually be another. He *did* want more for Emma; he must promptly reconcile himself to the idea.

Mr. Knightley went round to call on Miss Bates, unsuccessfully attempting to put all things Hartfield out of his mind.

He was received by Miss Bates, Miss Fairfax, and Miss Bennet.

Miss Bates thanked him profusely for the apples and wood he had lately given them. "We are provided with such kind friends! I do not know anybody in my situation more comfortable! I am so thankful!"

He spotted a look on Miss Lizzy Bennet's face that showed her views were rather different, but Miss Bates continued. "And we have had such a round of visitors this week! I told Jane and Lizzy; have you ever seen so many visitors in three days? It is quite something! Only this morning we had Mr. Perry—though of course he came around for poor Jane's sake—and then Mr. Cox and his wife, then Mr. Churchill—and now yourself. How we are blessed."

"Yes, I just saw Churchill at Hartfield," Knightley commented. "He is making the rounds, I see. I wonder how long he will stay before his aunt requires his presence in London."

"He did not say anything about leaving today," Miss Fairfax said in her sedate voice. "But I suppose one never knows."

"I do not think him at all likely to leave until he wishes it," Miss Bennet said. "And he does not wish it at present. He seems to be mightily pleased with all of Highbury, judging by his glowing comments on all he has met."

"A most cheerful young man," Miss Bates agreed. "I have never seen such a cheerful young man. And so handsome! I am so happy for Mr. and Mrs. Weston to have such a charming son."

"It was good of him to finally visit," Mr. Knightley allowed. "Miss Fairfax, are you acquainted with him? I believe he mentioned living in Weymouth, and I know the Campbells were fixed there for some time."

"I—Yes, we are somewhat acquainted."

"Then you have the advantage of knowing him away from his family. What do you make of him?"

"He is... much as he is here. That is, generally pleasing and being pleased."

"Ah."

Lizzy shifted impatiently, tucking her feet under the chair. Jane Fairfax, Lizzy was coming to believe, truly was as placid and serene as she appeared. It should not continue to bother her—Jane was entitled to her own temperament, given by God and nature! Jane Fairfax was, in some ways, not unlike her own sister Jane—but so reserved! Perhaps it was the reserve which annoyed Lizzy. It spoke of a deeper understanding, of deeper thoughts, and yet Jane gave never a hint of her true feelings or thoughts. Her comments could have been made by any woman.

Mr. Knightley did not stay long, and Jane became absorbed with a book. Lizzy tried to do so also. She had begun reading a new chapter that morning, but the many interruptions of visitors had left her disinclined to continue.

Lizzy went to the bedroom, the one she shared with Jane Fairfax, and set to writing a letter to her family. She did not immediately see the ink bottle, however. She remembered that Miss Fairfax had bought more ink from the itinerant ink seller only two mornings ago. Miss Bates had heard him hawking his wares in the street and sent Jane down with their bottle and a few coins to pay for a refill.

Thinking it was most likely in the writing desk, Lizzy began opening the small drawers and cupboards in it. It was a most beautiful piece of furniture: the woodgrain was bright and polished smooth, the handles and legs fine-tooled, and a design of leaves and flowers was carved on each tiny door and drawer. It was from Jane Fairfax's mother, she'd been told, one of the few luxuries of past finery.

In one drawer, which stuck slightly, there was a sheaf of creased letters stacked haphazardly and shoved in diagonally, as if in a rush. Thinking only to straighten, and to check if Jane had put the ink in there, Lizzy took the letters in her hands to smooth and straighten them.

She did so absently, and then realized with parted lips that they were addressed to "My dearest Jane," and signed, "Frank."

"What are you doing?" Jane Fairfax demanded. She quickly shut the door.

"Oh—I am so sorry—" Lizzy saw the offending ink, which Jane must have dropped in the drawer along with the letters when their first visitor arrived unseasonably early that morning. She dropped the letters in the drawer and shut it; she held out the tiny bottle. "I was looking for this."

Jane's lips compressed, but it was clear that there was a wobble she was trying to conceal. "You read them?"

"No. I only saw your name... and his." Lizzy wrung her hands. Poor Jane; how harshly Lizzy had judged her. "I will never speak of it if you do not wish it. But...you must be under a terrible strain, and if it would relieve you at all, please know I can keep a confidence."

Jane Fairfax looked away, and unshed tears glistened, grew, and overflowed silently. "Please leave me."

"Of course." Lizzy went back to the parlor, shutting the door gently behind her.

Miss Bates was placidly looking out the window, watching the neighbors and townsfolk pass by. "Is anything the matter with Jane?" she asked.

"No. She wants to lie down before dinner."

Miss Bates wagged her head sadly. "Poor Jane! She puts such a good face on it, but she is clearly still exhausted from illness and from grief over her grandmother. I do *so* wish that she might stay with me forever! I fear being a governess will be a sad trial for her health. The Campbells were so kind; they would have kept her forever, but Jane is proud, just like her mother." She sniffed, eyes misty. "When Miss Campbell, Jane's particular friend, married this year, Jane determined she could no longer live on their generosity. It was inevitable, I suppose. Providence knows."

Lizzy sat down with her book but did not read. Jane Fairfax and Frank Churchill! Was it a secret engagement, a growing intimacy, or just an illicit flirtation? Jane did not seem the sort for any of those scenarios! An engagement was most likely, if he was *writing* to her. But then young men did not always behave as they ought. And then too—to greet her in Highbury as nearly a stranger!

It was a mystery, without doubt. Lizzy hoped for Jane's sake that it would work out. Lizzy had no illusions about the life of a governess and would not wish it upon anyone. No, the thing for Jane to do was to marry, if she could, and if Frank Churchill were the one, so be it. If Jane never married, she would live at the mercy of strangers or in growing poverty with her aunt. Her fate might actually come "to the hedgerows" Lizzy's own mother was always bemoaning when she described Mr. Collins turning them out of Longbourn.

There was something in what her mother said. Lizzy and her sisters had a small inheritance on her mother's side—to Miss Bates, it would be nearly a fortune!—but Lizzy's mother and sisters would never live within their means. If conscientious choices were not made, if no sister married well... the situation would not be pretty.

Lizzy still did not regret Mr. Darcy. The arrogance with which he moved through life!

But she found herself regretting the *idea* of Darcy. A good marriage was perhaps not to be scoffed at...

Lizzy laughed out loud. To think I should come to sympathize with Mama!

Miss Bates smiled upon her. "I like to see a cheerful face. You are so good to stay with us, Miss Bennet, I can never be sufficiently thankful."

{ 19 }

ONE PERSON *NOT* THANKFUL FOR Lizzy's visit to Highbury was Mr. Darcy.

He rode his horse hard on the London road, having left after an early breakfast of cold beef, fresh bread, and coffee. Highbury was only sixteen or seventeen miles from his London house and he had a great desire to be elsewhere. He had not packed his things, or had his valet do so, but he probably would upon his return.

Mr. Darcy had gone through a cycle of disappointment, embarrassment, and frustration. It would have been far better if Elizabeth had never come to Highbury. Or if he had not come! He had been satisfied in London; he had put her out of his mind.

But *no*, Providence had put them both in Highbury and her effect on him had seemed trebled. He still had no intention of becoming a fool by offering for her, but without the reminder of her family, he'd slipped. He'd been able to imagine a future with her at Pemberley and put all unpleasant thoughts of duty aside.

The post road to London had a good surface and he went at a smacking pace, except for every now and then when he slowed to navigate a post chaise, or to pass a farmer in a tumbril, or to allow the mail to thunder by.

The sky was cloudy and he could taste the London air as he drew near the city. It was a distinctive odor of trash, waste, smoke, and humanity, but it was London.

No more mental circles. He would finish his business in Highbury and then take Georgiana and go home to Pemberley.

For rightness' sake, he must explain to Lizzy the circumstances of Wickham's "grievances," but after that he would go home. Darcy had planned to make a visit to Hunsford and Lady Catherine, but that would have to wait for late summer or fall. He would not go there when Elizabeth would end up a stone's throw away at the parsonage to bewitch him all over again.

At his town house, Darcy greeted his butler, shortly. In answer to his query, "No, I'll only be staying the night and then back to Surrey. A few tasks to discharge."

After changing into town dress, Darcy went around to Bingley's place and found that he was out, taking his sister Caroline for a turn in Hyde Park. Darcy decided to wait, the butler having respectfully informed him they were expected back shortly.

Darcy made himself comfortable in the study with Bingley's newspaper, asking the butler to inform Bingley of his need for a word when he got in. Some twenty minutes later, he heard feet, doors, and voices.

"Darcy!" Bingley said. "Thought you were down at Knightley's place. What brings you?" He clapped him on the shoulder. "Devilish good to see you. I've got something I wanted to talk to you about as well."

Bingley poured them both a glass of red wine, but Darcy was feeling rather like a student about to make a confession at school. He waved it off.

"What did you want to say?" Darcy asked. "My errand can wait."

"Bugger." Bingley took a large, fortifying gulp. "I am thinking of proposing to Jane Bennet. I know," Bingley raised a hand to forestall whatever objection he thought Darcy was about to make. "I know everything you would say. You've said it, after all. But since you left London, I've had plenty of time to think. And perhaps all my thinking would've come to nothing—my thinking usually does!—but Caroline visited Georgiana, who... Dash it all, I sound like the veriest gabster. In short, I heard from Georgiana that you were in Surrey with Miss Elizabeth Bennet. That got me thinking and talking to Caroline, and it came out that Jane is in London. In fact, she wrote us, and Caroline concealed it from me. Can you believe that?"

"Well—"

"I've just been to pay a call on Jane this morning; didn't tell Caroline yet. And Darcy! If you could have seen how glad she was to see me! And it wasn't in my head, either. Nor was she acting complaisant for her mother's benefit; for her mum wasn't there. Perhaps Jane doesn't care for me as I do for her, but I believe she cares enough. I mean to propose."

"Charles—"

"Don't try to talk me out of it, pray don't. For I daresay you could do so, you have so much sense and gravitas and authority! Everything you say sounds true as you say it, but I made up my mind this morning that I must not be persuaded again. Jane's aunt—perfectly capital woman, by the way, nothing to blush for—let slip that Jane had been quite excited about visiting her new friends in London, and if that does not mean me, I'm a lobcock."

Darcy waited.

"Well?" Bingley demanded.

"I wanted to be sure you were through. I have absolutely nothing to add to what you've said. I will only apologize for interfering before. I had your interests at heart, but I think it would have been better if I had been less busy. Your happiness must be your own affair; it is too great a burden for me."

"Yes, exactly! My happiness must be my own affair." He paused. "You really are not going to tell me all the objections of family and connections?"

"No. There *are* disadvantages to the match, but you are aware of them and thus to ignore them is your choice. And not necessarily a bad choice; I hope you will be very happy."

"I *shall* be very happy when Jane says yes! You may think me a coxcomb, but her look and voice today assured me she would!"

"I think you a humble man who was too easily taught to distrust your instincts. Your statement makes my own errand erroneous, however, so I will take my leave."

"Wait—you were going to talk about *Miss Bennet*?"

"There is no need, if you are going to propose."

"But what message had you? It is too strange; you cannot leave me in suspense."

"It is..." Darcy hesitated. "It is only that Miss Elizabeth has given me reason to think that her sister was quite cast down when you left Netherfield. 'Heartbroken,' was the word she used. I felt it my duty to let you know that my judgement in the case had been wrong. However, circumstance has proved it unnecessary."

"Heartbroken! My poor Jane; I could kick you for encouraging me not to go back to Netherfield. I know Caroline was at the back of it all, but you did help. Caroline keeps insisting that Georgiana should be my bride! Your sister Georgiana, can you believe it? I forgive you, however. I have the picture of Jane's delight this morning locked in my brain and nothing can dislodge it now."

Bingley then bored and wearied and stung him very much by expatiating at length on Jane Bennet's perfections and beauty.

Darcy felt this was a punishment he was probably owed and bore it as well as he could.

He declined staying for supper, however, and returned to his own town house. Georgiana was not there, so it felt very empty and lonely. The dining table was long, and the candles made it look even longer and emptier when he ate. *What would Elizabeth think of this place?* he wondered.

The large centerpiece on the table belonged to his mother's time. It would feel odd to eat here with just Lizzy. Perhaps she would have dedicated the second parlor, on the lower floor, to be a family dining room.

His cook had made several dishes, but only one course because Darcy did not find it pleasant to sit to more than one remove by himself. Lizzy was informal. She would probably ring for the nutcracker to work on these walnuts when supper had finished.

Darcy shook himself. No, she would not be coming here. He had grown too used to indulging such thoughts and ideas when his mind wandered. He really must exercise self-control and train his thoughts away from her.

He ate another of the bitter walnuts, distracting himself with thoughts of Georgiana.

Still, when he left the dining table and retired to his study, he eyed the ornate Stuart chairs against the wall, thronelike and demanding, next to the simpler but massive Jacobean cabinet. There was a desk, walnut and fine, but perhaps a lady would prefer furniture of less antiquity and more fashion...

He'd done it again. Darcy passed a weary hand through his hair. Perhaps it was more than Elizabeth. Perhaps he was simply ready to marry, and that readiness was bringing on all these thoughts of a woman's opinions and alterations.

He tried to picture another woman in the study with him, perhaps with a book or embroidery circle...

He *could* do it; he could picture Caroline Bingley or Emma Woodhouse or even his cousin Anne sitting opposite the fire from him. But it brought no thrill of joy.

If he decided to marry—in his mind he skirted right past Elizabeth's rejection—he probably *ought* to marry Anne. It would be a strategic alliance, uniting Rosings Park and Anne's inheritance back into the Darcy family. His aunt would be ecstatic. Anne would be an undemanding wife. They understood each other; they had known each other from childhood.

It was markedly unexciting.

There was Miss Woodhouse. He did not love her as he did Lizzy; but could he love her, given time? Could she? It was one of her good points that she seemed completely indifferent to him, had certainly cast out no lures or indulged in any flutters. She also was an heiress and of an excellent old family. It would be a respected match; applauded on all sides. She was intelligent too; though rather flighty and...and...

Darcy sighed. He should not decide anything now, depressed and disappointed as he was; the decision would have to wait.

{ 20 }

JANE FAIRFAX WAITED ANXIOUSLY for days, dreading the moment Lizzy Bennet would divulge her secret.

Jane did not suspect her of malice, but Jane had grown up in a hotbed of gossip. It seemed inevitable to her that Lizzy would pass on the shocking item she had discovered. Probably she would only tell Miss Woodhouse or little Miss Smith in "strictest confidence" and Jane knew exactly how far to trust *that*. Perhaps Lizzy would not even mean to divulge Jane's secret engagement but would give them away by a look or tone of voice.

Jane ate her boiled egg every morning with dread and salted it with apprehension. If her secret engagement to Frank Churchill became known, his aunt would *entirely* disinherit him! He would be left with nothing except his father, Mr. Weston, who was a very decent man, but had saved up for years only to buy his current house, Randalls. Mr. Weston did not have an estate to leave to his son; he did not even have a *cottage* to leave to his son.

And Frank, though wonderful, had not been brought up to have an occupation. It would be ever so difficult for him to change his ways now.

Nor did Jane know whether to write to Frank while he was staying so nearby. They had done so while he was away—the only danger then was in getting to and from the post office and hiding his letters at home. But now he was at Randalls with his father and stepmother, and Frank, though he was clever and quick with misdirection, was none too careful in other ways.

He had not called again since that day Lizzy saw the letters, but Jane knew she would see him at the Coles' party this very night. She slid her silk evening gloves on over her fingers, which were rough and dry from the coarse soap her aunt used, and caught the threads. The Campbells had always had lovely soft soap that did not dry and redden her hands.

Was she evil to contemplate that if all went well and she married Frank, such luxuries could again be hers? And her aunt's! An unknown but large portion of Jane's joy in the engagement was the thought that her aunt would not be destitute as she grew older.

No, indeed.

When Frank's aunt, Mrs. Churchill, eventually died—she was already very unwell—then Jane and Frank could marry and they would have more than enough to care for Miss Bates. She could spend half the year living with them, and the other half here in Highbury, if she so desired it. Everything would be delightful...

But now Jane truly *was* evil, for she had just thought with hope about a lady's death.

At her aunt's urging, Jane plaited and curled her hair for the evening and even offered, at the last moment, to do Lizzy's. "I was used to doing my dear friend's hair, Mrs. Dixon, and hers is similar in curl and texture to your own."

Lizzy thanked her and watched in the mirror while Jane expertly twisted strands, pinned, and twisted a few ringlets around her finger.

"You are very good; I don't think even my sister Jane does it better."

"Your sister is named Jane? I did not realize." She took another pin and twisted it in her hands. "Please, you will not... It would be *ruinous*..." She deftly pinned another strand behind the small knot of hair on the back of Lizzy's head.

"I would never," Lizzy said quietly. "I am not a tale-bearer."

Jane wished she could be certain!

The Cole family lived in Highbury proper, and thus it was only a short walk for the ladies, though the Coles' home was far larger and grander than the building where Miss Bates had rooms.

However, when the ladies reached the street, a carriage was waiting for them.

"Why, again!" exclaimed Miss Bates. "Mr. Knightley is so thoughtful—"

"But it is not the same carriage, Aunt," Jane said. She felt a swoop of her stomach which was answered when the door opened.

Mr. Frank Churchill, elegant, irreverent, and her secret fiancé, jumped down to hand them into the carriage. He looked handsome in a wine-colored evening coat. "Good evening, fine ladies. My mother sends you the carriage and her good wishes... and me! She was concerned that Miss Bates and Miss Fairfax might be chilled to the bone at this time of night."

He bowed and smiled, handing Miss Bates into the carriage first, as befit her age. Then he handed in Lizzy, and last Jane herself.

Normally his antics, squeezing her hand, whispering how beautiful she looked in her ear, would have caused her to color up and maybe give him a reproachful look. But with Lizzy looking on and *knowing*... Jane was stiff as a board and did not return the squeeze or even seem to hear his words.

In the carriage he was light-hearted and friendly, but Jane could barely hold up her head. She simply *must* tell him how things stood. She despised deceit of every kind and had been most unhappy at the thought of a prolonged secret engagement. The subterfuge it incurred! That was bad, but it was a thousand times worse when someone knew the truth.

The Coles' party had already begun when they arrived, and Jane found a place to hide beside a fake potted palm to recover. Mrs. Cole had decorated her ball room in the faux-Egyptian style which was all the rage just now, so besides the potted palm there were black and gold fixtures, alligator legs on the low tables, and even the bust of a mummy on a stand.

The room was not quite the size of the ballroom at Hartfield, but it was certainly large enough for dancing. Jane would have to remind Frank not to bully her into dancing since she was still in partial mourning for her grandmother. Some might say she and her aunt ought not even come to a party before six months were up, but Highbury was such a close community, no one wanted Miss Bates to remain lonely for so long.

"Penny for your thoughts?" Frank asked, appearing beside her with a glass of orgeat and handing it to her.

"We must be careful," Jane said. "You cannot appear too particular."

"And yet you faulted me for making Emma the target of my gallantry at the last party!"

"There is a difference between caution and making half the town think you're in love with her."

"You are very harsh today. Whereas I do not think anyone would notice even if I were to steal a kiss from you behind this very outlandish tree."

"Do not dare." Jane backed up to the wall. "I must tell you that Lizzy saw several of your letters to me. She is aware of...well, I do not know precisely, but she must be aware of us, and I am so mortified."

"Ah. That's not ideal. What were you about, to let her see your letters?"

"She sleeps in the same *room* as I do. I should like to see you—" Jane took a deep breath. "I mistakenly shoved the inkbottle in with the letters when I was called away; she looked for it."

"My sweet, lovely Jane... you must never attempt to be a spy. You would be guillotined before the day was done."

"It is not funny."

"It is a little. Never fear, my timid dove, we will be fine." He bowed and moved away.

Jane did not feel particularly better; especially when he approached Lizzy and began a conversation. Had he no shame?

She loved him, surely, but she sometimes wondered why. She had known him at Weymouth and had been, as the cliché went, swept off her feet. He had been musical and witty and charming. Then he had been attentive and passionate and—whenever he sensed she was closing off—suddenly sincere in such a way that took her quite off guard. He had depth under his flippancy, and it was those glimpses—along with her dear friend Miss Campbell's encouragement of it all—that she had fallen in love with.

Would she have allowed herself to be in love without those late-night conversations with her friend? Without the laughing and blushing and disclaiming—and all the times Miss Campbell told her how he had stared at her when she wasn't looking? All the times Miss Campbell assured Jane that his voice blended with hers in a duet as if it was meant to be? All the times Miss Campbell described how happy she would be when Jane was married to him and brought up to her true position in life?

Jane hovered behind the palm and watched Frank gamble their future with a smile and a smirk.

Lizzy had not seen that tête-à-tête between Jane and Frank, nor would she have tried. She was preoccupied by other things.

There was Mr. Elton, returned after little more than a month with a new wife. Her feathers nearly brushed the hanging chandelier.

There was Harriet linked arms with Emma, whose chin was higher than usual.

There was—and this took precedence in her thoughts—Mr. Darcy entering with Mr. Knightley.

She had hoped he might still be gone from Highbury on his errand to London. Oh, why had he come tonight? He was a proud man; she would bet her life on that. A proud man who had received a harsh refusal to his proposal, who had no pressing reason to stay in the neighborhood, and who detested country parties with strangers had no reason to remain. Why come at all?

And why did he look at her with a certain disappointment mixed with regret and even—dare she say—gentleness?

She expected to be met with haughty reserve if he spoke to her at all. Instead, he bowed over her hand and inquired, quite humbly, if she might find a moment to speak to him, at her convenience.

Everyone was engaged in their own conversations around them. Lizzy, fearing his strange manner would make her lose her nerve—he had a very intimidating presence when she was not angry with him—gestured to the strange mummy bust. "Perhaps we may go examine it."

Under the pretext of studying the details of the piece—the top of a sarcophagus but partially open to show a lump that was ostensibly a linen-wrapped head and neck and shoulders—Mr.

Darcy began to speak. Lizzy mostly kept her eyes on the aforementioned details, so it was an odd juxtaposition of plaster, paint, and hieroglyphics that became fixed in her mind with Mr. Darcy's brief explanation.

He explained how Wickham had squandered his inheritance from Darcy's father, a large sum of money, and how he'd returned to demand a position with a church. He wanted Darcy to give him the living that had just come open, as if his profligate career had nothing to do with the matter. And how, failing that, he'd seduced Darcy's young sister into an elopement, which had only been revealed at the last moment.

When he revealed his sister's age—fifteen!—and Georgiana's heartbreak at Wickham's treachery, Lizzy's eyes flew to his face in shock. He spoke softly but distinctly. His face was mostly impassive, but she could see pain and guilt in the lines of his forehead. If she was any judge of physiognomy, he was telling the truth.

"I only share with you some of the dastardly things he has done so you understand why I spoke and acted as I did. He has had more than his due from my family and tried to take more in the blackest of ways."

"But he—he seems so genuine," Lizzy said, turning back to the mummy. She was comparing her memories of Wickham's earnest face—too earnest? too suave?—with Darcy's pained one.

"You will no doubt become acquainted with my cousin Colonel Fitzwilliam when you go to Hunsford. He is also Georgiana's guardian and can confirm the truth of my explanation."

Lizzy felt flushed and dismayed. Her mind still flitted from memory to memory of Wickham, trying to find a way for him to be exonerated, for his character to be upheld, but no single act of kindness, uprightness, or fortitude came to mind. His looks certainly spoke of sincerity, but with a grandiose, self-pitying manner that seemed glaring in retrospect. How indiscreet he had been. How... manipulative?

Lizzy wanted to press her hands to her cheeks to cool them, but if anyone was watching, that would look so obvious. They would think Mr. Darcy flirting with her!

She simply could not consider this dispassionately with Darcy standing beside her, so close that his body warmed her arm through her shawl. "I—I need time to think. Thank you for the explanation."

He bowed slightly. "Of course. As for the other, I'm sure that you will hear from your sister soon."

Lizzy's eyes once more could not stay glued to the mummy. Her mouth and eyes opened in hope and surprise, but he was already moving away.

Good heavens. What could he mean? Had he spoken to Bingley about her sister's broken heart? Was that good or bad? She desperately hoped it was good but was afraid to hope.

Mrs. Weston, motherly and kind, joined her. "I believe sarcophagi are usually stored horizontally. It is somewhat off-putting to have it upright like this. However, the hieroglyphics are fascinating. I wonder if these were painted randomly, or is it truly a copy of the tomb of an ancient king?"

"Good questions all," Lizzy said, pulling her gaze back from following Darcy across the room to where he'd been pulled into Emma's orbit along with Harriet, Mr. Knightley, and several others.

"Are you quite well?" Mrs. Weston asked. "Mr. Darcy looked serious just now."

"Yes, I know." Lizzy felt again that some explanation must be offered the older lady, particularly as she had seen the end of their explosive conversation in front of her house. "Mr. Darcy is acquainted with my family—particularly my older sister—and we have had some disagreement about her." Lizzy tried to laugh lightly. "His friend is also in the mix... it is a sad tale of misunderstandings and cross-purposes, but I hope—perhaps—all will end well."

"Ah. That does explain why he often refers to you as Miss Elizabeth, rather than Miss Bennet. I had rather thought he must have met you *en famille* to have that habit."

"Yes, precisely."

"I hope, if you have any other difficulty, you will not hesitate to speak to me. You have not your mother at hand, and as I feel quite a friend to Emma, I hope you would view me as a potential source of help. If you have, for instance, a large decision to make, you may wish to speak to an uninvolved party."

Lizzy colored. There could be no doubt that Mrs. Weston wondered if Mr. Darcy had proposed, perhaps even if they were already secretly engaged. Which was *ironic*, considering it was Mrs. Weston's own stepson Frank Churchill who was secretly attached to Jane Fairfax!

"I can only assure you that Mr. Darcy is as likely to marry any unattached lady in the room as me." Lizzy's gaze trailed to where Mr. Darcy spoke to Emma. This, at least, she knew to be true. Lizzy may have been wrong about Wickham—oh, for half an hour alone to collect her thoughts!—but she could certainly not marry Mr. Darcy.

Mrs. Weston took this in good part and good-naturedly changed the subject, though she still wondered what had occurred. She could not forget that it was Emma's name in their conversation which had caught her ear the other day. Strangely, anger and consternation seemed to be the common thread in Lizzy's and Mr. Darcy's private talks, and Mrs. Weston could not help wondering what they could have to be so angry about.

Mrs. Weston spoke to Lizzy comfortably of winter, of books, and of music, but meanwhile she conjectured. Perhaps Lizzy had *expected* an offer of marriage the other day, and that had gone awry? Had Mr. Darcy expressed admiration of Emma instead? That could certainly make a young lady frustrated, if she felt misled.

Or perhaps the reference to Emma was merely chance. Perhaps he had proposed and been rejected? That seemed quite out of the way, for she knew Lizzy's situation to be middling at best, despite being a gentleman's daughter, and Mr. Darcy was an extraordinary prize to reject.

Unless Lizzy had placed her affections elsewhere... that would explain much.

While very curious, she was a warm-hearted lady, and did truly feel for Miss Bennet.

Lizzy was still in conversation with a thoughtful Mrs. Weston when Frank Churchill joined them.

"What are you two lovely ladies speaking of? Music? You must allow me to interject. I play nothing, but I am excellent at admiring and praising a young lady's performance, which seems to be a hefty fraction of the artform."

Mrs. Weston tapped him with a fan. "That is not true, and you have a fine voice."

"Thank you, my dear *mother*," he said in a playful, winning way. "I am ecstatic to know that you will be the sort to always put forward my good points."

"I do not think you need much help," Lizzy said.

He put a hand over his heart. "A coxcomb, you would paint me? I am too honest to deny it."

Lizzy smiled. "Yet you boast of honesty in the same sentence."

"Someone who can parse my sentences so quickly is to be feared above all things. I must instantly face down anything that frightens me. Miss Cole is demanding dancing; will you dance with me?"

She had no excuse to avoid dancing, which Lizzy wished to do for possibly the first time in her life. She accepted.

Mrs. Weston sat down to play.

There were some five or six couples, a respectable double line. Despite only being in the neighborhood for little over a month, Lizzy was acquainted with many in Highbury. Despite her own problems, she looked at the line of dancers with knowledge, interest, and uneasiness.

She did not know Miss Cole very well, but there was the new Mrs. Elton standing up just beyond her with young Mr. Gilbert. Mr. Elton had certainly not lost any time in returning with a bride! She looked very fine, though her nose and mouth were sharp as a hatchet, and she cast a snide glance at Harriet who had unluckily been placed near her. The new Mrs. Elton's feathers bobbed along with her and whipped about quite impressively when she turned.

Mr. Knightley was just beyond them, but against the wall; he did not dance. Mr. Elton and several other gentlemen stood aside also.

Lucky gentlemen to do what they wished without question!

Jane Fairfax also sat off to the side, as her mourning state precluded dancing.

First in the dancing line, however, were Mr. Darcy and Emma. How strange! Had Emma hinted him into it? Had he truly taken Lizzy's words to heart and thought of fixing his interest with

Emma? It was strange to see him dance when he so avoided it in Hertfordshire! Particularly at a private party where the dance was impromptu. Savage, he had called it.

But then, Emma was his equal in wealth, class, and station. She was even more of his status than Caroline Bingley, whom he had danced with several times at the Netherfield Ball. But to be so particular here...

Lizzy focused herself back on her partner, Frank Churchill, as the dance began. His light-colored hair and his teeth caught the candlelight as he grinned. A very dashing young man. If Jane Fairfax had communicated to him that their secret was found out, he was not perturbed.

"A wonderful party, is it not?" He lightly gripped her gloved hand and dipped and turned.

"Yes."

"My step-mother says neither you nor Miss Fairfax have yet visited to play the pianoforte. She truly does mean it, you know, she loves music and Emma—Miss Woodhouse, I should say—is not much addicted to it."

Lizzy shrugged half-heartedly. "Nor am I much addicted. My playing is lackluster. Miss Fairfax has not shown any great inclination to visit, else I would have accompanied her."

They separated for the dance and returned.

"Yes," he said. "She is not always as sure of a warm welcome as she deserves to be. Her life has taught her that things offered will often be capriciously revoked."

Lizzy gave him full credit for being able to speak on multiple levels while keeping perfect time with the dance.

"That must be difficult," she agreed. "I'm sure her friends wish more for her, but trust is not easily won."

"No. Perhaps she needs encouragement to persevere in taking hold of things offered. In practicing pianoforte, of course."

"Encouragement? But I am not well-acquainted with you or your character—"

"You mean the instrument, do you not? I can assure you it is top-notch." His confidence was unshaken.

"I should not know how to encourage her, but I would certainly not be a hindrance. It is not my place."

"Thank you; I suppose I cannot ask for more."

"You can and did," Lizzy said. "But that is as far as I am willing to go."

At the end of the dance, he bowed a little more deeply than necessary. "A wonderful dance, thank you. You are a strong-minded young woman."

Lizzy curtseyed; and Frank grinned again, before moving away and claiming Emma for the next dance. He did not even acknowledge Jane Fairfax as he walked past her.

An interesting gentleman. Lizzy was not sure she liked Frank Churchill, but she expected he might get what he wanted. He was certainly bold enough.

Lizzy moved aside and sat down on the bench beside Miss Fairfax, folding her hands in her lap. On the other side of the dancing area, Mr. Darcy was bowing to Emma at the close of their dance, while Mr. Churchill waited next in turn.

Mr. Elton, the dramatic parson, was only a few steps away from Lizzy. He whispered *sotto voce* to Mrs. Cole, the hostess, "Do you see how Mr. Darcy stares at Miss Woodhouse? I wonder if poor Mr. Woodhouse knows how his peace is to be cut up! I quite feel for him. Yet how could any young lady rebuff so eligible a suitor? I fear Miss Woodhouse may soon leave us."

Lizzy frowned at this piece of meddling. She had no idea what Mr. Darcy might or might not do, but she was sure Mr. Elton meant to create trouble for Emma.

Turning surreptitiously, Lizzy saw that Mrs. Cole was flushed, either with the wine, the crowd, or both, and her round mouth opened in surprise. She leaned close to Mr. Elton. "Do you think so? Do you have reason to think him particular? He has stayed in Highbury longer than he meant; he told me so himself!"

Their whispered conversation continued, but Lizzy could not quite make it out as the music for the next dance started up.

Mr. Darcy moved across the room toward them, and for a half a moment it seemed that he would come claim her hand for the dance. Before Lizzy could parse how she felt about dancing with him, or how she ought to feel, he paused a few feet away, turned back, and retraced his steps.

Mr. Elton and Mrs. Cole looked between the two of them and leaned their heads together to whisper again.

Lizzy looked away, blinking unexpected moisture out of her eyes. The stress of this stupid party! What she wouldn't give to be in her bed, with Jane Fairfax asleep, and finally able to think her own thoughts and cry her own conflicted tears into her pillow!

The moment brought back the first time she met Mr. Darcy, when he had snubbed her in refusing to dance, but Lizzy felt she understood him now.

He'd wanted her to know the truth of Wickham. Indeed, if Darcy's story could be believed, he had been quite magnanimous in his explanation, considering she had hurled such terrible accusations at him.

But that was it. He was not going to humble himself by pursuing her when her feelings were known. They were back to their first relationship, only now she had not the hot, instinctive prejudice against him to buoy her up when she was found wanting.

{ 21 }

M R. KNIGHTLEY NOTED THE INTERPLAY between Mr. Darcy and Miss Bennet with displeasure. He liked his friend Darcy, but how abrupt to make the poor girl think he was coming to dance with her and then changing his mind!

Darcy had been acquainted with her for some months, and it was not out of the way for Miss Bennet to expect him to dance with her, particularly as she was a stranger in the neighborhood and could not be expected to know many of the single gentlemen.

But Darcy had been in a curious mood the past week, making that quick trip to London, declaring he would leave the following day, writing and discarding a number of messages, and then asking if he could stay after all.

Knightley did not object, but it was strange. Darcy had seemed to swing between dour thoughtfulness and jittery impatience.

Knightley had wondered if perhaps Darcy had gone to settle some affairs with his man of business in prelude to offering for Emma.... but that was a speculation Knightley would never put to his quiet friend. Nor did it quite fit the circumstances.

Though truly, when Mr. Knightley had given it more thought, he mentally conceded that Emma might be very good for Darcy. She was as smart as he, and her liveliness would cheer and rouse him. His steadiness and self-discipline must balance her.

But the thing Darcy just did to Miss Bennet was rude. Harriet Smith at least had been asked to dance by young Mr. Cole, which was just as well, since it would distract her from the disdainful glances the new Mrs. Elton kept throwing her way.

Knightley looked back at Miss Bennet, and from this angle he could see her blinking back tears. He much disliked being described in glowing terms, but chivalrous was often used when he was not present.

"Miss Bennet," he asked, "may I have this dance?"

"Oh—there is no need," her voice was matter-of-fact. "I do not mind sitting down."

"Nor do I mind dancing; let us join the set."

"Well... very well, thank you."

If she had been suffering embarrassment or dismay before, there was no sign of it during the dance. He almost wondered if he'd completely imagined the whole; but he was not prone to it. No, she was simply made of sterner stuff than many young ladies, he suspected.

Miss Bennet was not quite so energetic a dancer as Emma, but she was graceful and before a few minutes had passed, he was smiling with real enjoyment. She did too.

"After all," she said, though perhaps more to herself than him, "what is spiritual turmoil compared to bodily enjoyment? We are made to be physical animals as well as mental machines."

"Indeed. And when one fails, the other may offer some succor. Which do you believe to be the strongest?"

She thought. "Brains or brawn? I have seen invalids with quite amazing powers of amusing themselves; also, those with excellent health forever depressed. There are those with sharp minds who are unable to find contentment, and fools who are prosperous. I suppose it depends on which beast we feed daily, and it is best to have them pull as a matched team, when possible."

"An apt analogy. I sense if you were a man you might have made a good parson, with an ear for a good homily."

A slight frown brought down her face.

Mr. Knightley stepped forward in the dance. "I did not mean that as an insult. I admire a clever woman."

"Thank you."

They finished the dance, and Lizzy thanked him again, but showed no disposition to cling. She at once joined a conversation between Miss Bates and Mr. Weston.

Later, when Knightley was departing, Emma quizzed him. "Dancing, Mr. Knightley? You never do."

"I am out of practice, but I hope I did not offend Miss Bennet's taste or the sensibilities of the room."

"Nonsense, you dance perfectly well. I hope—" Emma tugged at her evening glove, rearranging a finger, "I hope you will make this a new precedent."

"Indeed?" He felt a stirring of hope.

"Yes; gentlemen are always scarce at such events! Also, Mrs. Weston owned that she would enjoy dancing, though she feels her age makes her less eligible than the average new bride who might be expected to enjoy a few turns. And, of course, she cannot stand up with her husband."

"I think that's a great piece of foolishness; who more proper to enjoy a dance with than one's spouse?"

"Well, until fashion follows you into practicality—though I insist it would be very strange if married couples were to dance! What would be the point of a ball?—please promise to badger Mrs. Weston into dancing. She will say she ought not, but she would so enjoy it."

"Very well, Emma. Such amiable plans for your friend's enjoyment shall not be squashed by me. But please, do not promise me to anyone else. You are far too popular in Highbury for me to dance with all your friends."

"You did not seem to mind dancing with Miss Bennet. What did you speak of?"

"Well, as a matter of fact, we spoke of the relative power of animal versus spiritual instincts in the average person."

Emma's brow rose in disbelief. "While you were dancing?"

"Yes. My horses are here; I must bid you goodnight, Emma. I offered to take Miss Bates and her young ladies home."

Lizzy's friendship with Jane Fairfax had *not* got off to a promising start. If the friendship could be termed a friendship at all, if it could be compared to a baby bird as Lizzy had Mr. Knightley had once done, it was a hatchling that had squeaked miserably in its nest before falling resignedly silent. In fact, it might have starved to death from silence, reserve, and defeatism if not for the accidental discovery of the letters.

Their friendship would certainly not *starve*, now; that could no longer be its fate. The hatchling had been unceremoniously shoved out of the nest and would either learn to fly on its own or be dashed to a bloody lump on the rocks below.

Both girls wanted nothing more than privacy, the luxury to lie on their beds and possibly cry. Alas, it was not to be.

In the carriage, Miss Bates carried all before her on a tide of words.

"That was such a lovely party! Jane, you looked more beautiful than I could imagine, and I look forward to seeing you dance when we have put off mourning. How proud Mamma would have been to see you—But there, I shall not think of sad things. I am sure the brightness of the party is enough to keep my spirits up for many days. Brightness! So many candles. And the chandelier! I asked Mrs. Cole and she said Mr. Cole had it from a real India merchant from Brighton. India! And I'm sure the Egyptian things were very diverting. I liked to see you dance, Miss Bennet. And you, Mr. Knightley. Did not Miss Woodhouse look like an angel tonight? She and Mr. Churchill make a very handsome pair. She danced with Mr. Darcy too, who I am sure is very fine, only not from Surrey, so it is no wonder one cannot find him as agreeable. Do not you think, Jane, that Mr. Churchill would be the very man for Miss Woodhouse?"

Jane looked pained but before she had to answer, Miss Bates continued. "I think it. How wonderful to have so many fine neighbors!"

"Yes, Aunt," Jane replied.

Thankfully, they arrived home almost at once, and Mr. Knightley carefully escorted them across the damp walk that led to Miss Bates's stairs. The night was very dark, and the moon was completely obscured, so it was just as well he did. The unevenness of several of the stones made it an easy matter to catch the toe of a slipper.

Lizzy, of the three ladies the least familiar with the walk, did catch her toe and pitch forward. Mr. Knightley grasped her around the upper arm before she could really fall and helped her right herself.

"Thank you," Lizzy said. Mr. Knightley looked at her for a moment then nodded shortly and re-entered his carriage.

Going in the front door and up the cold, dark stairs to the parlor was a depressing business. There was a low fire in the parlor, laid by Patty before she retired for the night, but it was not very cheering. All three ladies automatically drew near as they removed gloves and stretched tired necks and shoulders.

Lizzy was dreading going into the cold bedroom with her cold relationship with Jane Fairfax, only to get in her cold bed where her toes would be cold through the night, despite the several pair of woolen stockings she would wear.

At Longbourn, their housemaid used a warming pan before she and Jane went to bed. Or if for some reason the housemaid could not come, Lizzy and Jane kept a few bricks near the fire which they could heat themselves and put at the foot of their bed.

There was not quite such comfort in Miss Bates's home.

Lizzy was too human not to compare this style of living with that of Mr. Darcy... But even as she moved to the bedroom and began to disrobe with numb-cold fingers, she knew she could never marry for money, particularly someone for whom she felt complete indifference, if not dislike.

But no—did she still dislike Mr. Darcy? The only thing she could say with certainty was that if his story was true, she did not really know him.

Jane Fairfax opened the door and entered as Lizzy wrapped her robe around herself. Jane was silent, and her presence seemed to suck whatever small warmth Lizzy had found right away.

Lizzy quickly shook her gown and hung it on a hook. The air by the window was even colder. Should Lizzy speak to Jane about the evening? Reaching out to her had done no good thus far.

This was the moment, could she but know it, that their friendship had either to flap its wings or die.

Lizzy was not one to go without a fight. However, she knew that prying would get her nowhere, no matter how badly Jane might need to unburden herself.

Instead, Lizzy chose vulnerability as she climbed into the bed and pulled the covers up around her shoulders.

"Tonight was difficult for me. I haven't told anyone, but... but Mr. Darcy proposed to me last week."

Jane's fingers stilled on her buttons, but then she kept working.

Lizzy continued, "I turned him down for several reasons, but my mother will be furious if she ever finds out. We will not be very comfortably situated when my father eventually passes. She was *already* furious that I turned down our cousin, a little toad of a man with only a comfortable living."

Jane's hands stilled again over the side catch in the bodice of her dress. She also had a choice to make, and till now, had generally chosen to let the birds, the friendships, die.

Jane might have been friends with Emma. Mr. Knightley thought the lack was Emma's fault, but the truth was that Jane never gave Emma a chance. One cannot become friends without being known, and Jane had constructed a smooth, blank, cream-colored wall which she never allowed Emma to penetrate.

But regret did not always lend the power to change.

"I am sure that was difficult," Jane said. The bird grew nearer to the ground.

Jane's only true friend had been Miss Campbell, the daughter of the family who had brought her up. But Miss Campbell had married and was now Mrs. Dixon. Miss Campbell had not intentionally abandoned her, but Jane was of a quiet, reserved nature, and when the part of her that she'd given to Miss Campbell was broken off, it left her aching.

"It *was* difficult. It was extremely awkward, in fact. I thought he would finish his visit to Mr. Knightley and *go*. Also... I said such horrible things to him. I allowed myself to believe slander and lies—Yes, the more I think of it, they could have been *blatant* lies—and I cast them all at his head. Tonight he sought to clear himself, but it was painful, embarrassing, humiliating."

Jane eased her own gown off and pulled on her thick, serviceable night dress. "I—"

For a moment, Lizzy hoped.

"I'm sure that was difficult," Jane repeated. The hatchling friendship hit the ground with a crunch of feathers and tiny spray of blood that made even Jane, unknowing, wince. "Goodnight, Miss Bennet."

Jane gracefully threw back the covers and climbed into her own narrow bed, safe and cold behind her cream-colored wall. Lizzy sank down as well and they were both silent as Jane blew out the candle and the room went dark.

And when Jane cried that night, from stress, uncertainty, fear, and disappointment, some fraction of it was for the friendships that might have been and yet never were.

{ 22 }

THE FOLLOWING DAY BROUGHT a letter for Lizzy by post. She and Miss Bates were just eating a few slices of French bread with a *tiny* bit of honey for breakfast, bread which Lizzy and Miss Bates had procured the day before from Mrs. Wallis's bakery, when Jane returned from her trip to the post office.

"Oh, my dear Jane," said Miss Bates, "you really must eat before you go out. I know it is the thing in London and some cities for women to go out before they eat, but you are not strong yet; you know you are not strong."

Jane wordlessly delivered a letter to Lizzy, who tore it open in a frenzy of curiosity; it was from her sister Jane, postmarked from Gracechurch Street, London. The letter was neatly folded with a modest, pre-made wax seal which their Uncle Gardiner always had an abundance of, on account of being a businessman.

The salutation was a little wobbly for Jane's hand. Lizzy could just picture Jane sitting at their Aunt Gardiner's escritoire and writing carefully while she tried to ignore the shouts and pleas of her small cousins, who were no doubt colliding with her knees, demanding stories, or pulling at her hands, demanding attention.

"Do excuse me," Lizzy told them. "It is from my sister in London." She nearly ran to the bedroom and closed the door.

Sitting at the fateful desk with its (not so secret) letters, she spread the single folded page and read.

My dearest, sweetest Lizzy,

I know you have suffered with me in my disappointment—perhaps even more than I have suffered because you love so keenly and hope so fervently!—so I write to you even before my mother, to tell you that Mr. Bingley has proposed!

You may well stare, or sink into a chair, or cover your mouth in shock—I did all three when he proposed. In fact, I sat on my aunt's pincushion and sprang up at once, quite startling poor Mr. Bingley. But I must tell you how it happened.

He learned from Mr. Darcy of your being in Surrey—you did not tell me Mr. Darcy was there; you were trying to protect me, sweet Lizzy—and somehow that led him to question his sister Caroline. He had not until then realized I was in London! He felt quite incensed over her "duplicity," but I told him I had been here little more than two months and he must not be too angry. It meant all the more to me that he sought out information and discovered my uncle's whereabouts (not, I learn, from Caroline, who feigned forgetfulness of my uncle's direction), but through his own inquiries in the city. Having ascertained the name of Mr. Gardiner of Gracechurch Street, he visited me last week.

What I felt at seeing him again! I was shocked, I was pleased, I was hesitant... but I wanted above all for him to feel welcome. I was never so thankful for my dear aunt! She said everything that was proper until my tongue worked again. And then... it seemed but a moment until we were on as easy terms as when he left. I did not want to hope, but I could not help it. I spent only two days in horrendous uncertainty before he called again. He had not been here above five minutes when he asked if he could have a word with me.

I am so happy, Lizzy! You were right to insist I come to London, and I can never thank you enough for insisting on the visit to Surrey in order to get me here. You are the best and wisest and staunchest of sisters.

Now I must write to my mother! Bingley has already spoken to my uncle, and he will write to Father.

Yours,

Jane B.

Lizzy wiped tears of happiness from her cheeks and half-laughed, half-sobbed. Wonderful, sweet Jane! She deserved this happiness, this perfect ending to a broken relationship. And Mr. Darcy... had he done it? Had this happened before or after Lizzy spoke to him? Either way, he must be aware.

Lizzy needed to share her joy to be perfectly happy. After reading the letter through once more, she returned to the parlor and told them her news.

Miss Bates clapped her hands and exclaimed joyfully. She had absolutely no knowledge of either person but was certain they must be "the most deserving of young people!" How she liked to hear "of a young lady being happily settled!"

Jane Fairfax inclined her head. "It sounds a most eligible match." She *was* happy for this unknown sister of Lizzy's, but Jane felt she'd forfeited the right to enter strongly into Lizzy's joy by not entering into her discomfort the night before.

Lizzy laughed again, shaking her head. Really, she could not fault Emma for her impatience with Jane Fairfax, but nothing would bring down Lizzy's mood today. "It *is* eligible. Oh, I cannot stay still this morning. I must have a walk to work out the energy which surges through me at the thought of Jane's happiness. Miss Fairfax, would you walk with me? I do not care where! We can go to Hartfield, or Ford's shop, or play on Mrs. Weston's piano—you pick the destination, only I must have exercise."

Lizzy did not forget that playing the Westons' piano might be a fraught proposition for Jane Fairfax, but Lizzy did not greatly care at this moment. If Jane did not want to be her friend, Lizzy would not jump through verbal hoops to avoid upsetting her.

Jane finished her bite of French bread. "Just allow me to wash my face and hands, and I will join you. Perhaps we might walk to Hartfield to see how Miss Woodhouse and Mr. Woodhouse go on after the Coles' party."

"Yes; *oui;* I concur! Let us go."

It was a clammy, cold day. The clouds were high, but thick, as if layers of thin wool had been laid one on top of the other, and just when you thought you had a glimpse of sky through the weave, another petticoat slid into place.

"It may rain," said Miss Fairfax.

"It may! But my sister shall marry the man she loves, so I do not care." Lizzy spun around as she walked, and a shopper exiting the apothecary stepped around her in alarm. Lizzy grinned in apology. "And, in all practicality, I'm sure Emma will send us home in the carriage if it comes on to rain."

But when they reached the grounds of Hartfield, they saw another carriage pulling up to the carriage house and stables. It was a fine carriage with a crest, though they could not see what it was. It must have already disgorged its passenger, for the groom was unhitching the matched team of four horses and leading them into the stables. It was too cold for them to stand about if the visit was to be longer than half an hour.

"Oh, do you think they have visitors? Bother!" Lizzy said. "I want to share my news."

"The butler will turn us away if they are engaged. It does no harm to inquire."

But Benton was not to hand when they knocked. A footman let them in, and said uncertainly, "Let me check if Miss Woodhouse is at home to visitors. One moment, miss."

"Curious," said Lizzy. "It must not be a regular visitor, or he would know whether to show us up or send us away at once. If the visitor was expected, she would have given orders. If it was a relation, we would be denied. Therefore, the visitor is not family, not local, and not expected."

Emma was also making her own deductions, but she was landing woefully short. The unknown visitor, the lady who faced her, was probably in her fifth or sixth decade. She was grand, commanding, and stern. Her graying hair was intricately styled, and a quantity of diamonds were on her fingers and wrists. She was also a tall woman, taller than Emma, and though she had a cane, she did not seem to need it.

She took her time looking over Emma. Her eyes boldly and somewhat defiantly categorized Emma from her curls to her jade green slippers which went with her rather dashing and certainly fashionable dress.

Emma did not like being sized up in this way, but also was slightly concerned this was an unknown aunt or relation she should know of. "How do you do, ma'am? You wished to see me?"

"Hmph. You are Emma Woodhouse?"

"Yes, that's correct, but you have me a disadvantage, I'm afraid."

"I am Lady Catherine de Bourgh. Of Rosings Park."

"Lady Catherine..." The name was familiar, but Emma wracked her brain in vain. Had she forgotten to write a birthday card to one of her mother's many distant relations? It was tiresome, but usually Emma went through the list without missing any! "Please have a seat, Lady Catherine. I shall ring for tea and refreshments."

The woman narrowed her eyes and for a crazed moment Emma thought she might refuse or stomp away. What strange behavior! The old lady sniffed unhappily, leaned the cane against the settee, and spread her (somewhat old-fashioned) skirts to sit.

"As I said, I am Lady Catherine of Rosings Park, near Hunsford in Kent. It is twenty-five miles from here."

"Oh. Oh!" Emma was relieved when the memory surfaced. "You are Mr. Darcy's aunt, are you not? He is traveling to stay with you next, only he has delayed his trip. I am so sorry! No doubt you meant to go to Donwell Abbey, which is in the next parish. Your nephew is staying there with Mr. Knightley, but my sister is married to another Mr. Knightley, and so you may have been misdirected here. Hartfield is the chief house of Highbury, but Donwell Abbey is the chief estate in the Donwell Parish. It is quite close."

"I know exactly where I am, Miss Woodhouse, and where my nephew is staying."

Definite ill-will. What was wrong? Benton entered quietly, and Emma requested tea and cake.

"Also," Benton said, "I am informed that Miss Fairfax and Miss Bennet are here to visit. Shall I show them up as usual?"

Emma was not easily frightened, but she was feeling rather out of her depth. If she had a father like other girls, she should instantly send for him to act as a buffer to the austere Lady Catherine. But her father was a gentle and anxious soul. She was beginning to think that she must keep him from meeting Lady Catherine at all costs. The woman was like flint.

"Yes, please," she responded. "Please show them up."

Lady Catherine raised a hand. "I see that you are a lady, Miss Woodhouse, so I do not presume to tell you what to do in your own home. However, I am certain that you will want to hear my message alone. I strongly advise it.

"I am, of course, at your service, but I would not wish to slight my friends who have come on this cold day to visit. Perhaps if I had had word of your coming..." Emma smiled sweetly. "That's all, Benton."

"Miss Woodhouse!" Lady Catherine was now glaring.

"I will be happy to hear anything you may wish to say to me after my friends depart. Besides, you must wish to warm yourself and receive refreshments if you have traveled so far today! You must be quite done in."

"Do not presume to know my limitations; all who do so are taken at fault. And do not think that the presence of more young ladies will prevent me executing my errand. I am made of sterner stuff, and I am not easily put off."

Emma was losing graciousness. "I have no desire to put you off, nor am I making any assumptions of you. I do not know you, ma'am, and you have shown up completely unexpectedly. I hope I know my duty as a hostess, but you also must know what is due from a guest. Please let us start again. I am honored to meet any relative of Mr. Darcy; he has been quite a favorite these last weeks. What brings you to our neighborhood?"

If anything, her words only seemed to increase the angry creases around Lady Catherine's eyes. "He's been quite a favorite? Well—"

She cut herself off with a huff as Lizzy and Jane Fairfax entered. Emma had never been so happy to see either of them as she was just now and greeted them with great cordiality.

"I have another guest, as you can see! Allow me to introduce you."

Thankfully, Lady Catherine turned her protuberant eyes on Lizzy for some minutes. "You are one of the Bennet girls, of Longbourn? Your father's estate is entailed on Mr. Collins. I do not approve of entails away from the female line, but I cannot regret it for Mr. Collins's sake."

"Yes, these things do happen," Lizzy said. She was too excited by Jane's engagement to be bothered by this reminder of the entail.

She eyed Lady Catherine curiously. Wickham had (she was nearly certain now) lied about Georgiana Darcy and his involvement with Mr. Darcy. But his description of Lady Catherine as arrogant beyond belief was apparently on the mark. And it was Lady Catherine's daughter whom Mr. Darcy was supposed to marry. Lizzy wished that young lady had come; she was curious to see her.

How strange to think that if things had turned out differently, Mr. Darcy might be introducing her to Lady Catherine as his fiancé. *That* would be a moment to remember.

There was an uncomfortably charged silence.

Emma smoothed her hair. "I do not know if Mr. Darcy will call this morning, but it is possible. Mr. Knightley visits once or twice a week, if not more, and Mr. Darcy often accompanies him."

"And what is my nephew doing wasting his time in Surrey when he is expected in Kent? He has many responsibilities in Derbyshire as well." The irritability of this was undeniable.

"I could not say," Emma said coolly.

Lizzy had some small suspicion as to Darcy's purpose in remaining, but that had run out a few weeks ago; she was now as much in the dark as Lady Catherine.

The butler arrived with the tea things, and Emma and Lizzy hailed it with relief. Jane Fairfax seemed unmoved.

"I will take tea, but I do not want plum cake," said Lady Catherine. "At this hour!"

Lizzy did not think it an unusual hour to serve food to a guest and the growing look of annoyance on Emma's face showed she felt similarly.

Lizzy and Emma had not spent much time together since the disastrous affair of Mr. Elton and Harriet, but just now, united in difficulty, they made eye contact. The thrill of connection made Lizzy smile, and Emma straightened her shoulders and cocked her aristocratic head.

"Lady Catherine, please do let us know what *has* brought you to Highbury, if it is not your nephew. Do you have acquaintance in the area?"

"No, I do not. Most of my acquaintance live in town."

"I hope you enjoyed the countryside, then. The road from Hunsford would have taken you through the heart of Surrey.

"Dreadfully hilly. Rosings Park is known for its orchards."

"How interesting. Hartfield is known for its..."

"Exquisite shrubbery," Lizzy supplied. "And fountains. Whereas Donwell Abbey is particularly known for..."

Lady Catherine looked narrowly at the two of them.

"The strawberry beds!" Emma offered. "No doubt Mr. Knightley will make up a party in the spring to allow us first taste."

"I do not care about strawberry beds or shrubberies." Lady Catherine put down her tea. "This pittle-pattle is unbearable. What are young ladies of quality taught these days? No, I must make my mission known to you, Miss Woodhouse, and if you regret having a crowd to hear it that is your own affair. My nephew, Mr. Darcy, is engaged to my daughter, the honorable Anne de Bourgh."

Emma blinked. "Oh?"

"Do not pretend to be ignorant of my meaning. You are a lady of quality, as I have said, which I was not prepared to find. I shall therefore, with respect for your father's station, plainly tell you that it will not do. You are unobjectionable in most ways, but it has long been the plan to reunite the family estates by this union. You will understand how these things go."

Lizzy stared. This was directed at Emma, but Lizzy could not help feeling the ramifications for herself. "And yet," Lizzy said, "would your nephew possibly court or propose to Miss Woodhouse if he were engaged? It seems most unusual."

Lady Catherine gathered her cane and stood. "There is just such informality in the arrangement as one may pick at, but the intention is clear. A woman of *taste* and *virtue* would not push the point."

Emma was nearly gaping at the vulgarity and presumption of this lady. "How dare you insult me so?"

"Tell me plainly, Miss Woodhouse, are you engaged to Mr. Darcy? I have it on good authority that you were nearly so."

Lizzy could not have been more surprised than Emma.

"Whose authority?" Emma demanded. "In what possible way can you claim to know my concerns?"

"Why, on the authority of your own parson, Mr. Elton. He is on terms of occasional communication with Mr. Collins and passed on the news."

Emma stiffened with outrage. She rose to be at the same height as Lady Catherine. "Mr. Elton was a great deal too busy. He has indulged in groundless and blamable gossip. I will say nothing of the unknown Mr. Collins, but it seems quite odd that he should think it permissible to discuss me! And to pass on any rumors he heard! I must leave it to your conscience that you chose to listen to them."

"You are disrespectful, Miss Woodhouse!" Lady Catherine thumped her cane. "You say it is groundless gossip? You are not engaged to him?"

"No!"

"And will you promise not to become engaged to him?"

"Absolutely not, ma'am. You have gone quite far enough. If I love Mr. Darcy, or any gentleman, it is none of your concern. I absolutely loathe being discussed in the way you have described, and I shall only refrain from asking for an apology due to my respect for your age and station. I shall marry Mr. Darcy or not as I choose."

Lady Catherine was incensed, but the butler entered again and it was clear from the glare she cast in his direction that she felt somewhat constrained by the presence of a servant.

Lizzy shuddered to think what the old lady would have said to *her,* if she knew that Mr. Darcy had proposed! She'd given Emma a trimming, and Emma was far more eligible than Lizzy. The mere idea of the conversation, the outrage upon outrage that Lady Catherine would feel, made Lizzy laugh.

It was only one half-choked peal of laughter, but Lady Catherine, perhaps doubting her ability to cow Emma, turned on her. "Miss Bennet, do not think I shall forget how you supported your impertinent friend. It does you no service. I should hate to advise Mrs. Collins to rescind her offer."

"Excuse me, Miss Woodhouse," said the butler, "but Mr. Knightley and Mr. Darcy have also arrived."

"Well, of course they have," flashed Emma. "Why does not the whole neighborhood come today?"

Mr. Knightley and Mr. Darcy were entering even as she spoke; they must have been on the heels of the butler.

Mr. Knightley looked grave and confused, but Mr. Darcy appeared both enraged and mortified. Clearly, he'd heard enough to realize the purport of the visit.

If ever Lizzy could find a kinder feeling in her heart for him, it was now. How humiliating! Nor could he take his aunt to task before such an audience, even though he clearly wished to.

Mr. Darcy bowed in a choppy, barely controlled way to his aunt. "Lady Catherine. I am shocked to see you in Highbury. I—I have had the misfortune to overhear some of your errand, and I must insist that we speak in private. At once." He turned to Emma. "Is there a spare room where we would not be inconvenient?"

"You... you could certainly use the study." Emma gestured uncertainly. "It is downstairs, near the front of the house. Benton will show you."

"Just as well," said Lady Catherine, with her head high. "I have nothing more to say to this young lady. She has been less receptive than I hoped. I suppose I can only pray you do not throw off every vestige of familial duty to offer for this insolent young woman."

Darcy's cheek grew a deeper red with anger. "Miss Woodhouse, you have my deepest apology for being thus harassed in your own home."

He took his aunt's arm and led her inexorably out.

With the door shut behind them, Emma sank down onto the pink upholstered chair and pressed a hand to her forehead. *"That* was one of the strangest interviews I have ever experienced. What a dreadful old lady!"

Mr. Knightley winced. "Emma."

"No, you do not get to lecture me about proper respect; you did not hear her!"

"I heard enough. I am sorry that she confronted you. It was badly done, but you must not sink your own manners to match."

Emma waved him away.

Mr. Knightley turned to Jane Fairfax. "Can I do anything for you Miss Fairfax? You look very pale."

"No," her voice was faint, "she merely reminded me of Mrs. Churchill."

Lizzy could well imagine that just such a scene as this—though probably worse—was something that Jane Fairfax quite dreaded. Mrs. Churchill was leaving her fortune to Frank, and if she found out Jane had "enticed" him into marrying a penniless nobody, she would probably want to tear her eyes out.

Mr. Knightley looked very hard at her. "Mrs. Churchill? I did not know you were acquainted."

Lizzy broke in. "I am not acquainted with her at all, but from a few things that Mr. Churchill has said, I'm sure she is much of the same cloth. Some ladies have too much of their own way. Are you terribly angry, Emma? It is so strange that she should come all this way for a rumor!"

"I am more surprised than angry," her eyes sparkled, "but now you mention it, yes. How dare those men discuss me and my prospects!"

Mr. Knightley was distracted from questioning Jane as she explained the connection of Mr. Elton and Mr. Collins.

"What mischief!" Mr. Knightley pulled out his pocket watch, flipping open its silver case with a thumb nail. "Did she drive two or three hours here merely to berate you? I do wonder, Emma, if it might not have been better to tell her right away that you'd no intention of marrying or leaving Hartfield. It might have saved you time and pain."

"As to that," Emma said a little frostily, "I am growing a little tired of the surmises placed upon my married state. It would serve that woman right if I *did* marry Mr. Darcy."

She broke from her haughty tone to ask, in a softer voice, "*Would* it be wrong to leave my father, Mr. Knightley? It would, wouldn't it? He couldn't bear to be here alone, and he couldn't bear to leave Hartfield."

"Emma, my dear sister," Mr. Knightley stopped fidgeting with his watch and sat beside Emma, gripping her hand, "it would not be wrong. Quite the contrary. You can be sure that I should take such care of him. Your loss would be difficult; but he would not want you—could he but understand it—to give up love and happiness for him. He may not understand it, but *I* will support you in whatever decision you make. I will do everything a son could do to ease the change for him."

Emma turned her face toward his shoulder, two tears trickling down her cheeks.

Lizzy felt that she and Jane ought not to be present for this. Emma and Mr. Knightley had a family bond of many years; their closeness and understanding was palpable. Mr. Knightley made Lizzy wish, not for the first time, that she had an older brother. What a comfort that must be.

Raised voices were heard from below and Jane paled again. The first voice sounded like Lady Catherine and the next Mr. Darcy, though Lizzy could not imagine him yelling at his aunt. She must have said something truly reprehensible.

"I cannot stay," Jane Fairfax said. "I do not feel well. Miss Bennet, will you come?"

"Yes, of course."

{ 23 }

Mr. Darcy marched his aunt—carefully but firmly—from the study to the front door. "Please send at once for her ladyship's carriage."

"It is waiting, sir," said the butler.

Without another word, Darcy handed his aunt into her ornate carriage and shut the door. It was good she did not try to speak again; he was not in control of his temper.

Mr. Darcy passed a hand over his eyes. His aunt was an autocratic lady, the queen of her own demesne, but interfering in his life was beyond the line. Berating poor Miss Woodhouse and demanding her obedience! It was beyond belief.

Worse, Darcy felt it put him in a tight position. He, somewhat unexpectedly, liked and respected Miss Woodhouse. If he had never met Lizzy, she might have been the kind of woman he married. She was elegant, well-bred, impeccable lineage, accustomed to country life... even better, she had a sense of humor. She had employed no artifice or arts to keep his attention. She did not covet his wealth or estates.

But he'd met her *after* Lizzy, and his heart was already engaged.

Now though... what did he owe Miss Woodhouse? Having been rumored to be engaged to him, having been chastised and insulted by an elder member of his family, did he owe it to her to offer her his hand?

Surely not. It was not as though she had been compromised in some fashion. It was not *his* fault that a rumor had begun. His aunt's response was not his fault either, but as the leader of his family, it was his responsibility.

He trod slowly up the stairs. Even if he did offer Emma the protection of his name, he comforted himself, she would probably not accept.

He nearly laughed. How he had been humbled! Lizzy had taken his confidence, his arrogance, and cracked it like a walnut, leaving only the empty husk behind. He had been so certain of Lizzy. Her age, class, and lack of wealth made it obvious she would accept him. What a self-assured, blind puppy he had been!

Now, with Emma, he felt even less of a prize. But really, a proposal could not be thought necessary. An apology would have to do.

He met Jane Fairfax and Lizzy just as they left the drawing room. Both gave stiff nods and farewells. Darcy would have given much to have Lizzy meet his eyes and share some form of communion this awful morning.

She did not.

Her eyes hovered somewhere around his cravat and her murmured, "Good day," was as detached as if they'd never met.

Well, he could not blame her. He had censured her family pretty heavily, and now Lady Catherine had proved him a hypocrite.

Mr. Darcy entered the drawing room reluctantly, with absolutely no intention of proposing to Miss Woodhouse. Yet, before too many minutes had passed, he found himself so tangled in his thoughts and words that he nearly did so.

"That is... I regret that any action of mine should have occasioned such remark, or that gossip has traveled so far and caused such repercussions. Of course, the words of others are not either of our blame, but as my aunt has caused you this distress, I feel I ought to at least offer you the option of making it good."

Mr. Knightley rose. "I should give you a moment alone."

Darcy froze. Had he done it again? "No, please. I would as soon not trouble Mr. Woodhouse unless there is cause, but you could be considered family in this case."

Mr. Knightley winced a little, and Darcy wondered how badly he was expressing himself. He was a polished adult man; what had happened? It was as if Lizzy had cast a curse on him, making him seem as tactless to everyone else as he was to her.

Mr. Darcy steeled his spine to wait calmly for Emma's answer.

She waved a hand. "I appreciate the nicety of the sentiments behind this offer, but I would never hold a gentleman to such a bad bargain. You do not owe me anything except perhaps commiseration, which you have offered. You would not want to be stuck with me for such a thing as this; Mr. Knightley can tell you how dreadfully flawed I am."

Mr. Darcy inclined his head. "I would count myself lucky."

Emma studied his face and wondered. This was her second offer of marriage and as much unlike Mr. Elton as could be. Mr. Darcy would never languish over her.

If he only knew it, he had rarely appeared to such advantage. He was always a tall, well-built, handsome man... but in his embarrassment and uncertainty, instead of growing harsh and stiff, he was instead vulnerable.

"No, thank you," Emma said gently. "What an inauspicious start this would be! Perhaps... if we were better acquainted."

Mr. Knightley began to cough and they both turned to him.

"Excuse me." He cleared his throat. "May I have some of that tea, Emma?"

"Oh, of course, but I'm sure it is quite cold by now." Her moment with Mr. Darcy was done, and she instead chided Mr. Knightley over his bad timing in the visit this morning.

"Believe me, I am aware of it," Mr. Knightley said heavily.

Lizzy and Jane Fairfax waited for Lady Catherine's carriage to get to the end of the drive before continuing to walk. The last thing either of them wanted was to possibly be hailed by Lady Catherine.

When the fancy carriage had turned and gone out of sight, heading north on the road that would lead through Highbury proper and then toward the London road, Lizzy and Jane walked on. A spattering of cold raindrops flecked their cheeks and dappled the packed dry dirt of the road.

Lizzy tipped her head up to see that the clouds had got darker. "Oh no, you were right; it *is* come on to rain. We could go back and ask Emma—"

"Nonsense. It is not much."

"If you are sure...well, we will hurry. I don't much want to go back and bother Emma if we needn't."

As the rain spat at them, Lizzy marveled how her beautiful morning had turned to this. She was still glowing about her sister's engagement, but she would just have to be happy alone for now. How she longed to go on to Hunsford and see Charlotte!

Jane Fairfax was pale and actually took her arm when Lizzy offered it. It was well and truly raining now. Jane shivered and her hand was icy cold. It would be such a shame if Jane became ill again! Lizzy was ready to move on from Highbury, but she would rather not leave ruin in her wake.

"I am sorry I forced you to walk this morning. Perhaps—but look, a carriage." Lizzy waved her hand energetically, and the carriage stopped just opposite them. "I think it is Mrs. Weston."

"No," said poor Jane, "no, no, it is Mr. Churchill."

Indeed, she had spied through the foggy window of the carriage more acutely than Lizzy, for it was Mr. Frank Churchill who flung open the carriage door and jumped out with an umbrella.

"My dear, sodden ladies, allow me to be of assistance." He held the umbrella completely over them while they scrambled across the slippery mud of the road. His carefully arranged hair was nearly soaked by the time they were in. He directed the coachman to turn about where he could—or even at Hartfield since this lane was so cursed narrow—and to take them to Miss Bates's.

"Were you attempting to swim home?" he joked. "Miss Woodhouse was too churlish to offer you a ride? I suspected it; I knew her sweetness must hide blackest evil."

Jane raised a hand. "Please, Frank, no sarcasm today."

"Frank! She calls me Frank which I have not heard in months. Congratulate me, Miss Bennet, since you know in what desperate case we stand, and how starved of affection I must therefore be."

Jane turned her face away. "No more, please."

"No more? But no more of what? You will feel better when you have got warm. I hesitate to imitate your dear, voluble aunt, but you really must take better care of your health—"

"I'm afraid that is my doing," Lizzy interrupted, hoping to give Jane a moment to recover. "I wanted to walk, and I was overly optimistic about the weather."

"I never sneer at optimism," he said. "I live life on the stuff. I wish you could give some of your optimism to Jane. Since we returned to Highbury she is very grave; very silent; very low."

"Frank, please, no more—" Jane said.

"No more, I know. But I think you do not realize when you say *no more* you are robbing me of what small joy I have in being with you. No more of what—"

"No more of any of this!" Jane's eyes were shut. "I cannot and will not continue this deception. I am done."

Frank was startled out of his insouciant cheer. "You do not mean that."

"I do. I dread this coming to your aunt's ears and the loss of your future. I dread the disapproval of your parents. I dread what you will do or say. I dread everything."

"But is not the thought of our future happiness worth that present anxiety?"

"No."

"But Jane—" he tried to laugh, perhaps by habit, but it did not come. "Do think what this will mean. You cannot be a governess. You were never meant for it."

"I can do anything it is my duty to do. I am sorry, but I am done."

The sound of the rain on the roof and the horses' hoofs smacking and squelching in the mud was very loud in the sudden silence. Lizzy opened her mouth to say something, to say *anything* to break the tension, but she stopped herself.

She *could* perhaps fill this awkward silence, but she realized for perhaps the first time that she ought not. Some emotions were difficult, nigh on unbearable, but anesthetizing this moment with chatter would be worse. Jane was changing the course of her life, and she ought to be allowed to feel it, for better or worse.

Frank finally laughed, forcefully. "Very well. I won't tease you now. I should only get a cold shoulder; you are implacable when you have made up your mind. You are my good angel, after all."

At Miss Bates's home, Jane blindly took off her wet pelisse. Miss Bates was exclaiming over her state and thanking Providence for Mr. Churchill, but Jane did not seem to hear any of it. There was a blind, numb look in her eyes.

Lizzy pushed her toward the bedroom and shut her in.

Miss Bates was mid-sentence. She paused and peered at Lizzy through her slightly askew spectacles. "Is anything amiss? Anything more than a most unfortunate wetting, I mean?"

"No, but Jane was feeling unwell even at Hartfield. We were away before we realized it was coming on to pour. I am so sorry."

This was quite enough to explain Jane's malaise to Miss Bates, and she was quick to agree when Jane opened the door presently, in her dressing gown, to say that she needed to lie down.

"Oh dear, oh dear," said Miss Bates. "She is not at all well, I can see it. I should not wonder if she were to take to her bed for a week! And we shall lose you so soon after, Miss Bennet! I cannot believe it is already March. But please do not think me ungrateful. You have been a blessing to us. Yes, a blessing. Even if Jane should be ill again, you have helped me past the bleak feeling I had when my dear mother passed away. I can never be sufficiently grateful."

"But I have done so little," Lizzy protested.

"So little? When you have done errands for me quite every day! Every day! And been so cheerful and pleasant, to remind me of what I was missing! Cheerful and pleasant, I declare, every day."

"You have many friends who are willing to do that. I love my hometown of Meryton, but I must say that you have the most attentive and kind friends. You are universally liked, Miss Bates, and I am old enough to know that is no accident."

This was quite enough praise to throw Miss Bates into a paroxysm of humble half-sentences and thankful paragraphs.

Lizzy smiled at her, but she could not *wait* to see her dear, sensible Charlotte in Hunsford! Highbury had given her enough of drama to last her many weeks. First Mr. Darcy, then Emma and Lady Catherine, then Jane and Frank! It was more than enough.

There were only two things left. If Lizzy saw Mr. Darcy again before he returned north, which she had heard was soon to happen, she had two things to say to him. First, she must tell him how overjoyed she was at Bingley's restoration, and second, she must apologize for believing Wickham's lies and blackening Darcy's character in Meryton. She'd had ample time over the last weeks to think through his explanation and her own memories, and she could come to no conclusion but that she had been a complete fool about Wickham.

She also wondered whether she ought to put in a good word for Emma.

When Lady Catherine commanded Emma to renounce her relationship with Darcy, she had boldly refused. Was it possible that Emma cared about him?

It would not be *im*possible, for the more Lizzy considered, the more she realized that Mr. Darcy could be very appealing to a certain kind of woman.

{ 24 }

Mr. Knightley took off his dampened riding coat when they arrived back from Hartfield and requested the butler to have a fire lit in the library and brandy brought in. He and Darcy had gotten unpleasantly wet and cold on the ride home.

They had not spoken much.

"Unfortunate about your aunt's visit," Mr. Knightley had said.

"Mortifying," Darcy agreed.

Now they both retired to change their clothes—their sleeves and cravats were sadly soaked and their riding breeches splattered with mud—and came back down to the warm library.

Mr. Knightley poured the amber brandy into two tumblers and offered one to Darcy.

He swirled it meditatively, stretching out comfortably in an armchair with his feet toward the fire. "You have never married."

Mr. Knightley took in this statement and then threw back his whole glass of brandy. A waste, but he relished the burn on the way down. He suspected he might need it. He refilled his glass. "That's correct."

"Plan to marry?"

"I don't know. I am happy enough to leave Donwell Abbey to my eldest nephew."

"Hm. I have no nephews. Other than Georgiana's inheritance, my worldly goods would go to one of my cousins."

"Not a terrible fate, if you don't mind the fellow. I think," Knightley took another fortifying sip, "I think it far worse to marry a woman one doesn't love or respect than to allow an estate to pass to a cousin or to the distaff line."

"Yes." Darcy swirled the glass, sipped it. "So you are content with your state?"

"Content?" A slew of images passed before Mr. Knightley's inner eye. His excellent land, rich soil, rich crops. His tenants, all good men, and their families. Tea with Emma and Mr. Woodhouse. Evenings and meals alone. "In most ways, I am content. As far as marriage... I do not know. I have felt of late that perhaps..." He looked blindly at the empty glass, instead reliving his growing unease for the past months. He reflected on his strange irritability, his dissatisfaction. "Perhaps I may make a change. In fact, I think I will."

"Yes," said Mr. Darcy.

They finished their drinks silently. Mr. Knightley occupied himself with letters of business, and Mr. Darcy with a book. If neither was terribly productive, they neither of them were rude enough to comment.

Mr. Knightley had made up his mind by the night of the Westons' party.

It was much the same group as gathered weeks ago at the Westons' Christmas party, who were now clumped in sparkling knots in the elegant drawing room of Randalls. Tonight, however, there was no snow, but instead a clear starlit night that heralded good things for the planting season.

From Highbury with Love

Upon entering the drawing room—a room he was well acquainted with from his visits to Mr. Weston—Mr. Knightley noted that it was again a bit overly warm. Instead of smelling of pomander oranges like Christmas, however, the room smelled of lamp oil and of the dinner Mrs. Weston would soon serve—ham and beef and sugary cakes.

Emma and Mr. Woodhouse were both in attendance and he greeted that gentleman first after his host. Emma had distributed greetings here and there but had already formed a group with both Mr. Churchill and Darcy.

Instead of going to her, Mr. Knightley instead joined Miss Elizabeth Bennet who was standing uncharacteristically alone near the doors to the terrace.

"May I have a word, Miss Bennet?" he asked.

She smiled. "Of course. I am thinking melancholy thoughts, which is never safe at a party, please distract me. Have you been reading more Kant?"

"I'm afraid it is not philosophy this time. Would you accompany me just briefly into the antechamber? All the guests have arrived, so we may speak alone there while yet being in sight."

"Of course. But I am now very curious."

They threaded their way between the groups by the fire and the pianoforte, and the group governed by Emma where the dancing would later be.

The small room just outside the drawing room held several gilt-edged side tables and was a staging area for the servants when they brought in food. Several men had left their hats on one of the tables. Three candles burnt on the closest table, but it was not as bright as the drawing room.

Through the open door, the sounds of the party were still audible but muted.

Mr. Knightley had wondered if perhaps he would feel nerves. He'd thought ruefully of a dreadful episode in London as a youth when he had developed a *tendre* for a somewhat older, experienced woman.

He did not feel nerves.

"Miss Bennet, I understand your visit will end at the end of March. I have enjoyed furthering our acquaintance these last weeks. Indeed, I have found that we have a markedly similar view on many things. Furthermore, I admire your dedication and kindness to your cousin, Miss Bates, and your cheerfulness and good humor despite their somewhat straitened circumstances. All your actions here in Highbury speak to your high character and intelligence." He cleared his throat. "In short, I would like to offer you my hand in marriage, if you should choose to accept me."

Lizzy blinked. In the low light of the candles in the antechamber, she could not perfectly make out Mr. Knightley's expression, but he seemed both sober and sincere.

Good heavens. At the outset of his words, she had expected that he was merely building to a dedicated *thank-you* on behalf of Miss Bates. He seemed to be the sort who took responsibility for those he cared about, and though Miss Bates was not his relative or tenant, Lizzy had seen how much he did for her.

But then he had ended with a proposal!

It was her third (if she counted Darcy's aborted speech), and again she felt unprepared. Unlike the previous two times, however, she wasn't angry or disgusted. Mr. Knightley was rather older than herself, but he was a good-looking man, and more importantly, one whom she enjoyed talking to. He was intelligent and fair-minded. He was kind and considerate toward those less

From Highbury with Love

fortunate than himself. He was, in fact, an excellent gentleman, and even had a sense of humor.

"You have surprised me," Lizzy said slowly. "Thank you very much for the honor you do me in asking." She tried to collect her thoughts. He *was* an excellent man—*why* was he asking her to marry him? He could not be in love with her, could he?

She was not in love with him, at any rate, but she liked him very well.

Could she love him? Very possibly.

Her bumbling, awkward cousin Mr. Collins had once told her she would probably never receive a better marriage offer than his. This time, however, it was very likely true. She would never receive an offer from a man to equal Mr. Knightley.

"But you do not feel we should suit, perhaps?" Mr. Knightley offered with a smile, breaking into her rather long silence. "You needn't hesitate to say so. I am thirty-seven and you are..."

"Soon to be twenty-one," Lizzy said. He had a rather adorable smile. "But it is not that." Her mind churned with disparate thoughts. He was a significant landowner. Lizzy would never grow to be a poor old maid like Miss Bates. She would never see her mother and sisters in dire straits. But then, Jane was engaged to Mr. Bingley! Her family was already safe.

Lizzy immediately felt regret for even considering a marriage for wealth, which she had sworn she would never do. But she did genuinely like Mr. Knightley.

The fact that Jane was well matched actually relieved her mind. If Lizzy accepted Mr. Knightley, it would not be mercenary.

Then there was Mr. Darcy.

But no, Mr. Darcy had nothing to do with this, did he?

Mr. Knightley tilted his head, perhaps trying to get a better look at her. "You perhaps have wanted to marry for love, as many young ladies do. I do not feel we know each other quite well enough for that, but I think we would very well grow into it. And, of course, if there is already a gentleman who holds your affections, you have only to say so and we will return to the drawing room as friends. As I hope we have become these last weeks."

"Yes, I do consider you a friend," Lizzy finally said. "And I believe I am inclined, if you are perfectly sure you should not regret it, to say yes." She put a hand to her cheek, not quite able to believe what she had said.

Mr. Knightley bowed slightly. "You do me great honor. I should perhaps add that while you have seen Donwell Abbey, you may not be aware that my family's fortune has dwindled of late generations. I live in comfort, but not what some might consider elegance."

Lizzy laughed. "Yes, I know. Emma will not stop haranguing you about keeping your own carriage horses."

He sighed. "Exactly. I use the farm horses when I need them."

"That would not weigh with me," Lizzy said. "My father does the same, and generally I prefer to walk." Her mind still swam with thoughts, some serious, some frivolous. She simply could not focus. Why would Mr. Darcy keep returning to mind?

Mr. Knightley must have realized she could not offer much more at present. "I would not wish to rush you. Perhaps I might call on Thursday after you have had time to consider?"

"Yes, I—I had better consider. Thank you for your understanding. Perhaps it seems ridiculous that I should need to think," she gestured at his person vaguely, "as the advantage would be entirely mine, but it is no small thing—"

He shook his head. "Not at all. I have often thought you mature beyond your years, and this only confirms my belief." He offered his arm. "Shall we return to the drawing room?"

Lizzy took his arm, feeling rather disconnected from herself.

There was no denying it was flattering that Mr. Knightley had preferred her. Mr. Wickham's attention had flattered her vanity, but Mr. Knightley's character was proven, so it was the better compliment. She felt less shallow for enjoying it.

Marriage was a serious business, however. Could she move so far from Meryton and her family? Could she commit her life to Mr. Knightley?

The first question was easy. Yes, she could easily move away from her family. She would even be fixed near Charlotte!

They circled the brightly lit drawing room slowly, and Mr. Knightley guided them to the periphery of the little circle around Emma. There they separated.

Hm. If she accepted Mr. Knightley, she would also be fixed near Emma. Emma would probably *not* appreciate Lizzy becoming the mistress of Donwell Abbey and one of the leaders of Meryton society.

They had not argued since that one angry day, however. And when Lady Catherine had been raking Emma down about Darcy's supposed attention, they had had a moment of real solidarity. Perhaps she and Emma could truly be friends one day.

Mrs. Weston's butler announced that supper was served in the dining room and Frank Churchill immediately offered his hand to Emma.

"My lady, shall we lead the way?" he asked. "In town, one always pretends an indifference to the food, but I have already tasted the lobster patties, and so I shall be graceless and enthusiastic."

"I do not think you could be graceless if you tried," Emma said, tucking her delicate white glove around his arm, contrasting with his deep blue evening coat.

"Do you all hear?" he said gaily. "She has challenged me to be graceless. How shall I answer her? An overturned wine glass? A stumble and roll? Shall I tread upon your feet when we dance? You must dance the first with me and give me a chance to prove you wrong."

Lizzy winced, thinking of poor Jane Fairfax back at Miss Bates's, alone in the frigid bedroom. She had cried off from the party, which Lizzy had expected.

Would Jane finally cry when she was alone? She had not—though Lizzy did not expect it any longer—confided in Lizzy any of her thoughts or feelings since she broke her engagement with Frank. If she was miserable, she hid it well after that tragic, rainy afternoon.

Frank Churchill on the other hand, seemed to be livelier than ever.

Mr. Knightley's lips were a bit thin and his smile a little forced when he offered his own arm to Lizzy for dinner. "I cannot entirely like that young man," he said, "no matter how much I admire his father and step-mother. He charms everyone, yet he seems careless and, I fear, self-centered."

Lizzy did not want to speak of Frank. She knew too much about his "carelessness."

"Perhaps so. But think how dull if the party were only full of those who think before they speak! No ill-considered jokes, no sarcasm better left unsaid, no telling slip of the tongue; how could one bear such good behavior? No, I prefer at least two rattles, three rakes, and four coxcombs at any party."

Mr. Knightley's lips quirked as they slowly joined the procession to the dining room amongst the other guests.

They ended up, fortunately or unfortunately, just behind Mr. Darcy and his dinner partner. To Lizzy's surprise, he was squiring the new Mrs. Elton, the haughty woman with the sharp nose whom Mr. Elton had brought back from Bath as a wife. How had Mr. Darcy ended up with her? He did not seem to be speaking much, but Mrs. Elton did not need encouragement.

"Did you not notice that Miss Fairfax is absent again tonight?" she asked. "She is the dearest girl, but sadly careless of her health! She really must strengthen herself for she is going to be a governess, you see. I am so well-connected in Bath that I expect I will be able to do wonders for her. What is that?" she asked, as apparently he had interposed a quiet question. He did not seem to realize that Lizzy was just behind him. "No, I am not much acquainted with Miss Bennet. She is rather pert and bold, is she not? Not at all, to my way of thinking, what a young lady in her circumstances ought to be. But consider Jane, have you ever seen a woman with such poise? Such ladylike grace? Such a fine figure? And she is as humble and teachable as never was! So thankful for my mentorship, I assure you. But if you mean that Miss Bennet requires employment, you have only to give me a wink. I am excellent at finding young people good positions. My friends always say so." She tapped his shoulder with her closed fan.

Mr. Knightley turned away slightly, lagging back a step to leave some space and allow another couple—Mr. Shilby and Harriet, as it happened—to precede them.

"I am not quite to the point of hiring myself out," Lizzy said to Mr. Knightley, who had also heard the whole. "But I shall know where *not* to turn for help and discretion if I find myself at *point non plus*."

Mr. Knightley sniffed. "I did not approve of Emma's plans, but I admit, she would have chosen better for Elton than he did for himself."

"Yes. I wonder if she has quite forgiven me for crossing her yet?"

"Probably. For all her faults, she is not a grudge holder." He paused. "And I hope it goes without saying that... that I would far rather see you as Mrs. Knightley than as a governess." He smiled ruefully. "That is not romantic at all, is it? I have been a bachelor too long. I am not good at making pretty speeches."

Lizzy patted his arm. "The last man who made me pretty speeches was quite untrustworthy. Obviously, I *prefer* a shallow rip, but I can settle for an honest gentleman."

Mr. Darcy looked back at her and Lizzy bit her lip, wondering if she'd spoken too loudly. His brow was furrowed.

Lizzy had been thinking of Mr. Wickham's flattery and lies, but if Darcy had overheard, perhaps he thought *he* was the untrustworthy man who had last made her a pretty speech.

Lizzy sighed. Yet another thing to clear up with Mr. Darcy.

{ 25 }

DINNER WAS DELICIOUS—the Westons' cook was quite good—but Mr. Darcy did not enjoy the lobster, the ham, the beef, or the various molds, puddings, and creamed vegetables as he should.

He had been quite caught by this Mrs. Elton, who was already calling him *Darcy* with great familiarity and speaking in a loud, vulgar way. This was exactly the sort of thing he most disliked in social situations.

The only relief he felt was that Elizabeth had somehow ended up across the table from him. She had smiled at him once, when their eyes had met during the first remove, and he had felt a loosening in his gut. He had been able to eat then.

She must not have meant what he'd overheard, that she thought he was untrustworthy. He must have misunderstood. What bothered him more was the way she'd patted Knightley's arm and smiled at him in such a friendly, nearly familial way.

Gracious heavens. Was it possible that Knightley, when speaking of a change in his single state, was picturing Elizabeth Bennet?

But she had only been acquainted with Knightley a matter of weeks, a few months at most... which was as long or longer than he had first known Lizzy in Hertfordshire.

But then, she was so much younger than Knightley! But more unequal matches were made every day.

The crux of it was that she had rejected Darcy, and she had every right to accept Mr. Knightley if he offered for her. Indeed, the thought that she would prefer Knightley to himself stung slightly—but not as much as it would have several weeks ago. His ego—had it truly been so out of control?—had taken a hard knock at her firm, angry rejection. This new wound barely registered.

After supper, Mrs. Weston's younger guests begged for dancing. Darcy watched with rather shameful interest whether Knightley would dance first with Lizzy, but he did not. Instead, with a word in Lizzy's ear, Knightley left her and bowed to Mrs. Weston, their middle-aged host.

She was obviously surprised and delighted. She was a new bride, despite her age, so Darcy supposed that dancing was not out of the question for her. Clearly Mr. Knightley had realized and made a point, as one of the leaders of Highbury society, to make it possible for her.

Watching their small drama, he was aware of Lizzy's extremely happy smile for the small interplay, and even Emma, resplendent in white opposite Frank Churchill, cast Knightley a glowing look of appreciation as they joined the set.

Darcy felt uncharacteristically chastened. Was this what Lizzy wanted in a man? Knightley knew his own worth but was affable and thoughtful. He was never above his company—even visiting the dreadfully talkative Miss Bates every week—and generally treated everyone with respect and consideration. That was only the gentlemanly way, of course, any true gentleman would do the same...

But with a rising dread, Darcy looked back at his own behavior in Hertfordshire, and to some extent here in Highbury, and compared it with that of Mr. Knightley. There was only one conclusion: Darcy's pride—that bastion of his family's superiority and benevolence—had led him far astray.

Had he forgotten until this moment what true gentlemanly behavior was like? Had he ever known? He had allowed his consciousness of his own position and worth to make him disdainful, arrogant, and even contemptuous of those around him.

Darcy writhed inwardly as he thought back to Lizzy's words. She forgave his bad manners far more easily than he could forgive his own.

How could he not have seen until now how badly he had behaved?

Lizzy danced the second dance with Mr. Knightley, which was pleasant, but was relieved when Mr. Darcy came to her at the third and asked for the honor of a dance.

"Yes, thank you," she said. "For now I will not have the trouble of finding a way to speak to you."

His eyebrows rose inquisitively, and she hurried on as they took their place in the lines of men and women dancers.

"Two things," Lizzy said as they touched hands and moved several steps to the left, beginning the first movements of the simple dance. "First, I have had a letter from my sister Jane, and she is deliriously happy. In anyone else, such effusions on her fiancé's perfection would be unbearable—I daresay you are subject to that on Mr. Bingley's side, as well—but from Jane I will accept anything. I believe I will give her a year before I put a stop to it, though in the normal course of marriage I suppose she will stop praising him by then."

Mr. Darcy smiled, though rather stiffly and unhappily. Perhaps her excitement with the evening—was she feeling a trifle giddy about Mr. Knightley?—had led her into too much freedom with him. He may have fixed things with Bingley, but that did not mean he liked the match. He was a *good* man, she had decided, but still not necessarily a *likeable* one.

They circled and came back together. Thankfully the music of the pianoforte and the voices of those watching and dancing quite covered their conversation. "The second thing is to apologize—most sincerely—for believing the slander against you and for, at times, encouraging it." She winced despite herself. "As I look back over the circumstances, I can see that I was very much at fault, very eager to think the worst of you. I hope you can forgive it."

He was obliged to wait a moment for the dance to bring them back together. "I think you are too hard on yourself. It is not in your nature to expect lies and deceit, and he imposed on you. In return, however, I must ask you to forget what my behavior was like in Hertfordshire. I was rude to you and unforgivably arrogant in my dealings with others. I shall do better in future; I hope you will think better of me in time."

Lizzy reassured him, but also felt a frisson of worry that he was leading back around to a second proposal.

Surely not! She was probably being unbearably vain to think he would still want to marry her! But if he *was* implying that... it would be unkind to lead him on.

"I already do think better of you. I hope that in the future, as we will be drawn by necessity into Jane and Bingley's lives, we may consider ourselves friends," Lizzy said with finality.

He inclined his head. He did not seem to want to talk and they finished the dance in silence. It reminded Lizzy of their first dance together at Netherfield.

Perhaps it was fitting that their relationship, marked by discord and misunderstanding, should be thus bookended by uncomfortable dances.

Lizzy could not avoid dancing with Frank Churchill. He had a devil-may-care gleam in his eye; she hoped he would not do anything drastic. He came to her after he had danced with Emma, with Miss Cole, even with Harriet Smith, and appeared on the surface to be bright and lively, but Lizzy distrusted his eyes.

"I daresay Miss Fairfax is laid down with a headache?" he inquired of her. His voice was quite normal in tone and she looked around at the other couples, startled. But no, she supposed that an inquiry about Miss Fairfax was not out of line.

"Yes," Lizzy said. "She didn't feel up to a party. She is still recovering from being ill, you know."

"No doubt." He finally lowered his voice. "I've half a mind to go back to my aunt and make a clean breast of it. I shall be thrown off and then Jane will see that I did care for her. Then I will spend the rest of my life in poverty, and she will feel unutterable guilty for the rest of hers." He smiled, but Lizzy didn't. "Don't all great love stories end in tragedy?" he asked.

"If you did anything of the sort, the blame would be yours. Nor do I see how that would prove anything worthwhile."

He moved his gold head impatiently. "Yes, I know. But it is not amusing to be jilted, Miss Bennet, when all that's wanted is a little fortitude. I was having a dashed good time with a secret engagement."

"Everyone must know their own necessities," Lizzy said. "Jane's don't include... well, I don't think Miss Fairfax cares for amusement as you do."

"She doesn't. Or me either, it appears."

Lizzy didn't meet his eye. She didn't know whether Jane still cared for Frank Churchill. She could not picture how they had ever become attached. Jane was so reserved and upright, Frank so playful and impertinent!

"But far be it from me," Frank said, returning to his usual manner, "to dance with a pretty girl and bore her with the future or the past. The present is where we ought to live, is it not? Eat, drink, and be merry, for tomorrow we die."

"Very Roman," Lizzy said.

"Oh, yes, you'd never think it to look at me, but I'm a dab at Latin." He sighed. "No, for me it must be *ad meloria*, which means, *toward better things*. There was a wonderful Latin duet that Miss Fairfax and I used to sing. Do you play or sing, Miss Bennet?"

"Not well, and certainly not in Latin." Was it possible that he missed Jane Fairfax for her superior voice? For the excellence of their joint performance?

"I already know Emma's powers," he said. "I wonder whether little Miss Harriet Smith plays? She has had an indifferent education, Emma says, but she may be musical. She would certainly make a picture at the instrument, and that is more than half of your truly "gifted" musician, is it not? I daresay if we were to be stricken blind, we should be quite surprised whom is actually a talented player with only the auditory sense to guide us."

"I don't think Harriet is particularly musical."

She was not surprised however, that he tried anyway. When the dancers declared themselves tired, a tea tray was brought in and Mrs. Weston suggested that a few young ladies might play for them. Frank soon bullied sweet little Harriet into playing.

It was perfectly bad luck that he should have picked on her just after the proud, new Mrs. Elton had been playing. Her voice was somewhat nasal, but there was no denying her fingers flew on the keys. Her husband, Mr. Elton, beamed with pride, holding himself with exaggerated dignity. His short clergy bands fairly quivered around his collar.

But all too soon, Frank Churchill had suavely thanked Mrs. Elton and insisted that she not exhaust her voice on such a dry, cold night. Then he bullied Harriet into playing.

Harriet was fine, probably much of a similarity with herself, Lizzy thought wryly, but nothing compared to Mrs. Elton, who visibly sneered at her.

"My dear Mrs. Cole," she said quite audibly, "we really must have a musical club. The true musician, such as myself, cannot have too much opportunity to enjoy *la musique*. We can invite whom we wish." An expressive movement of her eyes clearly mocked Harriet.

Harriet did make quite a picture with Mr. Churchill, both of them being blonde and so handsome. Harriet had played on her own at first, but he soon joined her. She looked quite thankful when he did. Her own voice sank to a thin whisper, admirably covered by his baritone.

His eyes flashed knowingly to Lizzy as he escorted Harriet to a settee and offered a hand to Emma.

Clearly, Harriet had been found wanting.

What a strange young man!

Mr. Knightley joined her on the loveseat with his own teacup. "You don't wish to play?"

"Not with Mr. Churchill," Lizzy tilted her head toward where he stood turning Emma's pages and singing with her. They sang quite well together, though nothing to match the exaltation of his performance with Jane Fairfax.

"Would you play for me, someday? I am not fastidious."

"Of course, but I fear you should tire of my scales. I never seem to move much beyond them, and while chivalry may endure any amount of torture, my father assures me that scales upon the pianoforte are something akin to the rack."

He smiled and settled in next to Lizzy, and she couldn't help looking at him now and again. How would it be to be married to this gentleman? Very... comfortable, she expected. He was not dramatic and nor was she (generally). He was very handsome, in his own way. He would probably not be compared favorably with Mr. Darcy or Mr. Bingley, but there was seriousness and good humor stamped on his brow and face. It was a face she could easily come to love.

Lizzy felt rather lightheaded. Had she drunk perhaps a touch more wine than usual at dinner? She did not think so. Was it merely the warmth of the room? The strain of answering Mr. Churchill's veiled complaints about Jane?

Whatever it was, she felt a little reckless. She dug her hands into the cushion she sat on.

"Mr. Knightley," she said. He did not respond. "Mr. Knightley?"

He looked over to her; he'd been contemplating Emma and Frank, frowning. "Pardon me, yes?"

"I believe, if you are quite certain of your offer, that I do not need those two days to consider. I would be honored to accept your hand."

Mr. Knightley smiled a little sadly and raised her gloved hand to his lips. "Thank you, Miss Bennet. I think—I really do think, that we could be very happy."

{ 26 }

NEARLY A WEEK LATER, Emma felt the morning breeze grow icy against her suddenly hot cheeks as Mr. Knightley walked with her around the rear garden of Hartfield. Her footsteps on the gravel path faltered.

Her face froze.

"I am sorry, I do not perfectly understand," Emma said. "You are going to propose to Miss *Bennet?"*

"I have already done so and been accepted. I waited to publish the news until I heard back from her father, which I did this morning. As one of my closest friends—you and your father, of course—I wanted you to be the first to know."

Emma blinked. "Yes, I wish you... I am sure..." She turned away a little blindly and cut a spray of early white spring flowers. She had come out to cut flowers, hadn't she? And then been plunged into this shocking conversation.

"Miss Bennet?" Emma repeated. "How is that possible?"

Yes, he had danced with Lizzy on several occasions, she remembered. He had complimented her mind and her independence. He had sided with Lizzy about Harriet and Mr. Martin. But...

"I do not quite understand," Mr. Knightley said. "How is it possible that she accepted me? You must ask her."

"No, no. I only meant—you have surprised me. But why should that be?" Emma tried to smile, but quickly turned to cut more flowers. "You've admired her for some weeks, haven't you? Even Mrs. Weston had suggested the idea after her Christmas party."

What was there to shock and—truth be told—horrify her about the match? Emma tried again for a smile. "Poor little Henry will be quite cut out. I quite think of Donwell as his own."

"Yes, but... Emma, are you unwell?"

With a deep breath and an effort that made her chest ache like she'd swallowed a stone, she fought back the suddenly developing tears. "No, of course not. I am merely shamefully amazed and wishing I had guessed it. My matchmaking senses have failed me again. You must see how mortified I am."

He shrugged. "It has only been arranged since the Westons' party on Tuesday. I know it will be a change for our family circle—your father so dislikes change, it will be hard for him—but I hope you will find it a good thing. As she is already your friend, I hope that will soon reconcile you to Henry's loss."

"Of course. I wish you every happiness in the world. You must—" Emma grasped for words, for she desperately needed to be alone. "You must be eager to tell the Westons."

"Yes, I believe I will stop in while I am on this side of Highbury."

"You should go at once. Then Mrs. Weston and I may comfortably gossip about you!"

"I hope you will call on Miss Bennet soon; I hope you will be good friends again."

"Of course!" Emma said again. "We have never stopped."

He did go, finally, and Emma handed the flowers to the housekeeper on her way up the stairs. "Put them in some water... I have the headache."

In her bedroom, finally, she closed the door and flung herself at her four-poster bed. Why Mr. Knightley's engagement should make her cry her eyes out, she did not know, but there was no other possible response.

Mr. Knightley was not supposed to marry. Like her, he would remain single, and they would remain fast friends all their lives. He would walk over to Highbury; she would raid his strawberry beds and play with his dogs. He would complain that she spoiled them for hunting.

Emma did not like change at the best of times, and this was the worst of times. For Mr. Knightley should never marry, unless... Unless it was to *her*.

She stilled on her bed, her sobs quieting. But, truly? Did she love Mr. Knightley more than as a dear friend? If she imagined herself the one who would have the banns read and say vows with him...

The warm glow that rose in her was matched by a stab of agony. Yes, *she* should be Mrs. Knightley, no one else! He was hers as surely as she was his. And she was too late.

In her agony, Emma forgot that Harriet was coming over at midday. She was roused by a knock on her door and the maid saying that Miss Smith was arrived and had gone into the drawing room as usual.

"Should I tell her you is unwell, miss?" the maid asked. "I already said as how you had lain down with a headache this morning."

"Yes... No, please tell Harriet I will be down directly." Emma splashed cold water from her basin on her face and dried it carefully with the soft hand towel. She must begin to accustom herself to the news.

Harriet sat primly and properly in the drawing room. She had that accursed book of riddles in her hands and seemed to be perusing it again happily. She had the temperament to enjoy a riddle all the more for already knowing the answer and she had no issue with repetition, which was generally the bane of Emma's childhood.

"There you are, Miss Woodhouse. I am so sorry you do not feel well," Harriet exclaimed, rising to kiss Emma's cheek. "Have you heard the news about Miss Bennet and Mr. Knightley? Is it not wonderful? You must tell me if this was one of your plans, like the way you arranged for Mr. Weston and Mrs. Weston—for I had no idea of it!"

Emma sank down on the chair her father usually used, large and soft. "I'm afraid I did not either. I just heard the news from Mr. Knightley."

"I called upon Miss Bennet, of course, since I thought she was to leave Friday and I wanted to wish her goodbye—and *they* told me the news. Miss Bates is quite giddy over it all. I think she could hardly be happier unless Jane Fairfax had got engaged. Miss Bennet has just received a letter from her father this morning giving his approval."

"The wonder would be if he *dis*approved of such an excellent catch as Mr. Knightley!"

"No, I am sure he would not, it is just the formality. I am very happy for her! She is not at all afraid of Mr. Knightley, is she? Or—or intimidated by him, as one might be. I hope not; I think it an excellent match."

"If your idea of an excellent match is that one spouse is not afraid of the other, I am afraid you have low standards."

Harriet's face fell, and Emma realized she was allowing her broken heart to make her quite sharp. "I'm sorry, my dear. You are quite right. I daresay they shall deal... extremely well!" She forced the last words out. "But come, I have not spoken to you since the Westons' party. Was it only my partiality, or did young Mr. Cox look at you rather particularly when you danced?"

Harriet blushed. "Oh, only the best of friends could think so. I am sure he only danced with me since the younger Miss Cole and Miss Fairfax did not attend. The ladies were in short supply."

"Perhaps." Emma sighed. "I wish I could see you happily married, Harriet! I have been an utter failure at matchmaking, an utter failure even at perfectly normal awareness. Would this one thing be too much?" Emma spoke more to Providence than to Harriet.

If Emma's own chance for happiness had fled—the pain of that had not yet begun to settle into grooves—could she not see Harriet happily established?

Harriet's eyes filled with tears, glistening beautifully. "I would do anything in my power... but I think you have looked at me with the eyes of a friend and not the eyes of the world! Please do not take this upon yourself. You have done everything a friend could do and more! And indeed, I value your friendship far more than any possible man! You must know this is true."

Sadly, Emma did know it. She opened her mouth and shut it again. Harriet had indeed rejected Mr. Robert Martin because she valued Emma's friendship more.

For the first time, Emma felt a flash of true self-doubt. What had she done to her sweet friend?

"Please don't cry, Harriet," Emma said. "I am all on end with Mr. Knightley's news, but you must not take anything I say to heart. I value our friendship also, and I shall doubly lean on you as I come to terms with Mr. Knightley's match." She turned a sudden almost-sob into a laugh. "At least she cannot possibly be as dreadful as Mrs. Elton."

"Oh, no, indeed. Though I suppose people will think it odd," Harriet mused. "For she is so much younger than he, and she is not precisely well-off, is she? Not like you, I mean, though she comes from a good family and has a portion. She is certainly not poor or unknown... I suppose Mr. Knightley does not care either way. He is so smart and she so witty, I am quite sure they will be very happy."

"Harriet," Emma was desperate, "I am so sorry to excuse myself, but I find my headache has not gone away after all. I really must lie down again, please excuse me. Give my regards to Mrs. Goddard."

{ 27 }

DARCY WAS ALSO AWARE that Lizzy would be leaving Highbury on Friday, and like Harriet, called to take his leave. He arrived a little past noon, when the weak sun had struggled out from behind the clouds, giving the town of Highbury a little more color, bringing out the reddish hue of bricks and the warm tones of wooden signs and posts. It gave more life and color to the drab town than usual, and he tried to convince himself that this weeks-long foray into humiliation had not been in vain.

He trod up the stairs to Miss Bates's rooms, allowing the maid to precede him. He was resolved to be upright, polite—at long last!—and to put the relationship behind him after this. He would go back to London, and back to Pemberley, and his life would move on. He had erred, and he regretted the loss of Miss Bennet bitterly.

However, he was not one to sulk or brood on his losses, nor did he believe in a person's fated destiny or any of the romantic nonsense from Mrs. Radcliffe's novels.

It was time to move on.

"It's Mr. Darcy, mum," the maid announced him.

The three ladies of the house were present, and also Mr. Knightley.

Darcy was not always quick to decipher mood and atmosphere, but there was certainly something rather jolly about the little grouping. Mr. Knightley sat with Lizzy on the loveseat and it looked as though he may have just released her hand, or she pulled it out of his.

Plain, spinsterly Miss Bates was flushed with her hands clasped at her bosom.

Elegant Miss Fairfax smiled benevolently at the whole.

Darcy bowed, feeling awkward and disliking it. "I have just come to bid Miss Bennet farewell. I have decided not to travel on to Hunsford and Rosings Park just now, but to return north, so I came to say *adieu*."

Knightley stood and clapped him on the shoulder. "I am glad you should come by while I am here, so that I can share the news."

Lizzy's face, just beyond Knightley, flashed a look of pain, of half-protest, and she began to raise her hand but stopped herself.

Knightley said, "Miss Bennet has been kind enough to accept my offer of marriage, and we have this morning received her father's blessing. We didn't expect word quite so soon; I thought I would've had to write you."

Mr. Darcy was less stoic than people generally believed. He did not have iron control of his emotions. He merely had a temper which did not rise to most bait, a heart which was not touched by most beauty, and a sense of humor he only indulged with his close friends. It was not necessary for him to often control his face in a way at odds with his internal state.

This was such a moment.

"Oh? Oh. I see." Darcy's eyes flicked instinctively to Lizzy, whose face was fixed in a wince, a sort of apology, perhaps. Miss Bates was all old-maidenly smiles. Darcy extended his hand jerkily to Mr. Knightley. "Congratulations. You are a blessed man."

Lizzy stood and Darcy took her hand as well, wishing her happy.

If he'd thought his heart had taken a beating at her rejection, it was nothing to this. For it was not merely pride this time, but the pain of realizing that there was absolutely no future chance with Lizzy.

Lizzy had seen that small amount of confusion and pain in Darcy's face. It was only a momentary stall, a fleeting hesitance in his hand and eyes and face, and it wrung her heart.

It was bad enough that her brilliant engagement should be rubbed in Jane Fairfax's face. Lizzy had hoped she wouldn't hear back from her father until she was in Hunsford with Charlotte. Obviously, Mr. Darcy and Jane Fairfax and everyone would eventually know... but Lizzy had planned on being out of the way when the news broke.

She'd certainly never intended for Mr. Darcy to find out like this! She had quite thought that it would take longer than six days for her letter to get to Meryton and to her family and then for her father to write back. Honestly, she'd thought perhaps her father would be so surprised that he might not write back right away. He was not a *prompt* correspondent at the best of times.

She'd told him she would still leave on Friday for her visit to Charlotte, and that he could direct his letter for her to the rectory of Mr. Collins.

But Mr. Knightley had judged it better to send a courier with a letter both from him and herself, and her father must have written nearly at once! Mr. Knightley had offered to visit them in Hertfordshire at Mr. Bennet's convenience, or, if Mr. Bennet would prefer, Mr. Knightley offered to host him and his family at

Donwell Abbey if he would like to see Mr. Knightley's situation firsthand.

Lizzy had fully expected that Mr. Darcy would be gone by the time an answer arrived, or that Mr. Knightley would tell him privately...

But Mr. Darcy bowed over her hand, with a telltale twitch in his jaw, wishing her well. There was a furrow between his eyes and a flavor of disappointment in his words of congratulation.

Lizzy felt like a wretch.

Jane Fairfax did not, in fact, resent Lizzy's engagement to Mr. Knightley and, indeed, was gently pleased for her. She was not so self-centered that she could not divorce herself and her troubles from the string of visitors they received once Lizzy's engagement became known.

That is, Jane *was* comfortably divorced from the proceedings until Frank came to congratulate Lizzy and say goodbye.

He bowed and kissed Lizzy's hand. "I hear you shall soon be the lady of the community! How quiet you have been; I had no notion of this development! Worse, Emma tells me she had not either and that was a raw blow. You must be a better queen to your poor subjects! And do remember me, your poor knight-errant, when you have entered your exalted station."

His eyes cut to Jane and she stiffened. Let him not bring her into his raillery! Her ragged nerves could not take it.

Miss Bates had stepped out to visit a friend, and so it was only the two young ladies and Mr. Churchill.

He kissed Lizzy's hand again, which was rather unnecessary. "If you *are* to be the queen, perhaps you can put in a good word with your ladies-in-waiting."

Lizzy pulled her hand away. "Thank you for your good wishes. I am sure I shall see you at times in Highbury, and I always like to be on good terms with people if I may."

"Oh, yes, though I do not know I shall be here very often. Perhaps I shall see you in London. There is not much for me here, eh, Miss Fairfax?"

This was too much for Jane. "Your father and step-mother, surely? Do not be petty and punish them for our... difficulty."

Frank came over and put a hand under her chin to raise her face. "My beautiful Jane, you have lost the right to censure me. Besides, I – petty? You must take it back! Witty, passionate, selfish, yes—but not petty. Come, we never have the chance to speak any more, and Miss Bennet is apparently the soul of discretion. Will you not put this behind us? You love me, you know you do."

Jane did not know that. She moved her chin away from him, afraid he would kiss her or something equally improper.

She had admired Mr. Frank Churchill when he became acquainted with the Campbells, her adopted family. His suave attentions, his intelligent, playful smiles, his sincere compliments—for once offered to *her*, not to wealthy Miss Campbell—it had been intoxicating. The first time he stole a kiss, she felt it must be love.

"Frank." Jane touched her handkerchief to her eyes. "I do not relish the thought of being a governess, but... it would be the height of selfishness to marry you in order to escape that fate. You know it would be. We have been friends, and I value that, but this," she gestured between them, painfully aware of their audience, "it will not do."

Frank's face—that face she thought she knew so well—quivered for a moment between pleading and scorning, between warmth and coldness, and coldness won.

"Far be it from me to stay where I am not wanted." He bowed to Lizzy. "Miss Bennet, your obedient servant. Good day."

{ 28 }

EMMA WAS SITTING LISTLESSLY by the small cascading fountain east of the house when Frank Churchill came down the lane looking very stormy. He had not yet spied her, and he whipped his cane viciously, nipping the heads off the green weeds and occasional head of grain that had re-sprouted along the roadway with the spring rain.

He paused to look up at Hartfield and she rather thought he would pass by. He had already stopped by that morning to visit with her. He'd sat with her and her father and they'd discussed Mr. Knightley's engagement. (It would take many such conversations and all her efforts and enthusiasm to even *begin* to reconcile her father to the coming marriage. And Emma did not have much enthusiasm or goodwill to muster at present.)

Frank rubbed his mouth and glared back the way he'd come. Then he stepped out hurriedly, heading toward her front door.

"Mr. Churchill," Emma called then. "How do you do? Did you forget something?"

"Ah, Emma, Miss Woodhouse, I should say. No, I did not forget something, but I am glad to catch you outdoors. What were you doing?"

"Nothing of any import. I am a sad waster of time, as Mr. Knightley could tell you."

He rubbed his hands. "Much as my father says of me, I believe. Miss Woodhouse, you and I have much in common."

"I suppose we may. What then?"

"We have been friends these past weeks, no? And you seem to know everything, so perhaps you have a suspicion of why I came to Highbury this year?"

"I—I assumed for your father's sake."

"My father... yes, of course." He squared his shoulders. "It was also for another reason, a desire to settle my future happiness. I think—yes, I do think—Miss Woodhouse, would you marry me?"

Emma cocked her head at this and couldn't help but laugh in surprise. It felt good to laugh. "Would I marry you? Are you seeking the information as an academic exercise or for keeps? Although we have danced and chatted these few weeks with great enjoyment, I admit to being unsure. If you are looking merely for information, I can say that there is nothing in you that would *prevent* my marrying you."

His face, though a little grim, lightened with humor. "It is well that I am not madly in love with you, or your manner would drive me to drink! How cool you are! How you laugh at me! Emma, the goddess of the neighborhood, has received so many proposals that she laughs in the face of supplicants."

"*Is* this a proposal?"

"Good Lord, I am worse off than I thought."

Emma laughed again. "Yes, you are. What a hand you are! *Are* you serious? You are not in love with me."

He smiled. "I like your forthrightness, Emma, that you may be sure of. Do I love you? Maybe I do! You seem to understand me better than—better than some others. I wish I could ask if *you* love *me*? But no, that is not the gentlemanly way. I cannot say that I entirely do, but I find you pretty and clever and entertaining; why not be in love? Do you ever find it—*intolerable*—that life should go on as it is? That you cannot and will not take another blow sitting down, you must rise and face it down?"

Emma paused momentarily on *pretty*—she was generally held to be *beautiful* in Highbury—but it was not a point of serious vanity for her, so she was able to let it pass. She was struck more by an answering pang in her own heart. *Intolerable* was a succinct way of putting her emotional storm of the past few days.

She had not suspected Frank Churchill had any deeper feelings to pull at him so.

"I do understand. And no one would take either of us seriously, were we to describe it so!" Emma said. "For we are the cheerful ones, the blessed ones. We have been given everything. What could we possibly have to repine?"

He twirled his cane and bowed grandly. "Well, then, Emma, from one blessed child of Highbury to another, shall we join our course and make of it what we may? I am sure we should do a smashing job of it, besides setting an extremely high bar of fashion and good-breeding in our little burgh."

Emma laughed at him though there was pain at the back of it. Her own pain, in fact, felt so universal, that she did not stop to think what "blow" had come upon Frank.

"Mr. Churchill, I believe we might deal extremely. However, I do have a caveat, which is my poor father. Whatever my friends may say, I do not believe he could bear it if I left for good! But you do not have lands or a home at present—except for your rooms in town which I have been told are shockingly extravagant!—so would you consider living part of each year here at Hartfield?"

"Why not? Quite a funny one is your father. I've no objection, though someday, when my aunt dies, I shall have responsibilities—But do you know, it has just occurred to me that in marrying you I shall probably displease my aunt, although you are not so objectionable as—well, as nearly anyone else. Still, if she threw me off, would you still accept me?"

"What silliness," Emma said. "I am not so ill-bred as to imagine it is a fortune that makes the man. You would be a gentleman of consideration no matter what your circumstances."

"Liberal understanding, indeed! Well then, Miss Woodhouse, shall we do it?"

"Why not?" Emma echoed. She felt rash. Also, a little sick, rather faint, but also very excited. "Indeed, why not? However... Oh dear. I do not think I can possibly bring the idea to my father today. He is already much excited. Should you object to a secret engagement for a week or so?"

"A secret engagement?" Frank's eyes sparkled. "Not at all."

{ 29 }

LIZZY REREAD THE LETTERS from her family at the desk in the bedroom, the fateful desk which no longer held Jane's secret letters.

At least, Lizzy suspected not. The fire had burned suspiciously bright one morning, and Jane kept leaning forward to poke at it with the heavy iron poker, tucking in suspicious scraps of cream-colored paper, which did not quite look like the twists of paper Patty used to light the fire.

Lizzy felt unsettled, uncertain. She hoped the letters would help her identify the cause.

Her father had written her a short letter giving his acceptance ("if she was sure of herself") and cryptically expressing his grief at losing her.

Lizzy's mother had written a longer letter that was chock-full of curiosity, advice, and congratulations on her new connection.

I am sure I do not know how you did it, Lizzy, for your father says this Mr. Knightley is quite a landowner, of an old family! Bingley is as nothing to him! Not but what Bingley has such a sweet temperament, and I think rather more fortune than your Mr. Knightley, but we do not repine. Mr. Knightley is far better of a catch than I ever expected you to achieve.

I hope you will not do anything stubborn or pettish to put up his back. Your father says you still want to visit Charlotte before you wed, but I say this is a great folly. Many marry with only three weeks to read the banns, and I think any unnecessary delay is the height of foolishness. Men do not like to wait and what is the use in making him impatient? I am sure he is rich enough to send you to visit Charlotte anytime!

If you will be swayed by what I say—but you never do, so why I should think it, I cannot imagine!—you will do everything just as Mr. Knightley wishes.

Now, about your trousseau, do not be allowing Mr. Knightley to know what will be best for you, for who could advise you as your mamma could? We must go to London while we are in Highbury, and I will see about ordering from your aunt's milliners and dressmakers for both you and Jane!

Now, your father had no idea of going to Highbury—"Why should I wait on my future son-in-law?" he said, "He is the one gaining one of my progeny. Should he not wait upon me?"

But your father will have these funny moods, my dear, and you may rest assured that I spared no time in convincing him of the necessity of a visit. Miss the chance to see Lizzy's establishment? Miss the chance to travel to a part of the country we have never been to, where we shall be considered a family of first importance, as Mr. Knightley is a significant man of the district, besides a magistrate of Donwell Parish?

Of course not!

We shall come for several weeks in May, and stay at Donwell, which Mr. Knightley particularly desired us to do. I am so excited I cannot even tell you. Kitty and Lydia will stay with my sister—they would be sad to miss the last balls with the officers!—but your father and Mary and I shall come. Oh, Lizzy, you and Jane have made me so happy, I have never felt so well. If I could only find three more such men for the younger ones, I should have nothing left to wish for. Perhaps you may find a good match for Mary. For whatever your father says, I'm sure she is quite as pretty as you and far more accomplished.

There was more in that vein.

Lizzy had reluctantly agreed with Mr. Knightley's suggestion, and with her parents' urging, that instead of heading to Hunsford and Charlotte, she should remain in Highbury at present.

She did *not* on the other hand, agree with her mother that she ought to marry in three weeks, nor did Mr. Knightley ask her to do so. He had mentioned summer, and that sounded well to Lizzy. Her parents would visit and all would be settled here, then she would spend time with Charlotte and at home in Hertfordshire again before returning for good. Perhaps August.

Lizzy did not entirely look forward to her mother's advent at Donwell, but she knew it was an embarrassment that could not be avoided. And truly, her mother was not that bad, just a little silly. Lizzy had not been embarrassed of her mother before the coming of Mr. Bingley and Mr. Darcy, for everyone in their neighborhood was well acquainted with Mrs. Bennet.

Mr. Darcy...

She had not thought she could hurt a proud, stony man like that, but she had done so. In fact, new evidence would indicate that he was not at all proud and stony; that his tall, imposing exterior hid a heart of flesh after all.

Lizzy shook her head. It no longer mattered.

It being a blessedly dry, warm spring day, Lizzy put on her shoes. She desperately needed an outing, fresh wind on her face, the exertion of body instead of mind and heart.

"I am going to stop by Ford's and then Mrs. Goddard's school to visit Harriet," Lizzy told Miss Bates and Jane. "I am hoping she will walk with me. Would you like to come, Miss Fairfax? It looks to be a beautiful day."

She looked up, startled, as if the idea of a walk was very strange. "I do not think so. I am a little tired today."

"Oh, but you must not stay in, my dear Jane," Miss Bates said, pushing her spectacles up her nose. "The doctor says you really must walk more. And perhaps I say it as should not, but really Miss Bennet must not go around unaccompanied! What would Mr. Knightley think of us?"

"I walked out before and he did not think any the worse of us!" Lizzy objected. "And also, you have not once called me Lizzy since you heard of the engagement. I have really not changed, you know. I am still your cousin."

"Oh, such sweet manners! Such complete condescension!" Miss Bates sighed happily. "You are the kindest girl imaginable, but I hope I know what is due to the future Mrs. Knightley! You have no idea how happy it makes me. Why, you are like family! Well, I don't precisely mean *like* family, for a cousin, even second or third, *is* technically family—where was I? Oh, Jane, you simply must walk, my dear, you must not stay inside to keep *me* company."

Jane obediently put her knitting away and donned her outdoor things.

Lizzy executed her errand at Ford's, a new pair of gloves, with a little of the pin money her father sent along for her prolonged stay. Jane Fairfax browsed absently, and indeed, was so lost in thought that she had to be called thrice before she responded to her name.

The speaker was haughty Mrs. Elton. "My dear Jane, I have not seen you since church last Sunday! You really *must* walk more, you know. I have been looking about me for a governess position for you, and I believe I have found the very thing! I shall call soon to give you all the details. Now, do *not* tell me again that you are not ready for a position! If you will but do as the doctor bids you—and myself, for my friends call me a miraculous physician!—you will perfectly well!"

Jane Fairfax smiled as one trapped. "Thank you for your kind efforts. I suppose I am ready for a position. I really have no," she sniffed and wiped her nose, "no reason to delay further."

Lizzy moved away, but their voices were still audible.

Mrs. Elton slapped her wrist. "That is the spirit! I am so happy to hear you say so. At your age, you want to be doing, though I still say it is a crime for a beautiful girl like you to be wasted as a governess!" She looked around for support for this opinion, and her eyes fell on Lizzy.

"Oh, Miss Bennet! I did not immediately spy you hiding over there." She surveyed Lizzy, from Lizzy's perfectly serviceable bonnet to her rather worn shoes. Ever since Mrs. Elton had heard about the engagement, she had looked at Lizzy with puzzlement. After her first vulgar moment of disbelief, she had vacillated between graceful condescension and ladylike scorn.

Lizzy found her somewhat amusing. "Hello, Mrs. Elton! I am selecting gloves, for mine are sadly worn, and I hear that Mr. Churchill is coaxing his father to give a ball in town soon. Shall Mr. Knightley and I see you there?" Lizzy was not above using her new status to poke at the woman.

Mrs. Elton exhaled a long, slow breath from her nose. "You and Mr. Knightley?" She laughed, a little sharply. "I suppose I will attend. I do dote upon Mr. Churchill. *There* is a young man who knows how things ought to be done. A little town bronze for this backward little village, no? In London—though you have never had a season in London, have you, my dear Miss Bennet?—it would not at all be the thing to rent a room for a private ball, but one must make allowances for village life, mustn't one?"

Mrs. Elton waved a careless hand as she moved further into the store, and Lizzy and Jane were soon on their way down the street.

"*Do* you need a position soon?" Lizzy asked Jane. "I believe your aunt would rather you stay with her always."

"Yes, she would, but it is not practical."

That was all that was said until they reached Mrs. Goddard's school and found Harriet putting on her bonnet, quite ready for a walk.

"Oh yes, thank you! Such a lovely day and Miss Woodhouse—Miss Woodhouse has been very busy of late. But I was about to walk out with my friend, Miss Bickerton. She is another of Mrs. Goddard's boarders. May she join us?"

Lizzy had no objection. They meandered two by two back towards town, but as they passed the Richmond road, Harriet and Lizzy were both beckoned by the green shady recess beneath the elm trees and the excellent surface of the wide road that led away from town.

"We will turn back as soon as we reach the Hitchens' field," Harriet said. "It will be beautiful if the bluebells have bloomed. Even if not, we may enjoy the yellow gorse that grow along the road!"

Harriet, to do her credit, had not been talking incessantly of Lizzy's engagement. Miss Bickerton did not have such self-control.

"I am quite in a tizzy," she said, "to think I should be walking with Mrs. Knightley as shall be! They say that Donwell Abbey is nigh on four hundred years old!"

Harriet broke in, "Is it not closer to two hundred? Miss Woodhouse told me one ought always to underestimate the age of an estate, rather than overestimate. She says boasting of such things is tasteless."

Miss Bickerton ignored this. "And though he does not have ever so many servants, our teacher says with a new lady mistress he will hire more. Probably he will even buy his own carriage and horses to keep for her! Shall you ask for a matched set, Miss Bennet? White! You must ask for white to go with a blue carriage."

"Too bland," said Lizzy. "I shall require a black team with a crimson carriage."

Miss Bickerton, walking a step ahead with Harriet, looked back, eyes like saucers. Even Harriet's sweet face looked scandalized.

Lizzy laughed. "I would never ride in such a thing! You are making me laugh. Mr. Knightley shall not greatly change his life for me, nor would I ask it."

That was when they saw the gypsy encampment.

Lizzy was fascinated, for they did not get many gypsies near Meryton, perhaps because it was farther north and sometimes colder. Or perhaps because it was some ways off the main North Road.

It was a collection of tatty wagons and bony horses, laundry hung on branches, and two campfires sending smoke trails through the trees. A pot over one fire must've held some sort of stew, for Lizzy could smell garlic and onion in the air.

Several children sat hunched near one of the fires, and several, even smaller, raced among the trees.

"Oh!" Harriet gasped. "We must turn back."

Lizzy supposed she was right, though she doubted they were in danger.

Miss Fairfax had also halted abruptly.

One of the children spotted them and being nearer, ran up. He held out a grubby hand. His dark hair was shiny and bare, and his feet were also bare, though it was chilly in the shade.

"Got a shilling, mum? Just a shilling or two, eh?"

Miss Bickerton screamed.

Lizzy flinched, and of course, the rest of the boy's family looked up.

Lizzy was inclined to give Miss Bickerton a sharp smack to calm her down if she screamed again, but before she could say anything, that young lady took off running.

Rather than running back down the road, she ran up a steep embankment on the other side of the Richmond road, away from the makeshift camp, leapt over a hedge and disappeared.

"Good heavens," Lizzy said. "Whatever is she doing?"

Harriet whimpered and began to follow, but Lizzy seized her arm. "No, for heaven's sake. We must simply turn back."

"Yes," agreed Miss Fairfax.

But several of the men (and the women) had had a rough laugh about Miss Bickerton's flight and already a crowd of children grew around the remaining ladies.

"Give us a shillin', miss? Maybe even a quid? Yeah, miss?" These children were a little older than the first, several of the skinny boys were nearly Lizzy's height. They crowded closer and they smelled of camp smoke.

The three ladies turned to go back, but they were surrounded. Lizzy began to walk, but Harriet was so frightened, she didn't move. Lizzy pulled at her arm.

Harriet pulled out her purse and gave over a shilling to one of the medium-size girls. "P-p-please let us go."

But they only pressed closer at the sight of the purse, probably due to the unaccustomed encouragement of three shrinking ladies and the spectacle of the running one. Lizzy was not afraid, but she was uncomfortable and a little uncertain. Several teenage boys and a large older woman joined the group, loudly adding their voices to the comments.

"Haven't you all three got purses, eh?" the lady asked. "Haven't you got a shilling nor two for those as is in need? Haven't you got charity? Good Christian charity to the poor, yes?"

Lizzy was between Harriet and Jane. She put her arm through each of theirs. "We really must keep going."

Jane looked faint but was game. Harriet was terrified. Lizzy began to all but drag them forward, feeling the occasional hand touching her skirt along with the clamor of begging and (more humiliating) laughter.

The begging, and certainly the laughter, were not bad-natured, but Lizzy was out of her element, and extremely annoyed with her two faltering companions.

{ 30 }

DARCY WAS LEAVING HIGHBURY the same way he'd arrived, on horseback. His things would follow him in a job carriage.

Having just taken the London road for his flying trip to London to speak with Bingley, he decided to take another route, a little longer, but more scenic. And that was why he came upon Miss Bennet, Miss Fairfax, and Miss... well, he could not remember her name, but the little schoolgirl friend of Miss Woodhouse. They were surrounded by a motley group of ragged children, undoubtedly from yonder gypsy camp, and even Lizzy looked uncertain and vexed. The other two looked nigh onto fainting.

"Oh, Mr. Darcy!" Lizzy called, "Thank heaven you are here."

"Here, get on with the lot of you," he said to the children. "Don't plague these ladies."

He trotted nearly into the midst of the group, who split apart like smoke and drifted away at once. He dismounted and Lizzy sagged a little with relief.

"I have never been so happy to see you! I thought you had left town already. Do, please, take Miss Fairfax's arm, and then I can help Miss Smith."

Darcy did as she asked but soon caused her to switch with him, for Miss Smith was much weaker, her eyes rolling and her body sagging at unexpected moments. He kept his horse in hand with his left hand, and supported Miss Smith with the other.

"All well?" he asked. "No injury?"

"No, we are perfectly fine!" Lizzy snapped. "But Miss Bickerton must make a spectacle of herself screaming and running away quite theatrically, which of course drew more notice. And Miss Fairfax kept her head, but she was already a little tired when we set out, and the excitement overcame her. I am so sorry, Miss Fairfax, but we will be home directly. Miss Smith... I say, Harriet, do buck up! They are gone."

Mr. Darcy wrapped his arm around Miss Smith's waist—how much he would rather it was Lizzy—and kept her from falling as she stumbled over a stone.

"I will let Mr. Knightley know they are in the neighborhood," Darcy said. "I am sure he will clear them out."

"It was not precisely their fault," Lizzy said conscientiously, "at least not at first."

"Regardless, I suspect they will leave before ever we convey the news."

He and Lizzy supported Harriet to Mrs. Goddard's school—which was by far the closest—and Miss Fairfax and Miss Smith were made much of. Miss Bickerton had run straight back, screeching, and told them the whole.

Mr. Darcy took his leave of Lizzy in front of the school. "I am glad I should have happened along to help you."

"Yes, a merciful providence was at work. Also, I am thankful that I should get to say goodbye properly before you leave. I—" she faltered. "I wanted to apologize. I did not mean to mortify you by my acceptance of Mr. Knightley, or the manner of announcing it. It was unexpected and, I fear, painful. I hope that we can be friends, as we will no doubt see one another through Mr. Bingley and Mr. Knightley."

Mr. Darcy took a last look at her. There was something more open and forthright about her just now. She was also pink from exertion, a little windblown, and... and he really should not look at her this way since she was going to be married.

He bowed over her hand. "I hope we may be friends also. Goodbye, Miss Elizabeth."

Darcy rode back to Donwell Abbey to inform Knightley of the occurrence and came back with him to show him where the camp was.

Really this last occurrence was for the best. He must begin to accustom himself to how things would be.

Besides, if Lizzy had not gotten engaged, how long would he have harbored a sentimental hope that things might change between them? How pathetic that would have been! How distracted he might have been. No, better that the door should be firmly shut. He did not doubt his ability to squelch his feelings over time.

"I must congratulate you again, Mr. Knightley," Darcy said, conscious that he had been a little stiff when he first heard. "Miss Bennet is an excellent young lady. She showed courage and great presence of mind today."

"She seems a formidable girl."

Knightley did not realize *how* lucky he was that she had accepted him, Darcy thought. Knightley did not realize how easily Lizzy would whistle a fortune down the wind. Somehow it seemed intolerable that he should take his blessing in stride.

"I know for a fact that she would never marry for position or wealth, so her acceptance is a true commendation of your character."

"My thanks, I suppose, but how would you know that?"

"Well... as it happened, I was an unwilling observer to a little drama in Meryton, when her cousin, who is to inherit her father's estate, proposed to her and was rejected. He is a silly, pompous man, the parson for my aunt, Lady Catherine, and I see him all too often. Lizzy's rejection was taken rather hard by her family. Unfortunately, the man himself had too much sense to be quiet about it, he told me the story himself."

"His misfortune was my gain, then."

Darcy's evil genius compelled him to continue. "Her mother will be most satisfied with you. She has grand dreams for her daughters. I don't envy you that connection."

Knightley looked over to him, searching. "Is this a warning? My thanks, but her father's letter was unobjectionable. I can't believe, based on Miss Bennet's behavior and conversation, that her family is low."

"That is perhaps why I've ventured to warn you. The eldest two daughters are something quite out of the common way, but their family... is not. Still, you live far enough away that it will not be much of an issue."

"Even if I lived close, I would not shun my wife's family or keep her from them."

"No, of course not. Only—" Darcy wanted to be understood— "it is no pleasant thing to welcome a vulgar mother-in-law to the family. It might make any man think twice."

"Any man, perhaps, but not a *gentleman*, I would hope. When a man of independent resources has made up his mind, all matters but those pertaining to the actual person of his wife must become immaterial."

It was a rebuke and Mr. Darcy felt the full weight of it. "My apologies. I should not have spoken."

Mr. Knightley furrowed his brow in thought and then his eyes widened. "Good Lord, was Miss Bennet the one you steered a friend away from? No wonder she pokers up around you."

"It was not Miss Elizabeth Bennet, but her older sister, Miss Jane Bennet. Does—does she *poker up* around me?"

"Definitely. She is too lively to be much discomposed by anybody, I believe, but I have seen her relaxed and genial in a different way when you are not at hand. She becomes more adversarial with you. On her guard, I daresay."

Mr. Darcy felt a pang of jealously that quite took his breath away; unlike anything he'd experienced in his life. That Mr. Knightley should have her as wife was still too strange and distant a thought to grasp, but that Knightley should know Lizzy's smiles and quips and conversation when she was relaxed and happy—as Darcy had apparently *not*—made him nearly ill.

It was perhaps the difference he had noted just now in the courtyard of the school. An openness and vulnerability he had not seen in her before. The thought that he would only ever receive it as a friend because of his own pride and haughty behavior haunted him as he bid goodbye to Knightley and rode on, alone.

{ 31 }

EMMA COULD NOT YET THINK with anything like equanimity about Mr. Knightley and Lizzy. It was an ache in her heart that occasionally stabbed painfully. Her secret engagement to Frank was a draught of laudanum or poppy, however. It did not heal the injury but dulled the pain of it.

It certainly gave her something else to dwell on, as well as a twisted sort of relief that Mr. Knightley and Lizzy would never guess how deeply she was injured. Nor would any of the surrounding neighborhood pity her at "losing" Mr. Knightley. How could they pity her when it became known that she was marrying the other darling child of Highbury?

And if a small part of Emma enjoyed the idea of taking the spotlight from Lizzy, she excused herself on the grounds of extreme circumstances.

Unfortunately, she had yet decided how to break the news to her father. And of course, it could not be made known in the neighborhood until Frank had her father's blessing.

Although Mr. Woodhouse liked Frank Churchill and his family—Mr. Weston was one of his old friends, and of course, Mrs. Weston had lived at Hartfield for twenty years as Emma and Isabella's governess—none of those facts would reconcile him to a change of this magnitude.

With this in mind, Emma had at last decided—strange as it might be—that she simply had to apply to Mr. Knightley for help.

She had gone to him with her difficulties and emotional hurts for nearly fifteen years; she could not stop now, even though she did love him.

He had not come to Highbury since the day he made the announcement, and so she did not see him until the day he invited a select group to go strawberry picking in his fields.

Lizzy came with Miss Bates and Jane Fairfax, of course. Lizzy was first in consequence now, and she was the one, with unspoken agreement, whom the whole party centered around.

It was hard.

The fact that Emma ended up taking the rather long walk to the strawberry fields with Mr. Elton was worse. He had not forgiven her for rejecting his suit and was all smiling complaisance and thinly veiled sneers.

She comforted herself that Frank would have escorted her but that he was trying to maintain their secret. He had offered his arm to Harriet, for which Emma smiled upon him. She had not forgotten that Mr. and Mrs. Elton were wont to be harsh with her dear little friend. To make things more difficult, who should ride up to the house when they were on the point of departing but Mr. Martin! Harriet's Mr. Martin!

He had immediately reined in and apologized for interrupting Mr. Knightley. "Didn't realize you had a party here, sir." He touched his hat. "I shall call another day."

"Hold on a moment, Martin," Mr. Knightley had said. He'd gone aside and they'd spoken for a moment.

Emma couldn't be sure, but she suspected Mr. Knightley had invited him to join them. Mr. Martin, to his credit, took care not to look at Harriet as he took his leave. "No, you are too good. I wouldn't force myself on your guests."

He rode off, and Harriet turned her fair head away, blinking a few times and needlessly fixing the blond curls that framed her face. Emma could not help a pang of real grief. She had taken Mr. Martin from Harriet and offered her nothing, *nothing,* in return. Of course the poor girl was still had a *tendre* for him!

Mr. Martin was not a gentleman, but he had a strong jaw and good-natured features in a coarse sort of way, just the sort of man who might appeal to a lonely girl.

But there was more suffering to come. All three of the other young ladies had had that "harrowing" interlude with the gypsies and everyone (but mainly Mrs. Elton) were agog to hear about it. Emma tried to display interest, but really, must they go on and on?

If she had been capable of impartiality, she might have recognized that Lizzy only spoke about it in humor, Miss Fairfax not at all, and Harriet only in answer to questions.

Emma was not capable of it.

Thankfully Mrs. Elton latched onto Jane Fairfax and began sharing all sorts of horrid details about a family who needed a governess.

Emma slipped away to pick the early ripened strawberries on her own. She had never felt so alone at an outing like this.

Mr. Knightley had brought his dogs and she saw the beautiful little Dalmatian nosing about further down.

"Here, Betsy," Emma called. She smoothed a hand over the dog's velvet head and inky black ears. "You are the only one who notices me."

These were *her* people, *her* town, and *her* Mr. Knightley... and yet she was the least important!

Emma hated the pettiness of her thoughts yet could not overcome them.

Had Mr. Knightley even looked for her when they reached their destination? Emma felt bruised and shallow and disgusted with both him and herself.

When Emma returned to the chairs and shade which Mr. Knightley's servants had put up for them, Frank was the only one lounging there, idly eating strawberries which some member of the party must have already brought back.

His eyes were on the fields which stretched away on the low hillocks and rises beyond them, he seemed to be watching the Eltons and Jane Fairfax.

"Emma, there you are," he said. "Listen. I have been planning a ball with my father—rented the room and all—and it would be strange if I canceled it now. How about if we announce our engagement then? Do you think we might bring your poor father around to the idea by next Friday?"

Emma sat. She was not in a rush, but then, everything was miserable and perhaps the announcement would make her feel better. "Next Friday? Perhaps. Truly, I must speak to Mr. Knightley about it. He always knows how to approach my papa."

Some of the others were returning, and Emma felt more dejected than ever watching Mr. Knightley's attentive behavior to Lizzy. He was attentive to everyone, but her eyes caught every smile, gesture, and item that passed between them.

Frank grew livelier with the advent of the crowd. He teased Harriet about her stained fingers. He helped Miss Bates when she dropped her strawberry pail and laughingly extracted a tithe for his services which she was only too happy to give.

"So helpful! Such an old butterfinger I am!" said she.

He debated with Lizzy the relative merits of strawberries versus cherries. He agreed with everything Mrs. Elton said about Jane Fairfax's new situation, but as Mrs. Elton's gaze was frequently turned toward Jane, he made such expressive gestures of eye and eyebrow, that even Emma was amused.

"Finally our goddess has laughed," Frank said, when one of his respectful remarks was accompanied by such an accurate impersonation of Mrs. Elton's supercilious head movement that Emma laughed aloud.

"I declare," said Frank, "that Miss Woodhouse has been too sober by half all morning. I have come up with a game. We must each try to amuse her. You may each say one thing very clever, two things moderately clever, or three things very dull indeed. And she must promise to laugh beautifully at each one."

Harriet clapped her hands. "I shall think of one of our riddles!"

Mr. Weston chuckled. "I believe I have a conundrum or two."

Mrs. Elton turned up her nose. "I must confess to despising parlor games. They are tedious even in a parlor, and insupportable in the great expanse of nature. I am quite the naturalist."

Lizzy shrugged. "We must all please ourselves on an outing of pleasure; you must not stay if you had rather walk about. I am happy to play a game."

Emma was annoyed by Lizzy's casual assumption of responsibility for the party, even if it was merely to diffuse the rudeness of Mrs. Elton's snub. That was Emma's role!

Miss Bates giggled and pushed up her spectacles which were sliding down her rather shiny nose. "Well, I need not be uneasy. 'Three things very dull indeed.' That will just do for me, you know. I shall be sure to say three dull things as soon as ever I open my mouth; you all know I shall!"

Emma could not resist.

"Ah, but that is the difficulty. You will be limited as to number—only three at once."

Miss Bates did not immediately catch her meaning and laughed, but after a moment she blushed. Her plain face grew blotchy and pink. "To be sure," she murmured. "Yes, I see what she means, I will try to hold my tongue. I must make myself very disagreeable, or she would not have said such a thing to an old friend."

Emma immediately grimaced in the silence that followed this little speech. Perhaps if the others had gone on at once, her words would not have hung in the air so.

Mr. Weston slapped his knee. "I have one, though I think it rather for Miss Bennet than Mis Woodhouse. What do you get when you cross a lizard and a zebra?"

Lizzy squinted at him. "I haven't the slightest idea. A most unusual pair of gloves?"

There was laughter, and he raised his hands. "No, no. A *liz*ard and a *ze*bra—a Liz-zee! A most congenial creature!"

Lizzy laughed, "Why, thank you! If only I had stripes."

Emma felt vaguely ill. She fanned herself with a hand. "The sun has shifted. May I trouble a few of you to move a bit so that I may find a spot in the shade?"

The gentlemen sprang to their feet to help. Mr. Elton took the opportunity to ask his wife to walk. "I am sure I have nothing to say to please Miss Woodhouse or Miss Bennet, or any young lady! But my lady and I are not so weak as to be bothered by a little warmth."

"Of course, my dear," Mrs. Elton agreed. "This sort of game is all about flattery and I cannot feel it does any young woman credit, but then I myself am a stranger to vanity. At least my friends say so."

Frank laughed as they left. "What a well-suited couple. He didn't know her above two weeks before they married and therefore their compatibility is quite lucky. One never really knows a woman until they have seen her at home. Her manner in London, or at one of the seaside towns, for instance, has nothing to do with her true person."

"Or a gentleman's manners with his true person, for that matter?" said Lizzy.

"No, gentlemen may try to dissemble but we lack the talent. How many a man has committed himself on a short acquaintance and rued it all the rest of his life!"

Lizzy scoffed. "I think, for those who have married in haste and repented at leisure, you cannot possibly claim that men have been the worse off. Women have always the greater risk, the greater loss, if they have misunderstood their husband's character."

Miss Fairfax, who had seldom spoken before, looked to Lizzy. "You are right, no doubt, and such things do happen. But I think that for most, there is time between acquaintance and marriage to realize one's mistake and draw back. Do you not think so, Miss Bennet?"

"One hopes."

Jane continued, "I think that it is mainly weak, irresolute characters who will suffer an unfortunate acquaintance to become an oppression forever. Those of stronger character will brave unpleasantness to preserve their future. Don't you think so... Lizzy?"

Lizzy smiled at her quite blindingly. "I completely agree, Jane."

Emma felt an understanding pass between them and again felt out of things.

Frank looked to Emma. "Dash it, the future governess may be right. Will you promise to find a wife for me, Miss Woodhouse? I cannot be trusted to choose for myself and I have certainly not a strong enough character to save myself if I err. I put myself entirely into your hands."

Emma smiled, more because she knew she *ought* to thrill at the meaning in his words than because she did. "I will do my poor best. I believe I may have just the person."

Mr. Knightley invited his guests to return to Donwell Abbey to get cool and have further refreshments.

Miss Bates rose. "Oh, yes. Thank you. So considerate, so helpful. Especially with such tiresome company as I must be. I am so sorry, Mr. Knightley."

The poor woman had felt the full weight of Emma's cruel joke at her expense. She had been unusually silent, except when her humble but sadly repetitious mind prompted her to rehearse out loud the insult she had been given.

On the walk back to the house, Mr. Knightley caused Emma to wait for a moment, after entrusting the overwarm ladies to good partners.

"Emma," he began. "You know I do not like to censure you, to scold you, but how can I let this pass? How *could* you speak so to Miss Bates? To make fun of her in that way is beneath you, and certainly beneath what she deserves."

Emma rolled her shoulders. "Oh, I know, I know. But she is such a blend of good and ridiculous. I was hot and tired and you know how she goes on and on, saying the same thing a dozen ways to yesterday! I daresay she did not understand me."

"She felt your full meaning; she keeps mentioning it. Imagine that she was once a young lady like you or Miss Bennet or Miss

Fairfax! She is not so clever, but she does not deserve to be mocked to her face. As a spinster of limited means, who will sink lower as she grows older, you have a duty to treat her with respect! She used to honor you with her notice, and now you scorn and laugh at her."

Emma sniffed and tossed her head. "Well, and what else do you reproach me with? Pray do not hold back, I am sure other aspects of my conduct were found wanting today. To think I missed seeing you at Highbury this past week!"

"You cannot turn me away from this by making me feel guilty. I perhaps have scolded you too harshly at times, and I am sure without the cavalier influence of Mr. Churchill you would not have behaved so. But this... It was badly done, Emma!"

She turned her face away from him, towards the south fields, away from the sun. When she raised a hand to wipe her cheeks, he thought for a moment that she was crying. Unsure what to do or say, he waited, but when she turned back to him, there was no evidence of tears except perhaps slightly reddened eyes.

"Very well, I confess you are right. I will ask her forgiveness." She hiccupped. "However, as you disapprove of me so thoroughly, my other errand today is probably futile. I had intended to ask for your help with my father."

Knightley gentled his tone. "You know I am always at your service. Even my harsh words, could you but see it, are entirely in your service."

"Do you recall your words to me after Lady Catherine visited? About marriage?"

Knightley felt himself growing uneasy. "Yes."

"Then I have another confession. Mr. Churchill has asked me to marry him, and I have accepted."

Knightley took Emma's arm, possible the least gently he had ever touched her, and halted her. "Good God. You are *engaged* to Churchill?"

"Yes. Go ahead and criticize me, I expect it. Though how you will disapprove when everyone will think it the most natural and fitting match in the world, I do not know."

"I thought your—your *flirting* rather marked today, but... Emma!" Mr. Knightley took a deep breath. "He is not—He is—I thought perhaps you had a preference for Mr. Darcy."

She shrugged. "Mr. Darcy seems a fine man in his way, but so silent! No, it is Mr. Churchill who proposed to me. And we shall suit, shall we not? We have so much in common in personality and background and family. We are a perfect match, are we *not*?"

Mr. Knightley found that he was gripping Emma's upper arm rather cruelly. "I am sorry. I am surprised. But he is not a good influence on you, even today—"

Emma held up a hand. She did not seem in danger of crying anymore. "No, I cannot allow you to disparage him to me. And he was not to blame for my lapse today! That was carelessness and ill-humor, I have already confessed I was wrong—you cannot place it at his door."

Mr. Knightley could and did place her unaccustomed rudeness at Frank Churchill's door. Knightley had disliked Churchill before, but knowing them to be already engaged was a fresh blow. Knightley had reconciled himself to the idea of Mr. Darcy and Emma—at least he believed he had—but not to the possibility of the selfish and impudent Mr. Churchill.

Frank would encourage all the least amiable parts of Emma's character. Worse, he would fail to appreciate all the genuinely excellent qualities in her!

Emma looked at him. Did her intelligent eyes, she who knew him so well, see too much?

"Emma, if you are sure you want to marry Frank, I will do everything in my power to reconcile your father. But please, be sure."

"Is there any reason I should not marry him, besides your belief in his weak character? Please tell me, Mr. Knightley, if you know of any reason I ought not."

Mr. Knightley felt his heart give a great bound, both painful and exhilarating, and it was all he could do to contain it. *Because I am in love with you.*

He had never allowed the thought to form wholly in these past months, as it began to condense like a cloud of mist in the fields of his mind. He had never allowed it to germinate in his mind in so many words; it was a seed he had locked away.

He loved Emma as a sister, as family. He loved her as a young person he had seen grow from youth and who had become his equal in intelligence and understanding—though not perhaps maturity.

But this past year he had begun to love her as more, only he had known how odd, how unlikely it would be—he so much older than her! And so he had protected himself from her inevitable coming marriage by making his own choice, and now he had no standing to stop the disastrous one she was engaged on.

How dared he propose to Miss Bennet for such a reason? How had he been so self-deceived?

Still, his thoughts returned to Emma. Would her marriage truly be disastrous? Or was that his own biased heart speaking? Were Frank's faults so large or was it merely that Frank was young, handsome, and full of vitality?

"Emma, I apologize that my surprise betrayed me into harshness. If you wish to marry Frank, I have no objection."

She turned her face down and now wiped away a tear or two on her cheeks. "Thank you."

He hated that she had felt so alone and uncertain of his help. "I will always be ready to help you. Let us talk to your father tomorrow."

She gave a watery smile and they resumed their walk.

{ 32 }

EMMA FELT A GROWING DREAD when the day of disclosures came, and Mr. Knightley joined her in her father's sitting room.

It was always quite warm, for her father much preferred a big fire and no draughts, and she felt perspiration bead on her back.

Mr. Knightley gave her a reassuring smile and squeezed her hand as they sat opposite Mr. Woodhouse.

"We have not seen you so often since you got engaged," Mr. Woodhouse said, sipping some very weak tea. "Miss Bennet is a nice girl, but it is very sad. You must admit it is very sad to cut up the peace and traditions of a neighborhood like this! And so soon after Mrs. Weston left us. I fear you will regret your decision."

Mr. Knightley cleared his throat. "But you will find that I will be visiting quite often, sir, I will not forget you. And if none of us married, how should we carry on our names? How should we ever have new little 'Emma's or 'Isabella's to brighten the world if no one married?"

"Isabella has five children," Mr. Woodhouse protested. "It is enough. And more than enough too, for they worry her dreadfully. She writes that little Emma has a ticklish cough, and she is sure it may be typhus."

Emma shook her head. "You know I read you John's postscript that it was only the croup. My tiny namesake shall be just fine."

"I have no opinion of John just now," Mr. Woodhouse muttered. "An excellent father no doubt, but he has not called on Perry during any of his last three visits, despite the children's sickness. I cannot like that!"

Emma decided to brave it. There was no leading up to such things with her father and the sooner she said it, perhaps the sooner the curdling feeling in her stomach would subside. "Papa, I have something of importance to say. Having seen how happy Isabella is, and now Miss Bennet with Mr. Knightley, I have decided to be married."

He turned wide, disbelieving eyes on her.

She felt it unnecessary to specify whom just at first. The idea alone would be a shock. "I know I have often said that I should not, that I had no reason to marry, but I have changed my mind. However, you need not fear, I will stay at Highbury for the present. My husband will too. You and I will go on as before, only with more cheer and comfort."

He blinked at her. "Married? Oh, my poor Emma. You cannot know what a tragic thing marriage is. Your poor mother! God rest her soul. I want you to have every happiness, but I do not think marriage can be considered a good thing for my poor, dear girl! Look at poor Mrs. Weston!"

"But Mrs. Weston is very happy, Papa. And it is funny you should mention her, for that brings me around to the name of the man. It is Frank Churchill, Papa."

"Mr. Frank Churchill? But he is frequently so flushed! He takes no care of going from hot rooms to the cold outdoors. He does not care about exertion. He cannot be considered healthy!"

Mr. Knightley broke in, firmly. "That is merely his complexion, I am sure he is the healthiest young man. He is rarely unwell; just like Emma, for you know how rarely she ails. And as he has no estate of his own at present, Emma says he is content to live part of the year here at Highbury."

"But what of the *other* part of the year?" Mr. Woodhouse asked, looking suddenly much older. "Please do not expose yourself to the rigors of London, my dear! I could not bear to lose you as I did your poor mother. That Isabella must stay in such an unhygienic environment is terrible enough. You know how she suffers!"

"But she does not," Emma protested. "She and the children are very happy there. But that is beside the point. I shall not need to go to London with Frank. He may very well go up part of the year while I remain here. You know how I love Highbury. I have no great desire to go to London."

Mr. Knightley frowned. "You had not told me this part of the plan, Emma. I can't think it judicious to have a young man on the town without his wife season after season. But I suppose there is time and to spare for thinking that through."

"Yes. What worries me more," she purposefully brought this up to distract her father, "is whether his aunt will approve of me! Frank tells me she has often threatened to cut him off if he should marry to disoblige her. I should hate to cause it."

Her father clasped her hand. "No one could disapprove you, Emma. You are perfect."

Emma winced, thinking of Miss Bates, who had excused herself to avoid Emma's visit of reparation. "Hardly that. But if Mrs. Churchill should cast off poor Frank, we would support him, would we not, Papa? You know that Mr. Weston loves him dearly but does not have lands to pass on. Mr. Churchill will be quite part of the family!"

"I have never desired sons," Mr. Woodhouse said. "Boys are so violent; so uncontrolled; so gluttonous!"

"Well, he is not twelve, sir," Mr. Knightley said, "so I do not think you need worry about that. In fact, I see it is nearly time for your morning walk, your three turns. Will you take it with me, sir?"

"No... I, oh no. I am discomposed. I am feeling a spasm in my back."

"Perhaps we may walk it away, sir. Let us warm our muscles, gently, in the open air."

"Oh, no, I cannot. Emma, you must send for Perry at once."

Emma shook her head at Knightley. "Of course, Papa. I will send your man to help you into bed. I think you ought to lie down."

"Yes, I fear you are quite right. Too much excitement—Oh, what a tragic year it has been."

"Things will calm down eventually, Papa," Emma said. "Do sit quietly until he comes."

She signed for Mr. Knightley to follow her out into the passageway.

"It is no use urging him to exert himself," Emma said. "He will feel better for a little cosseting."

"You are probably right. It will be fine; the hardest part is over. I was not much help to you, but you may count on me to support his spirits and urge the merits of the plan at every turn."

"Yes, it could have gone much worse." Emma wished again that she might feel better about it, more excited. "I do appreciate your presence; it helped."

Mr. Knightley tucked her hand around his arm. "Then may I interest *you* in three turns in the garden? I think your complexion, far from being flushed, is sadly pale."

Emma's breath caught in her throat; her heart hurt. Was this what maturity felt like? "Yes, please."

Emma found the meeting with Frank's father and stepmother, her own dear Mrs. Weston, far easier.

Emma came to visit—something she did generally once or twice a week—and Frank joined them, sending a servant to fetch his father.

When they were all assembled, he took Emma's hand. "I am happy to inform you that I have asked Emma to marry me, and she has accepted."

Nothing could have been warmer than Mr. Weston's hearty congratulations, his red face, his shining eyes as he slapped Frank on the back. He blew his nose a time or two and told Emma she couldn't have made them happier.

Mrs. Weston was more reserved, but she hugged Emma tightly, rocking her back and forth for a moment as she used to do when Emma was small. She eventually pulled out a delicate handkerchief and wiped her own eyes.

"Now you will be my daughter in title, not merely in my heart," she said.

And if Emma was a little less laughing and a little more silent than usual, Mrs. Weston was too biased of an observer to note what this might mean. She was too invested in the thought of "Frank and Emma," a phrase which she had repeated quietly to herself for some weeks, to note any little details that might challenge the prevailing relief she felt.

{ 33 }

WHEN HARRIET RECEIVED an invitation from her friend Beth Martin to come stay with them for three weeks in July, she did not know what to do. Miss Woodhouse had given her advice the day they visited, and Harriet had not brought it up again since.

Seeing Mr. Martin on the day of the strawberry party had been difficult. He had not even seemed to see her. It had been so different from the kind and attentive way he had always greeted her in the past. Even after she had rejected his proposal!

Harriet folded the letter into her worn reticule and made ready to go to Hartfield to consult Emma. However, halfway there, she had a thought. She was not given to great reflection, but as she passed Ford's and then the bakery and then the rooms where Miss Bates lived, she paused.

Miss Woodhouse was Harriet's dearest friend, and that could not change. Miss Woodhouse had noticed Harriet, selected her, mentored her, treated her with every sign of friendship. That could never be equaled.

But... in this instance, as Miss Woodhouse had firmly stated that she would not give Harriet any further advice on visiting the Martins, perhaps Harriet might consult... Miss Bennet? The idea felt slightly daring, slightly disloyal.

Miss Bennet was also Harriet's friend, though, was she not? And she was the soon-to-be Mrs. Knightley! That would make her the lady of Donwell Abbey and the landlord of the Martins. She would have an interest in them. Indeed, as Mr. Knightley was friends with Mr. Martin, Miss Bennet might in some fashion become friends with them herself, unlike Emma.

The incongruity of these two ideas did not trouble Harriet overly, however, since she rarely spent time in comparison and contrast, which was her chief dislike of all essay and rhetoric lessons.

With great trepidation, as might a spy who is fearful of being seen, Harriet looked up and down the street before darting across the road and into the stairwell that led up to Miss Bates's rooms.

Miss Bennet was sitting with Miss Fairfax and they welcomed Harriet, though Miss Bennet soon said, "Are you feeling quite well, Harriet? You keep looking furtively at the door."

"No! Oh, no, I am perfectly fine. I was merely—" She screwed up her courage. "Miss Bennet, I have received a letter from my friend, and I am not perfectly sure how to answer it. I was wondering if, perhaps, you would advise me. If you do not feel it an imposition! However, oh dear, I feel sure it is. Pray forget it."

"No imposition," Miss Bennet said gaily. "In fact, you have made me curious and so you cannot leave me in suspense. If it is not confidential, you must certainly show me now!"

Miss Fairfax rose, "I was on the point of lying down; I will do so, then you may be private."

"No, no," poor Harriet said, pulling the slightly crumpled sheet from her reticule. "I do not want to drive you from your own parlor! It is only a small matter. I am not so grand as to need privacy."

But Miss Fairfax only smiled weakly. "Do call me for dinner, won't you, Lizzy? Don't allow me to sleep through."

"Of course." Lizzy smoothed the letter in her lap, and it was all Harriet could do to remain quiet while she read it. Miss Woodhouse said silence was a mark of good breeding. The *right* silence, at the *right* moments, she had said.

Harriet supposed this was a right moment.

Lizzy was a fast reader. "I see. Since you already did me the honor of letting me into your confidence about Mr. Martin's proposal, I can understand the difficulty."

"Exactly! Miss Woodhouse says I must go if I wish, but that I ought not if I feel I may not be perfectly safe from a recurring affection for Mr. Martin, which would make us both miserably awkward. I would not for the world upset him, or his sisters or his mother, of course. Do tell me what I ought to do!"

Lizzy looked at the letter and back at Harriet. "And if my advice differs from Miss Woodhouse?"

"Oh—Well—It hardly can, because she has only advised me to be sure of my own mind, and that is what I am not. To be sure—both of you are so much quicker than I! So much more learned!"

"Yes, but Harriet—it does not follow that because Miss Woodhouse and I are both ladies that we must agree. There is not one right course of action here, do you see? It is not a choice between right and wrong, but of opinion."

Harriet began to pick at a loose thread on her glove. "To visit or not visit? I suppose I see what you mean. Does this mean that you will not advise me?"

"No, on the contrary, I believe I am too vain to give up an opportunity to give advice." Lizzy laughed ruefully. "But that is not to my credit, and you must take what I say lightly. Harriet, I saw Mr. Martin look at you a few days ago—it was after he'd spoken to Mr. Knightley and was riding away—and I think he is still very much in love with you. The option before you is not merely to visit or not, but to encourage Mr. Martin or not."

Harriet could not speak if she tried.

Miss Bennet continued, "If you are determined to refuse him again, you should not visit, it would be unkind to him. But if you feel that perhaps you regret your refusal, that after several months of reflecting, you find you still care for Mr. Martin and his family, I think you should visit."

"But Miss Woodhouse says— They are not the sort of people I *should* like. Farmers, you know."

"But you *do* like them, do you not? And Mr. Knightley likes them. I like them, what little acquaintance I have! Perhaps as Mrs. Knightley I can prevail upon Emma to relax her standards slightly," Lizzy sighed, "or perhaps not. But you must think whether *you* would like to live with them for always."

"Oh..." The idea opening before Harriet was breathtaking. As she generally agreed with whomever she had spoken to most recently, Lizzy's words seemed to sweep away a large part of Miss Woodhouse's warnings. "But what if he does not ask me again? What if he has changed his mind?"

Lizzy put her finger to her lips, nibbling a nail. "I do not think he has changed his mind, but there *is* the possibility he may not ask again. I do not know his temperament. I think you might do what you can to encourage him."

"I cannot! I should be ever so nervous. I would be on tenterhooks the whole visit. I do not know how to encourage Mr. Martin."

"I don't believe it would take much, just your general complaisance and perhaps a hint..." She trailed off. "No, I see what you mean. It would not be a challenge for me, but that is not your nature. What a dreadfully anxious visit you would have! No, it would be best if you were certain before your visit. Perhaps a letter? Of course, why did I not think of that before? In general, a woman does not write to a single man or vice versa, but he wrote his proposal to you, and I believe the rules of etiquette would allow for a second note from you responding to his proposal."

Harriet felt her cheeks warm while the rest of her felt cold. "But what could I say? It is so forward!"

"It is not the easiest thing, I admit. Perhaps you could say merely that your 'sentiments have changed,' and if his are unchanged, you would be very happy."

"Do I dare? I am not much of a writer. And I do not know... *ought* I to marry Mr. Martin? Oh, do you think it possible?"

"I think it very possible. Women make far worse matches every day. Besides, I liked the look of him."

"He is very handsome, I know. I did not find him so at first, but his features are so exactly *him,* one cannot help but find him handsome after one knows him..."

Lizzy smiled. "I think you need to ponder that idea a little more, and if you still feel that Mr. Martin, simply by being himself, is one of the handsomest, kindest gentlemen of your acquaintance, you must either write or visit with the intention of accepting him the next time he asks."

Lizzy had barely finished breakfast the following day before Harriet brought her letter around for approval. She seemed to be in a rush. Perhaps she feared she would lose her courage or that Emma would confront her if she waited.

Her penmanship was of the sort that might be termed *adequate schoolgirl,* but the letter was not so bad.

Dear Mr. Martin,

I have enclosed this note in my letter to Beth and asked her to give it to you. I know it is very forward to write to you, please forgive me. Beth has invited me to visit in July—but I suppose you know that!—and I should very much like to come. Your mother and sisters were so kind during my last visit.

But before I agree, I feel I ought to tell you that my sentiments have changed from what they were when I wrote you last. That is, they have not precisely changed, but my understanding has. If you should not like me to visit, I shall not.

Yours sincerely,

Harriet Smith

"Is it a good letter?" Harriet wrung her hands. "It is short, but Miss Woodhouse said that is not so bad."

"It is a good letter," Lizzy said. "You do not exactly clarify your change of heart, but I believe it is more than enough."

Harriet clasped it to her chest. "I have never been so frightened."

"I hope you never will be again."

She left at once, and Jane Fairfax raised her fine eyebrows. "You have taken on a great responsibility."

Lizzy finally felt that she had achieved some sort of connection with Jane. It was tenuous, and Jane still drew back behind her walls at times, but something had broken loose when Frank had disparaged deceptive women and marriage.

Lizzy grimaced. "Yes, I know I have. I am as bad as Emma! But do not reproach me, please. You did not see Harriet's face when she first received his proposal."

Jane smiled faintly. "You and Miss Woodhouse are rather similar, it is true, but that is not a bad thing. You are both lively and confident, witty and elegant. You are more like each other than you are like me."

"For you are ignorant and haggard? Do be serious."

"I am. My tone of mind is different than yours or Emma's. I am not so ready to laugh, or to talk, or to amuse. Emma has tried at times to befriend me, I know she has, but I never reciprocated."

"She has not my tenacity, perhaps," Lizzy said. "Rank stubbornness, my mother says. I do not think it too late, however, if you wished to become friends with her. I suspect Emma, because of her place in society, is lonely." Lizzy grimaced again. "And I may just have deprived her of her best friend."

As it happened, Lizzy saw the result of Harriet's letter only two days later. Mr. Knightley had called to ask if she would take a walk with him, and as they were walking on the Donwell Road away from Mrs. Goddard's school, they saw a horse galloping toward them.

It lessened to a trot and a walk, and then Mr. Martin doffed his hat.

"How do you do, Mr. Knightley? Miss Bennet!"

"Fine," said Mr. Knightley. "Did you have aught to discuss? I seem to keep missing you."

"No, no. I was on my way—elsewhere. Good day!"

He flew on and Lizzy seized Mr. Knightley's arm. "Good heavens, did you see his face? I believe I know what he is about. May we turn back for a moment?"

They turned back toward the school and Mr. Knightley teased her. "You have a look of Emma about you just now. Have you been matchmaking?"

"Yes! But you may not censure me, for it is a match you approve of also. Let us go closer that we may see."

Mr. Knightley grumbled that he was not a peeping tom, but gamely kept pace as Lizzy all but raced down the road. She hoped that Harriet might come out to Mr. Martin, as he could certainly not be shown into her private rooms...

"Yes," Lizzy sighed. For there on the plain gravel walk in front of the school stood Mr. Martin, looking very trim in his best coat. Harriet stepped out the front door and turned to dismiss the maid who'd summoned her. She didn't have on a hat or bonnet, and her blond hair shone in the fitful sunlight and shade that the tall trees cast.

Lizzy and Mr. Knightley were too far to hear Mr. Martin's words, but he drew close to her and said several things.

Harriet's eyes were downcast, her cheeks red, but she nodded several times.

Mr. Martin tipped her chin up with a hand, the other tentatively touching her cheek. Then he bent and kissed her.

Lizzy suddenly felt that perhaps she'd been too nosy, but before she could turn away, she saw Harriet standing on her toes to reach him, her hand slipping around his neck as she kissed him back. They broke apart, laughing, and Mr. Martin embraced Harriet, swinging her in a circle so that her feet left the ground.

Lizzy turned away then, drawing Mr. Knightley after her. She sighed. "I am very happy for Harriet."

"As am I."

Lizzy looked at his profile. She could easily imagine kissing Mr. Knightley. He was good-looking, etc. But did she feel anything like the incandescent happiness which had been so obvious in Harriet and Mr. Martin, even from afar?

She feared she did not. Nor did he for her. She'd once thought only love would do for marriage; had she changed so much in the past year? For a moment Lizzy felt a stranger to herself.

Not all marriages had to be that way, of course. Maybe it could grow.

They walked on toward Donwell Abbey and he retrieved the dogs he usually walked with.

"What is this one named?" Lizzy asked. A frisky black and white dog pranced around his feet. "Did you call her Bea?"

"I—" He broke off and stroked the dog, no longer meeting Lizzy's eyes. "No, her name is Betsy. Emma named her. Shall we walk back through the fields?"

{ 34 }

M R. KNIGHTLEY DREADED Mr. Churchill's ball, where the announcement of Emma's engagement would occur.

It was not that he had not thought of trying to rectify things, but it was the height of dishonor for a man to renege on an offer of marriage.

Still, if ever there was a woman who he believed might understand, who would be reasonable, it was Miss Bennet.

But... he could not bring himself to do it. She would be everything gracious, he believed, but he had offered for her in good faith and could not bring himself to break his promise.

And if he forfeited his honor to be with Emma, what would he really be offering her? And furthermore, he would not be gaining Emma by jilting poor Lizzy. Emma was already engaged to Frank. She loved Frank, or if she did not, she soon would. She certainly did not love Mr. Knightley, not in the way he wished.

So, he put away all such thoughts and placed himself the rather onerous task of diverting, encouraging, and reconciling Mr. Woodhouse to the changes coming to him.

The night of Frank's party arrived and it was fine. The shifting clouds of the midafternoon gave way to a sparkling starry night. All the carriage drivers and grooms would have plenty of light.

Mr. Churchill had rented a room in the Crown Inn in the center of town. It was an easy walk even for Miss Bates and Miss Fairfax, though Mr. Knightley called around to walk with them down the dim street to the Crown.

Emma had planned to arrive early to help with any last-minute details of the ball, but Mr. Knightley had not felt it incumbent on him to do so. Mr. Woodhouse would not be there, though he had reluctantly agreed that the announcement should be made.

The hotel was full of light and noise. The ladies detoured to a small room where they changed from their sturdy boots to dancing slippers and by the time they returned, Frank was on hand to greet them gravely but with a glint in his eye. He was no doubt eager to acquaint everyone with his prosperous suit.

Mr. Knightley found his air repugnant.

Frank led them into the ballroom where it seemed the whole party had already arrived, and three musicians tuned up on a small, raised platform. Mr. Knightley escorted Miss Bates to a grouping of chairs near the large fireplace, though only a small fire burned, for it was a warm night.

Frank Churchill lingered behind talking to Lizzy and Miss Fairfax. Mr. Knightley tried not to resent him.

Lizzy distrusted Frank Churchill's expression as he bowed over her hand and smirked at Jane Fairfax. Lizzy was beginning to feel downright protective of Jane.

Lizzy had not met Frank Churchill under the best of circumstances to judge his character, but he was certainly not making a good show of things.

"I am so glad you have both come," he said. "I feared perhaps you would have the headache. Women so often do, it seems."

"Better than gout, the manly ailment," Lizzy retorted. She would have gone on, but Frank delayed them.

"Mrs. Elton has been boring me rather heartily with talk of a family in London who need a governess, but I suspect her enthusiasm has carried her too far."

"It has not," Jane told him. "I have been writing to the family Mrs. Elton recommended to me. I daresay I shall accept a post with them; they seem perfectly unobjectionable."

Frank narrowed his eyes. "Playing the victim, my dear?"

Lizzy slipped her arm through Jane's. "No, how should she? She is to be congratulated on facing the future with boldness. Come, I see Miss Smith is trying to get our attention."

She steered Jane toward Harriet. Lizzy had had a note from Harriet but had not spoken to her since the day she'd witnessed the reunion with Mr. Martin.

Harriet stood happily with the two Miss Coles, though her hands in their white evening gloves occasionally tugged restlessly at one another. She smiled at Lizzy. "Oh, Miss Bennet, is it not a beautiful party?"

They chatted for a moment before Harriet caught her eye and they moved a little apart. "Miss Bennet, I am so delighted. I know I have done right when I have also made Mr. Martin so happy. The only fly in the ointment—as Mr. Martin might say!—is that I have not yet told Miss Woodhouse."

"Oh." Lizzy was a little disconcerted. "I would not inform her at the ball. You must do so privately. She will be very happy for you. Sooner or later."

"Yes. I—I think she must be, for she has always my happiness at heart, and I will explain that I *am* happy."

"Yes. But for now," said Lizzy, "dance and enjoy yourself. Do not borrow trouble from tomorrow."

"What is troubling you, Emma?" asked Mrs. Weston quietly, looping her arm through Emma's. "Frank is going to announce your engagement, and while you look lovely, as always, you cannot fool me. Your limbs seem to droop through the dances, and your jaw is locked in a smile. It is your father, isn't it? Mr. Knightley says he was quite cast down when you asked him about the match. But my dear, Emma, you know your father! He sees every change as a tragedy."

Emma felt tears prick her eyes. She wanted very much to sit in Mrs. Weston's lap as she had done as a child and admit that she had eaten too many sweet buns and made herself quite sick.

"I am a little troubled for him, but you are right, it is his way," Emma said. "I suppose it is also that *I* do not like change, even when it is good! Frank and I, Mr. Knightley and Miss Bennet, Jane Fairfax going away..."

"Yes, I suppose that may be." Mrs. Weston was dubious. "Miss Fairfax's future does trouble me. But in Mr. Knightley's marriage you are gaining a friend, not losing one!"

"Yes. I think perhaps I have the headache a little."

Emma roused herself to dance and speak to nearly everyone. She spent extra time with Harriet, for her guilty conscience continued to prick her that she had so totally failed her friend. Harriet seemed perfectly happy though, even a little giddy. Emma tried to watch where her gaze fell, to see if any particular gentleman was the source of this effervescence, but she made no discovery.

Emma also made a point to sit by Miss Bates for a quarter of an hour. Emma had tried to visit but had not yet been admitted. How terrible that she had hurt Miss Bates so deeply! It was humbling that Emma could not even offer an apology until Miss Bates was essentially a captive audience at a party.

Emma seated herself next to Miss Bates and when that lady smiled at her for a moment it was as if Emma was a little girl again, come to visit old Mrs. Bates and receive the odd sugar-candies that they sometimes had on hand.

But then Miss Bates seemed to recollect the recent past. Her face fell and she blushed; she mumbled; she excused herself.

Emma put a hand on her arm. "Pray wait just a moment, please."

Miss Bates seated herself again. Miss Fairfax was on her other side and Emma did not exactly relish making her apology with Jane looking on, but she knew she did not deserve to be choosy. She had insulted Miss Bates in front of her beloved niece; the least she could do was to make amends the same way.

Emma took Miss Bates's hand. "I am deeply sorry for how I treated you at Donwell Abbey. I was cruel and rude and heartless and I have no excuse. You have always treated me so kindly, and despite how I spoke that day, I *do* value your friendship. Please, please forgive me for acting so."

Miss Bates's gaze fluttered from Emma to the fire to Jane. Her free hand fluttered to her spectacles and back. Her lips fluttered over words that denied Emma's wrongdoing, forgave her for it, and excused it in the same breath.

But when she had landed from her fluttering, she was still accepting Emma's light grasp of her hand. "I—Oh, of course, my dearest Miss Woodhouse. I know I am such a silly old lady now, so talkative and dim! I was never witty like my dear mother or my sister! So foolish—"

"Now, I cannot allow you to abuse yourself," Emma said. "If you forgive me, I am thankful from my heart. You did not deserve to be treated so. Now, if you please, I have heard from several sources that Jane received a letter from a family in London! But sadly, every time I try to get the details, I am interrupted or entreated to dance. Do, please, tell me the news."

Miss Bates beamed through the misty glass of her spectacles. "Oh! It sounds just the thing for Jane. I have it just here, for I told Jane people would want to know. 'Everyone is interested in your position, Jane!' I told her. I will just get it and tell you the particulars. Oh, I have left it with my hat and boots."

While she went away to retrieve it, Emma offered an olive branch to Jane Fairfax. "I know it is properly your news to tell, but I thought your aunt would enjoy the telling of it more. I hope you do not feel slighted."

"No, not at all."

Jane was as close-lipped as ever, but Emma tried not to judge her for it. "She was always so happy to share *your* letters with me when you were with the Campbells. Although she much prefers your presence, the lack of letters to share has been a change. You have always been a faithful correspondent to her."

Jane inclined her head. "I feel it is the least I can do for her. She was very attached to my mother, you know. I believe my mother's death was more a blow to her than to me, for I was too young to recall. I try to keep her up to date on my life."

Emma leaned forward. "Do you know, I feel the same way about my mother? That it was more of a blow to my father, I mean, than to myself. Though if I were to say that to him, it would make him sad, so I do not. It is kind of you to write."

"It is kind of you to stay with your father. Many young ladies would allow pining or regret to cloud their affection and cheer."

Emma had rarely heard so many words from Jane in her life. "Thank you, but you must not think me better than I am. I do not like change—I have realized how much that is true, of late!—so it has not been the sacrifice for me that it might be for others."

"I am glad for you."

The words were simple, but heartfelt. Emma felt again that Jane Fairfax really was a most beautiful and appealing girl, with such a tragic situation. Really, perhaps Emma *could* be her friend, if it was not too late.

But Miss Bates was back with the letter and Jane sat back with a smile of appreciation for Emma. It was not the perfectly elegant expression Jane Fairfax often wore, but one more personal. Emma wished she'd seen it before today.

{ 35 }

LIZZY HAD RECEIVED MORE than a few congratulations during the evening. She had danced every dance; indeed, she found nothing made one so popular as an engagement. She had found Highbury a friendly community before, but now that she was engaged to Mr. Knightley, it seemed no one wanted to waste time getting on excellent terms with her.

Easily pleased, if not easily impressed, Lizzy had no fault to find with this program. When Mr. Knightley sought her ought for a dance, she related some of the amusing comments to him. "I had known you were well-liked, but now I know how well. Everyone is determined to find me everything that is perfect, which reflects well on you. I feel I must warn you that things will be different when you visit Meryton."

After the first round of dances, when the group paused for rest and refreshment, Mr. Frank Churchill called for attention. He stood near the front of the room, nearest to the door that led out to the vestibule of the hotel and the outdoors. Emma was next to him, but there was nothing unusual in that.

He cleared his throat once more and raised a hand to pause the last few conversations. "Before we go enjoy the feast I have ordered for us," he paused for good-natured hurrahs from the men, "I have an announcement. Despite the frivolous and foppish fellow you all know me to be, Miss Woodhouse has done me the honor," he paused and seemed to be looking for a particular face in the crowd, "she has done me the honor of accepting my hand."

A tense silence was broken by tentative and then more exuberant cheering, at least from the younger members of the party. The older members began to turn and congratulate Mr. and Mrs. Weston, or to comment amongst themselves. Harriet slipped to the front to embrace Emma, and the young gentlemen shook Mr. Churchill's hand.

Lizzy put a hand to her mouth to hide a gasp and she looked about for Jane Fairfax. Poor Jane! Where was she? There, over by the small, raised step where the three musicians sat.

Lizzy turned to Mr. Knightley. "Please excuse me for a moment." But she saw such a look of such pain and self-loathing on his face that she momentarily forgot Jane. His brow was furrowed. Deep, sharp grooves outlined his mouth. His lips were nearly white.

What had disturbed him so deeply? Clearly something about Emma and Frank Churchill.

But no, she must help Jane. She left Mr. Knightley and slipped like a leaf in the current of a stream to Jane's side.

Lizzy sat and wrapped one arm around Jane's waist, for Jane looked alarmingly pale. "It is not so bad. I am here, lean on me."

Jane shook her head faintly. "No, no. I am fine. I *ought* to be fine. I do not care so very—so very—" Her face screwed up in the unmistakable look of someone fighting back tears. "It is only... he *looked* at me so. Did he mean to hurt me? Oh, Miss Bennet. Lizzy. I really must get home."

"Yes, do not speak any more at present. I will take you home directly."

How exactly to do this, Lizzy was unsure. They had walked to the Crown Inn, and the distance was not far, but she wasn't certain Jane would make it. Jane had been terribly weak and ill when Lizzy came to Highbury and that was not long ago. Now Jane had had her heart and pride smashed in a most cruel way and she looked as if she might faint.

Mr. Knightley approached with his own pain—was it pain?—smoothed away. Lizzy would not have known the difference, but she now recognized a tamped, despairing look in his eyes.

"Miss Fairfax is unwell," Lizzy said. "We must get her home and to bed directly."

"At once. I will ask Mr. Churchill—"

"No," Jane whispered. "Do not bother him, please."

Mr. Knightley looked at her searchingly. "Well, Mrs. Weston then. She can call up her carriage quietly." He went and whispered to Mrs. Weston, who looked back to them in alarm.

Unfortunately, many of the party, first distracted from the feast by the announcement, now distracted from the announcement by this development, gathered around Jane.

"Poor dear, Jane!" cried Miss Bates. "I knew you were not looking hale tonight. I am shockingly to blame."

A servant offered to get hartshorn and water. Mrs. Weston sent one of them to bring her carriage around. Even Emma came over in concern. "Is there anything I can do, Miss Fairfax?"

This was quite the worst thing to happen to Jane. Lizzy could see her shrinking away from everyone, especially Emma. She could see her fighting to suppress sobs, could see her shuddering with revulsion at making such a scene for such a reason.

Lizzy whispered to Emma, "I think if we could clear out the crowd a trifle, it would help. Give her a moment to collect herself and get to the carriage."

"Of course." Emma clapped her hands. "We are quite crushing Miss Fairfax. I know we all care for her, but she needs air and silence more than fussing. Will you all set a good example with me and leave her to her aunt and Mr. Knightley for now? They will see her safely home." Emma made good on this start by leading the large part of the onlookers away to the adjoining hall which was laden with food.

Only Frank Churchill ignored her. He watched Emma leave, and though she cast a querying look over her shoulder, he shook his head.

He instead bowed slightly before Jane Fairfax, who was turned half away from him, her handkerchief found and pressed against her eyes.

"My dear Miss Fairfax, I am devastated that you find yourself unwell. If there is anything that I might do, though a relative stranger to you, I beg you will let me know. I hate to see a lady suffering."

There was such lying sincerity in his voice, belied only by a slight smirk and the knowledge which Lizzy had of the circumstances, that she could hardly believe his brazenness.

"No, no," whispered Miss Fairfax. "I simply need to go home."

"Of course. A shame you should feel so unwell during our announcement. I know you would have been the first to wish us happy. Did you not tell me in Weymouth that I ought to find a bride who was up to snuff?"

Jane hid her face in her hands.

Lizzy fumed. He was all but torturing poor Miss Fairfax. Had he set up this party and this announcement to hurt her? When Frank went so far as to turn his limpid, too-innocent gaze on Lizzy, she could not stand it. She jerked a step forward and slapped him.

Mrs. Weston and Miss Bates gasped; Mr. Knightley froze.

Frank Churchill raised his hand to the red spot on his cheek, incredulous.

"How dare you?" Lizzy hissed. "Neither Emma nor Jane deserve this. If you have any shred of gentlemanly behavior, you will go to the dining room at once."

"How dare *I*, Miss Bennet? You are the one—"

Lizzy raised her hand again and he cut off. Mr. Knightley gently put his hand on hers and lowered it. "I think Mr. Churchill was just leaving."

Frank still looked aggrieved as he left, as if he were the one misjudged. Or as if the misfire of his cruel, petty scheme deserved more pity than Jane's very real distress.

Mrs. Weston did not demand an explanation for what had occurred, for which forbearance Lizzy was thankful. Miss Bates was, for once, stricken dumb. They all three helped Jane to the carriage, where Mrs. Weston claimed the privilege of helping Miss Bates get Jane home and to bed.

"You can walk Miss Bennet back," she said to Mr. Knightley. Her eyes seemed to say more.

The carriage rattled away, and Knightley again offered his arm to Lizzy. The sky was still starry and bright, but it had grown very cool. It must be near midnight. "I have no great love for Frank Churchill but your anger seemed specific. Please do explain."

Lizzy didn't move. "I have never done such a thing before."

"I assumed not. Come, I am not angry, but I am confused."

Lizzy sighed and joined him, walking slowly down the cobbled road. "It is not entirely my story to tell."

"Then I must make surmises. Miss Fairfax's distress was acute and sudden. A past romance with Mr. Churchill? An expectation suddenly found false?"

"No, but you are not far off. A secret engagement, which she called off only a few weeks ago. I think the shock, the malicious edge, was worse than the disappointment. She has called him petty and sullen, and I am afraid this was a vindictive move on his part. At least in part."

Mr. Knightley's hand fisted. "That blackguard. How dare he use Emma to hurt Miss Fairfax? And he called himself a gentleman. "I knew he was not what he ought to be... but this! I could call him out for this."

A traitorous part of him was fiercely glad. He had solid reason to prevent Emma's marriage to Frank now.

Mostly he was angry, however. The man had deceived Emma! He had convinced her that he loved her and she him. What a horrible awakening it would be for her. One's first love was not always one's last... but Emma had been so against marriage. The fact she had made a change for Frank Churchill argued no small attachment!

"And it will be my duty to tell her," Mr. Knightley realized aloud. "What a wretched task! She will be skeptical, then she will defend him. Eventually, when convinced, she will be devastated. I have never fought a duel, but I could shoot a man for this."

"I beg you won't," Lizzy said. "You would have to leave the country, wouldn't you?"

"No, of course I will not." He closed his eyes for a moment. "What a ghastly mess. I cannot bring this to Emma."

Lizzy had not exactly forgotten the pain she saw on Mr. Knightley's face when the engagement was announced, but she had not had much time to think on it.

Now she did. "You already knew about Emma and Mr. Churchill. You were not surprised."

"No," he admitted. "As nearly a brother to Emma, she consulted me."

Lizzy digested this as they walked. She had forgotten to change back into her boots, and her dancing slippers were soaked through, her toes quite cold.

"But you are not her brother. And you hate the match." Lizzy stopped. She did not want to hurt him, but she had to know. "Mr. Knightley... are you in love with Emma?"

His clear, dark eyes cut away from her, and that was an answer to Lizzy. "Gracious heavens."

Lizzy examined her feelings and found she was... not injured. A little sad, quite a bit perplexed, but her heart was not breaking.

"No, Miss Bennet, please forgive me for not answering at once. I do love Emma, for since my brother John married and left for London, she and her father have been my family. But I did not propose to you while thinking of her."

"No, I don't suppose you did." Lizzy examined him. The poor man looked quite miserable. "You have only realized recently? And you could not tell me. No, I see. How awkward."

"I am not without honor. I hold myself ready to honor my promise and our marriage contract."

"Heaven save me from honorable men, they are as difficult as the other! Do you think it would be better to marry me, knowing yourself to be in love elsewhere? That, to me, would be less honorable."

He grimaced.

Lizzy shivered, her feet were so cold. "Let us walk on; I think I have had enough of doing this face to face." They continued, shoulder to shoulder.

Lizzy did not feel like crying, but there could be no doubt she was filled with a certain amount of disappointment, with lingering anger, and with frustration at herself.

When she was quite sure that she had her voice under control, she spoke calmly. "Mr. Knightley, I fear that we should not suit." She looked further down the street where Mrs. Weston's carriage had drawn up. "It shall be a trifle embarrassing, but if you will inform those you know that I have cried off, I would appreciate it. I will write to my father. And then... then I think I shall visit my friend Charlotte."

Her mother's response did not bear thinking of. Her father would support her, but still... it would be ugly. But far less ugly than marrying a good, kind gentleman who was desperately in love with someone else.

"Why have you not proposed to Emma?" Lizzy demanded. "Usually I would not pry, but I feel circumstances have given me a temporary right to interrogate you."

Mr. Knightley was silent for a long moment. "You have said yourself that I did not realize until recently, and that is true. She is very young."

"We are nearly the exact same age."

"Yes, but I only met you recently. I knew Emma when she was ten."

"Yes, if you had proposed then, that would have been quite Gothic. I could not have approved."

Mr. Knightley granted this a fleeting smile.

"I do not tease you to make you miserable," Lizzy relented. "But to show you that it is not so very dire. You have already allowed her to name your dogs, to help plan your home garden. You practically live at Hartfield. In fact..."

Lizzy pictured Mr. Knightley and Emma together, as she had seen them so often during her trip. *Did* Emma love Mr. Knightley?

"In fact, her engagement might be entirely your fault."

"*My* fault?"

"Well, I suppose if we venture into technicalities, I am to blame also, but I advise you not to play that card just now. No, you became engaged to me. What did she do? She accepted a half-hearted proposal from Frank Churchill!"

He frowned. "That did surprise me. I thought she was nearly on the brink of becoming engaged to Mr. Darcy. He all but proposed on the day his aunt came to Hartfield and she did not reject him! It was quite telling."

"Did he?" Lizzy could not bring herself to talk of Mr. Darcy to him. "Well, perhaps he gave her the idea that marriage was possible, but she did not accept anyone until you were engaged."

He shook his head. "I don't know that that affected her at all."

"Frank does not love Emma or he could not have used her so. And I sincerely doubt he made her pretty speeches or even a compelling case for love." Lizzy paused as they reached Miss Bates's door. "Take heart, sir. I think that Emma is in over her head and will be far less devastated than you expect to find out Mr. Churchill is not what she thought him."

{ 36 }

LIZZY RAN UP THE STAIRS ALONE and paused for a moment to press cold hands to her hot cheeks. She would only have these few moments alone to come to terms with her new predicament before entering Miss Bates's parlor.

Why had she ever accepted Mr. Knightley? Now it would cause far more uproar and talk! She would be scorned or pitied by his friends and her own. Oh—how foolish! She had thought a compromise on her own behalf could harm no one, but she had not reckoned on this.

Lizzy sighed deeply. She had been living in a dream of comfort, a dream of love. Now she was simply plain Lizzy Bennet again. That had been enough, and it would be enough again, but she felt rather empty just now.

She went into the parlor and found Mrs. Weston standing by the window and looking out. She was watching Mr. Knightley walk back down the street.

"How is Miss Fairfax?" Lizzy asked.

"She revived somewhat. Miss Bates is helping her into her night things and tucking her in." Mrs. Weston visibly composed herself. "I love my husband very much, and with the greatest will in the world to think well of my new son, I cannot put a good construction on what has occurred. I will not ask you to betray

Miss Fairfax's confidence, but please tell me, ought I to intervene? All is clearly not right."

Lizzy exhaled long and slow. "Someone must intervene, but I think not either of us. Mr. Knightley is aware of the basic facts and will, I believe, have words with Mr. Churchill tonight. I think that you might need to prepare yourself for an abrupt end of the engagement."

Mrs. Weston's fine eyes widened. "As bad as that? Oh, dear."

"I should perhaps add that Mr. Knightley and I have decided that we shall not suit. He will no doubt tell you when time allows."

"I am so sorry, my dear!"

Lizzy shook her head. "It was as much my mistake as his. Far better that we fix it now than repent it later. I'm afraid there has been a spate of mistaken romances in Highbury."

"Yes, I'm afraid so. Emma will be so disappointed! And Mr. Knightley must be furious with Frank." She put her hand to her mouth. "Oh. Mr. Knightley and Emma...? Why did I not see?"

Lizzy sank wearily into a chair and took the poker to stir the coals in the fireplace. "I did not see either, not until tonight. I think he will act, though he was not sure how to speak to Emma when he left me."

Mrs. Weston put a comforting hand on Lizzy's shoulder. "You have been very generous tonight. I am sorry it was required of you. However, if you have but a little fortitude left, perhaps we may make sure at least some good comes of this."

"I would be happy to do so."

Mr. Knightley returned to the party with slow strides. He would not make a scene, but he would not allow Frank Churchill to impose on Emma's good nature and trusting heart any longer than necessary.

The meal had been eaten, though many still lingered with wine or sweetmeats by the time he returned.

Others had returned to the ballroom and the dancing had resumed with five or six couples. Emma danced with Frank.

She seemed as bright and lively as ever, but Frank's eyes locked onto Knightley when he re-entered the room. His expression, if Knightley read it aright, was somewhere between guilt and belligerence.

Mr. Knightley, not wanting to create more of a scandal than would no doubt already occur—poor Lizzy! Poor Emma!—made the rounds among the elders of the party, reassuring those who asked that Miss Fairfax was fine, merely overtired and a little anxious. Mrs. Weston would return directly, never fear.

Knightley wanted to confront Frank as soon as the dance was done, but he realized he ought not. Frank danced next with Harriet Smith, then one of the Miss Coles, then one of the young matrons. How he should look so nonchalant when he'd caused the heartbreak of one young lady, and would soon cause the heartbreak of another, was inconceivable.

Mrs. Weston did return.

At first Knightley avoided her. Eventually, when the news spread of his engagement ending, and Emma's ending the same night—it would end, so help him—people would look back and analyze this evening. He wanted to provide as little fodder for gossip as possible.

Mrs. Weston was determined to exchange words with him, however, and he relented lest he foolishly have to avoid her the rest of the evening.

"I spoke with Miss Bennet." She raised a hand. "You were very much at fault there. No, do not get stiff, my dear sir. You have chastised Emma far more harshly at times. You sought to distract yourself and used her as a shield, but it is good you both realized it now. There will be time and to spare for analyzing why it happened—I am feeling all sorts of foolish for not realizing how the land lies—but the most pressing question is how you will break it to everyone."

"I do not think there is any good way," Mr. Knightley said. "My only concern is that people not think ill of Miss Bennet on my behalf."

"There will be a great deal of talk no matter how it is done. In my opinion, it would be best to wait until Miss Bennet has gone to visit her friend."

"If you think it best, I will not mention it at present."

"I do. I will leave you now, but pray call on me tomorrow if you can find a moment. We must discuss."

Mr. Knightley felt an evening of dancing had never lasted so long, but at last the families began taking their leave. Mrs. Weston button-holed her husband and gently but firmly requested that he take her home and not wait for Frank. "He will want to say goodbye to the last lingerer, and he may use one of the Crown horses to ride home."

Eventually it was only the maidservants cleaning and clearing away and Frank Churchill, standing near the door with his hands clasped behind his back.

"Well, Knightley," he said. "You remain. Would you like to have a pint in the taproom? I'm sure it is empty just now."

"You may have a pint if you wish." Knightley was already growing annoyed at Frank's attitude, which only lent a new layer to his anger.

A sleepy manservant fetched the drink, and Frank stretched out his legs, perched on one of the stools in the taproom. "Very well, we are alone and I have a tolerable idea what you will say. Miss

Fairfax would say nothing, but I suppose Miss Bennet gave you an earful, eh? She is not like my dear Jane, she will not suffer silently, oh no." He stroked his cheek, which she had slapped.

Mr. Knightley felt his teeth grind. "Please do not make stupid and unnecessary observations. Is it true that you were engaged to Miss Fairfax until a month ago?"

"Yes." He drank deeply. "But if a man may not enter a new engagement after a woman cries off, you will have taught me something I don't know."

"Do you have any real affection for Emma?"

"Of course I do. She is just like me. Elegant, witty, selfish, tied to her father's apron strings the way I am tied to my aunt's. She is a good sort."

Mr. Knightley's jaw tensed again. "Do not compare your conduct to hers. I gather that I am correct that you do not love Emma, but merely desired to hurt Miss Fairfax. No, sir, I am no longer interested in anything further you have to say. You will leave Highbury tomorrow but only after acquainting Emma with the details of what has been done, preferably in person. A note will do if you do not have the nerve. If she chooses to keep the engagement, I will say nothing. If she does not, however, as I expect, you will never again bother either of these young ladies."

Frank waved a hand. "What will you do if I decline? You may spare yourself the threats. I suppose you would tell my father or publish my secret engagement to Jane. That would very possibly ruin me, for my aunt would be incensed, but I don't suppose you care for that. No, I will go. Even tonight I began to regret the engagement to Emma. A very good girl of her sort, but she is so bold, so self-sufficient. I prefer a woman who desperately needs me."

Mr. Knightley's lip curled in disgust. He could just about picture how the engagement with Miss Fairfax might have progressed, and this detail only completed the picture. Frank must have enjoyed being Miss Fairfax's "savior," and felt that he could go his length in any number of ways without her censure.

It was beneath him to brangle, however. "Yes, well, I will await your departure. Mind you make it all known to Miss Woodhouse."

Frank raised his hands. "I have already agreed. I think I shall go visit friends in Weymouth again. Weymouth is the place for falling in love."

Mr. Knightley had not sat, and he now moved to leave. At the door, Frank added, "Speaking of love—I am rather adept at spying out these little things, you know—does Miss Bennet know you are in love with my dearest Emma? Perhaps you have your own confession to make."

Mr. Knightley did not deign to answer this but left with a curdled feeling.

{ 37 }

EMMA SAT LIMPLY IN THE drawing room, the late morning sun slanting in on her, with Frank's note in her hand.

Engaged to Miss Fairfax?

Found he could not hold her to the engagement?

Felt compelled to explain?

The feeling of vague sickness she'd felt since last night, of being overfull of sweets by her own greed, began to seep away. Emma felt her body relax in a new way, and though anger was coming, her predominant feeling was relief.

She laid the letter on the small writing desk and clasped her hands in her lap. She could reassure her father that she wasn't leaving him. It would make talk, which she couldn't like, but that was not *her* fault. The feeling of deep waters closing over her head receded. She could breathe deeply again.

And how *dare* Frank Churchill propose to her out of pique and then call it off the day after the announcement! Thank heaven they had not yet sent a notice to the *Gazette*. What a selfish young man! How could he convince her that they were two peas in a pod? The impudence of it was appalling.

And she had been taken in.

What a deep mistake she had nearly made! Why, she felt nothing for Frank Churchill beyond a casual amusement and a sense of family history. She had been a broken-hearted little idiot and her wild ride, which would surely have ended in a metaphoric broken neck, had been unexpectedly halted. It was *terrible* of Frank, but... thank heaven.

And poor Miss Fairfax! No wonder she had broken down after the announcement. Emma's friendliness for her, strengthened during their first frank conversation the night before, reached a new high. How dare Frank hurt poor, lovely, lonely Miss Fairfax!

Emma would do all she could to benefit and befriend her. Mr. Knightley had been right about that, as he invariably was. Emma rubbed her eyes hard, as one does after a nightmare.

Mr. Knightley had been correct about her rudeness to Miss Bates. He had been correct about Frank's unsteadiness. About Lizzy's merits. Why did Mr. Knightley have to be so correct so often—and yet completely wrong in his choice?

When Harriet came and made *her* announcement, Emma could only laugh and then sigh. "I *was* the cuckoo in the nest. How humbling and horrible. Do not look so fearful, Harriet! I have not lost my senses. Providence has made sure that I am *amply* humbled today and ready to hear your news. You shall not be persecuted by my poor judgement and pride this time. It is still not what I could wish—But you are emphatically not me. My dear friend, you are happy, and I am happy for you. Mr. Martin is an excessively lucky man."

Harriet embraced her, crying. "Oh, thank you, Miss Woodhouse. I knew that you would understand, yet I did not think I could be perfectly happy if you did not."

"Then please be perfectly happy, with all my blessings."

"Thank you! And you will be happy too, Miss Woodhouse! I was never more surprised than I was last night, but you and Mr.

Churchill are perfect—both so clever and stylish. I am so happy you will not die an old maid!"

"Well." Emma stood back from Harriet and touched her warm cheeks. "As it happens, I do not think Mr. Churchill and I are going to be married."

Harriet looked aghast. "No? It was only announced last night."

"I know! Oh, how impulsive and stupid I was! If only I had realized before... but it is too late. There will be *such* talk. But I really must not discuss it with you until I write to him. Oh, Harriet, you are wiser than me. Please excuse me, my dear, I must compose a letter."

It was only a little later that her maid came up to Emma's sitting room, the one attached to her bedroom, and knocked softly. "Mrs. Weston is here to see you, miss. And Mr. Knightley, and Miss Bennet."

"All of them?" Emma pressed her temples. There was nothing to cause a headache like dancing until the wee hours and then writing a letter of rejection to a man who essentially betrayed her. "I do not think... but no, I must see them. I will be down directly."

Emma was surprised to see that Lizzy wore a worn traveling dress and hat, as if she were going on a trip. Mr. Knightley looked his usual self, though tired, and she longed to smooth away the wrinkle between his eyes.

Mrs. Weston looked determined. "Frank has gone to Weymouth," she said. "I believe you know the rest, but I want to apologize, Emma. If I had had any idea of his previous attachment to Miss Fairfax, I would have warned you days ago."

Emma smiled weakly and embraced her old governess. "I know you would have. It's unfortunate that the announcement should have been made before all was discovered, but it is done.

As you have often told me, it is better to look forward than back. I have already written to Frank. I have ended the engagement."

Mr. Knightley stood stiffly by the door. "I am relieved to hear you have written, but I am so sorry, Emma."

Emma shrugged. "I feel a fool. How does Jane do this morning? It must have been a shock."

Lizzy assured her that she would recover. "She is still planning to join the family in London in a few weeks' time. Today she is more resolved than ever."

"Well, then," Emma said, "I appreciate the visit, but I must confess my head aches terribly. Can we delay any further discussion for another day?"

Mr. Knightley inclined his head. "Of course."

"No, there is more," Lizzy said, elbowing him lightly. "It will not take long. I am going on to visit my friend in Kent today. Mr. and Mrs. Weston have been so kind as to offer to send me in their carriage."

Emma tried to remember. "Oh? I thought you were to delay until your family came to Highbury."

"They are not coming after all," Lizzy said. "Because Mr. Knightley and I..." She waited as if for him to complete the thought, but he was resolutely silent. "We have decided that *we* also made a mistake. I have requested that we end our engagement and he graciously agreed."

Emma's eyes flew to Mr. Knightley, and he looked quite miserable.

"Yes," he confirmed. "Miss Bennet has no blame at all; I am very much in her debt."

"So, this is farewell for now," Lizzy said. "I wished to say goodbye and to tell you that—despite everything!—it was a fascinating visit. Perhaps someday I may come again, and we may start over as friends."

Emma felt as if her emotions were on the end of a pendulum, swinging wildly to and fro. "I would like that."

Mrs. Weston rose and took Lizzy's arm. "Come, my dear, let me escort you out. You have already said your goodbyes to your cousins, so I can send you on your way after the carriage takes me home."

Mr. Knightley made to leave as well, but Mrs. Weston looked significantly at him. "Take your time, sir. You need not show us out."

Mr. Knightley hesitated while Emma hugged Lizzy and bid her goodbye. When alone in the room, neither of them sat.

"What a mull we have made of things," Emma said. "I expected a certain amount of comment from you—for you told me what you thought of Frank!—but now with you and Lizzy... I am so sorry."

Mr. Knightley took in Emma's pale face and furrowed brow. "Please do not waste sympathy on me. You put a brave face on it, but you have been used badly."

Emma moved a shoulder indecisively. "I have also used others badly. Harriet, Lizzy, Miss Bates... You must know that I feel my own errors deeply."

Mr. Knightley wanted very much to embrace Emma, to tuck her head into his shoulder and let her cry as she used to. He did not. "I know you do. It is one of the things I admire about you."

Mr. Knightley opened the door and Emma accompanied him down the stairs to the front hall. "It may not feel like it now, but time will heal these wounds," Mr. Knightley said.

Emma shook her head. "I am not injured. Disappointed in myself, yes. And the gossip this will cause does not bear thinking of! But Frank did not touch my heart, and that is as much a testament to my foolishness as his perfidy. How could I become engaged with so little knowledge or true affection?"

Mr. Knightley shook his head. "I have no grounds to chastise you, for I did nearly the same thing."

"Did you? But you spoke so highly of Lizzy; I thought you in love with her."

"I continue to think highly of her, but no more than that." Mr. Knightley picked up his hat from the table and toyed with it.

"What a pair we are."

"Yes, a *pair*. How is your head? Do you need to lie down?"

"It is not so bad."

"Then, Emma..." Mr. Knightley looked about him. They were in the foyer of Hartfield, visible from six doorways and the stairs. The unused study was just off to one side. "Come in here for just a moment."

Emma followed him with furrowed brow.

"I must confess one thing more. When Lady Catherine visited and you asked me if it would be wrong for you to marry, I thought you were thinking of Mr. Darcy. *I* began picturing you with him from then on, and that is half the reason for my poor decisions."

"I was not thinking of him."

"I know. Emma, when I came to think more fully of marriage, I found that I could not picture you with Mr. Churchill, or myself with Miss Bennet. I can only picture you... with me."

Emma's chin quivered, and Mr. Knightley took her hand. "I told you I would always support you, but I would far rather support you as your husband than as your brother. Do I—do I have any chance of success?"

Emma's chin was quivering full well now, and tears grew in her eyes. Her head shook faintly, as if in disbelief.

"I am not good at making speeches. If I loved you less, I could talk about it more. I have lectured and corrected you so often; you know I always speak the truth. Believe me one more time. I love you." He brought her hand to his lips and kissed her fingers.

"Oh...!" Two tears trickled down Emma's cheeks. "I am the one who loves *you*, Mr. Knightley. I have been so envious of Lizzy I could not think. It was too late and there was nothing I could do. I could not bear it."

Mr. Knightley stroked her wet cheek with his hand. "Neither could I. But we have been given a rocky second chance. Shall we take it?"

"Yes. A thousand times yes."

Mr. Knightley finally kissed Emma.

She was just the right height, just the right everything. Mr. Knightley knew this had been worth all the pain; Emma had been worth every year of waiting, every day of miserable uncertainty.

"You know who I have envied?" he asked against her hair. "Mr. Martin. I have rarely seen a man so happy. When Miss Bennet dragged us back to watch their reunion... I could only think of you."

Emma clutched him tighter, her cheek pressed into his riding coat. "Poor Harriet! I have been so much at fault. And Miss Bennet! I do feel wretched that my happiness should come at her expense. She could not love you the way I do, but she did, perhaps, in her own way. Do you think I might find someone for her? Not that I would matchmake! But—"

Mr. Knightley kissed Emma again, running his hand over her smooth cheek, her silky hair. It was a far better method of stopping her than any he'd found yet.

{ 38 }

Mr. Woodhouse anxiously rolled the edge of the blanket which covered his legs and lap. "I don't understand this at all. Mr. Churchill is gone? You are to marry Mr. Knightley?"

"Yes, but you like him better, Papa, you know you do! And he may stay here with us and still care for Donwell Abbey. You know that will just perfectly suit you, for it shall be nearly the same as always."

"Yes... I suppose, but I do not know. I cannot understand what has happened to Mr. Churchill. One does not become engaged and then disappear. It is most inconvenient. What if something dangerous has occurred?"

"No, no, he is fine. He has gone to Weymouth and written to his father and to me. It is just a misunderstanding."

"It was not done like this when I was a young man. I cannot think it sensible. Not you, my dear Emma, you are everything perfect, but it is very strange. Are you certain you will marry Mr. Knightley? I think I had best send for Perry. But you must promise not to have cake at your wedding, Emma, that is all I ask. Oh... I do feel a spasm beginning in my stomach."

Miss Bates was no less confused, but Jane tried to reconcile her. "People make mistakes all the time, do they not? And if they were not allowed to fix them, then where should they be? Miss Woodhouse and Mr. Knightley are such old friends. I'm sure it is the most natural thing in the world."

She may have succeeded in convincing her aunt of this, but it could not be supposed that the general neighborhood would fall for it.

There was exclaim; there was conjecture.

"Mr. Churchill was so frightened of his aunt, they had to call it off."

"No, but did you hear? Mr. Knightley called him out, he left for fear of a duel!"

"Mr. Knightley fight a duel? Bah."

"But Mr. Churchill and Miss Bennet both left town the same day! I have heard that they both went to Brighton!" Knowing heads nodded.

"But no, I have heard that they ran off to Gretna Green, on account of Mr. Churchill's aunt."

"No, Frank Churchill is definitely in Weymouth, but Miss Bennet never returned to her family; I hear she is ruined."

"No, indeed," put in Mrs. Weston, whenever she heard this, "Miss Bennet is simply in Kent with friends."

This was held to be a pretty poor story.

Miss Fairfax also supported it, however, with occasional evidence in the letters that she and Lizzy began to exchange.

It was an *extremely* strange thing, that was all anyone agreed upon.

And when it become known, quietly, that Mr. Knightley had proposed to Emma and been accepted, people again nodded knowing heads. "Yes, they have both been disappointed."

"I always thought they should unite Hartfield and Donwell Abbey."

"But he is so much older than she!"

"No more so than Miss Bennet, and we know Miss Woodhouse!"

"His brother and her sister are already married, I always said it was inevitable."

"Bah, you never did. You're as surprised as me."

"They certainly look happier. I wonder, will Mr. Knightley still be magistrate after he marries? Mr. Brown's pig rooted up all my winter turnips, and so I shall tell him...!"

And what with one thing and another, the scandal was allowed to slip away. The rightness of the current match was impossible to argue, and when only three weeks later, after the banns were read, Miss Woodhouse and Mr. Knightley were wed, everyone grew acclimated far faster than they would have expected.

Miss Fairfax was one of Emma's attendants, and to some surprise, Miss Lizzy Bennet was another.

There were whispers.

"She came to attend for Miss Woodhouse? When she was engaged to Mr. Knightley only months ago? I never heard of such a thing!"

"But she does not seem unhappy. She is the same as always."

"She *was* visiting her friend; she is staying at the parsonage at Hunsford, I have it on authority from the rector there. I told you not to listen to those tales slandering a respectable young lady!"

Harriet was there, along with Mr. Martin, who signed the book on behalf of Mr. Knightley. Mr. Martin was quite awed by the honor done him and quite glowed when he took Harriet's arm at the back of the church during the short ceremony.

There was cake, but Mr. Woodhouse was kept well away from it.

Emma found herself pensive after the wedding and the wedding breakfast were all completed.

Mr. Knightley drove them both back to Donwell Abbey late that afternoon in Emma's carriage, though she now found she did not care a whit if he got his own carriage horses. Everything hers was now also his, and that was a very simple solution, was it not?

He swung her down from the carriage after tossing the reins to his groom.

"You are very quiet, Emma. Touch of the sun?"

It *was* quite warm, but Emma was not easily overpowered. "No, I am fine."

They would spend a week living at Donwell before moving Mr. Knightley to Hartfield, though Emma planned to be at Hartfield every day to visit.

"Do you wish we had a proper wedding trip?" Emma asked as they entered the cool of the Abbey's shadowy, quiet entryway. "I know you will always claim to be happy with whatever is necessary, but... *are* you disappointed?"

"No, of course not." He took off his hat and helped Emma to remove her bonnet carefully untying the strings for her, enjoying the novelty of being allowed this small intimacy. "This is new bonnet, is it not?"

"Of course it is new! One does not marry in an old hat, my dear sir. At least, *I* do not. How adroitly you changed the subject."

"Then let me be more clear." He took her hand and led her into the parlor. "I am not disappointed, because I know that we have many years to go to the seaside or to London, or anywhere. That we do not go now, out of kindness to your father and the many upheavals he has endured this year, is so little compared with what I have gained today."

She raised her face to his, her hand trailing up and down the sleeve of his morning coat. "You have gained me. I still cannot quite believe that you wanted to."

Mr. Knightley brought her hand up and kissed it. "Then you have not been paying attention."

"That has always been a fault of mine. You must take care to have my full attention before saying something important like that."

"I will do better." Mr. Knightley kissed her, knowing they were finally alone. He felt Emma's hand in his hair and he couldn't help pulling her closer.

After a moment, he leaned back and rubbed a thumb over her lips. "Now I have your attention, but I've forgotten if I had anything important to say. Today I am the one distracted."

Emma was all too happy to go back into his arms, and Mr. Knightley swung her around in a circle so that her feet left the floor.

She squealed in surprise, clutching at his arms. "Good heavens. Where is my staid Mr. Knightley?"

"I have wanted to do that for quite a while," he said. "I love you, Emma."

"And I love you. I have always respected you, trusted you, listened to you, but I do not know when exactly it turned to love." She kissed his hand and gave him a saucy smile. "But I daresay if you had begun dancing with me sooner, we should have got on a little faster."

Mr. Knightley laughed. "And now I know exactly how long your wedding day sentimentality lasts."

"I also take leave to inform you that having danced so little with me *before* our vows were said, you simply must make it up to me after. It is not the thing for married couples to dance at parties, but I find I want to dance with my husband."

"Did I not say as much about Mrs. Weston?" Mr. Knightley had had enough of the parlor. He tucked Emma's hand in his and led her to the stairs. "I said the same thing, you must own it."

She cocked her head. "I do not remember. If you did say it, you said it poorly, otherwise I would have seen sense. There is no one so appropriate to dance with as one's spouse."

"You are quoting me!"

"Am I? Where are we going? Should we change for supper already? I am not very hungry after that feast."

"Nor am I, but you are too provoking to handle downstairs. I would prefer to argue with you elsewhere." He turned to the right at the top of the stairs.

"It will not help your case."

"On the contrary, I think it will."

Epilogue

Dear Lizzy,

I am still having such palpitations, such spasms! Oh, if it were not for dear Jane and Bingley I should very possibly expire. I know you write that comment has died down after the wedding, but Mr. Collins wrote such a letter to your father about the whole affair! Mortifying!

I ought to have expected that you would throw away your last chance for matrimony, as that is what you did with the first, but I was foolishly optimistic! I am always an optimist, but it is difficult to stay cheerful in such a world, with such ungrateful daughters.

Now you write that you are ready to come home, but you cannot have thought! There was not merely gossip in Highbury. Do you think no one there has friends in other places? The story has spread to Meryton and I have such palpitations, I can hardly go into company. All of Hertfordshire is talking of it.

I do my duty to take Kitty and Lydia and Mary to the balls—they have so little time left with the dear officers of our regiment!—but I am regularly put to the blush. By you, no less, who have always lectured us about propriety! It is too awful, Lizzy.

No, you simply cannot come home yet.

You mentioned that our cousin, Miss Fairfax—though whether such a distant relation can be called a cousin, I do not know—but you say she is going to London to be a governess. I do not have any opinion of governesses, but you may as well accompany her there and stay with your Aunt and Uncle Gardiner.

It will be an act of charity to your poor cousin, and at least that is something for your reputation.

Your aunt and uncle may still wish for a companion on their journey this summer, though whether you deserve such a treat I must leave to your conscience.

But the answer is no, you do not! You are so provoking, Lizzy.
Your long-suffering Mama
F. Bennet

To my favorite daughter,

Lizzy, when I told you that I begrudged the man who earned your hand, I did not quite intend for you to throw him over. I suppose that is my mistake for being vague. I have often said precision of thought and speech is of utmost importance, have I not? I congratulate myself on my perspicacity, if not on the art of my letters.

I think you best had make a stay in London as your mother wishes. You went on one errand of mercy for your sister's sake—yes, of course I knew the reason you suddenly decided to go to Highbury—but now another for your own sake. I do not think you wish to be present with your mother in her current mood. If you imagine her outrage at the incident with Mr. Collins and treble it, you can imagine her daily state at the comments made in the village.

Of my love for you, I recommend at least another fortnight or five. Enjoy London, my dear.

Your exhausted father,
T. Bennet

From Highbury with Love

Dear Miss Bennet,

Thank you again for your kind letter to me. It was so lovely to see my name written on the post as Mrs. Harriet Martin! I cannot quite believe it!

It was lovely to see you at the wedding also. Did not Miss Woodhouse look like an angel? Or rather Mrs. Knightley, as she is now!

And Mamma—did I tell you that Robert's mother insists I call her Mamma just as Beth and Mary do?—anyway, she says that you must be a very good-humored young lady to lend countenance to the wedding so that no one would think Mr. Knightley had aught to be embarrassed of. She is so very observant and wise about things like that! Though she has not met you in person, she says that my descriptions of you give her the highest opinion of your good sense. It is wonderful to have a mamma one may speak to just at any time.

She is teaching me ever so many things. I can make the most wonderful pickles now, and Robert says I am a natural at baking. He loves my barley breads and Sunday puddings! But that is only because Mamma has taught me how to listen to the dough to hear it sing. Robert also encouraged me to name the three new laying hens, and I have named them Lizzy and Emma and Jane!

He laughed about my names. He laughs so often these days. I cannot tell you how wonderful marriage is. I have heard all my life that a decent marriage is all I am fit for, but that makes it sound so much less pleasant than it is. But then, I suppose, to anyone besides Robert, it would be less pleasant.

And now I smell that my bread must be nearly done, so I shall say goodbye.

All the best,
Harriet Martin

P.S. On a sadder note, I must tell you that I have finally found out my parentage and I am not the daughter of a gentleman as Miss Woodhouse so long thought. I feel I ought to tell you because I did become acquainted with you, in a sense, under false pretenses, and I hate shams. But I am not terribly worried, for Mamma says that you would not care a whit, and that at any rate, what I am now trumps whatever I might have been.

Darcy,
Thank you for your felicitations on the event of my marriage to Emma.

I am a lucky man, far luckier than I deserve, on several fronts. I nearly made a bad mess of my future and was granted a fresh start at the eleventh hour.

You carefully do not ask about Miss Bennet, so perhaps you have news of her elsewhere, but I will just venture to say that she was everything gracious about the matter. And truly, from her countenance at the wedding breakfast, you would never guess she was involved other than as a friend. How she truly feels I am no longer at liberty to ask, but as far as appearances go, she is as well as can be expected. I did not act wisely there; I shall always regret that.

Jane Fairfax and Miss Bennet will be settled in London for some time, and I hope you will look in on Miss Bennet if you come to town. It will be hot and unpleasant in the city over the summer, but if you are there, bear it in mind. You once told me Miss Bennet was something out of the common way, and you were quite right.

I hope I didn't cause you pain with my ill-timed proposal, in addition to the other problems I caused.

Your chastened friend,
George Knightley

From Highbury with Love

Dear Miss Fairfax,

I shall be happy to pick you up at the stated time in Highbury and then convey you to your new post in London; however, I have a better idea. Why do we not go a few days sooner, so that you may become acquainted with my aunt and uncle? They are the dearest people, and of course, my nieces are the best little girls in the world. They will happily tell you so.

Then you will have some acquaintance in London, even after I go home. I hope that you would never need a place of sudden retreat, but it might ease your mind to know that you have a welcome room on Gracechurch Street. Or even just a place to visit on your occasional day off! Do say you agree, and I will tell my uncle the day.

Lizzy

Darcy,

What are you about, to hide Georgiana away at Pemberley all summer? I hear this is your plan and I do not love it, nephew, I do not. (Good gracious, I sound like Lady Catherine, which I swore never to do! You must be the one who brings out the worst in us.)

The season is over and of course I would not keep you in London all summer—quelle horreur!—but my daughter would love to see Georgiana, and since she will be presented next season, I am reserving lessons for her with the best dancing instructor in London. Georgiana should join us.

Since I will be presenting Georgiana as well as Nancy, you really must oblige me in this. I've barely clapped eyes on her since Michaelmas, and I want to see that she achieves a certain amount of confidence before I must introduce her to the ton. Just promise me a few weeks!

I do not know if I can prevail upon Harold to come to town and occasionally dance with the girls, but I know my dear Richard will oblige me. And if you come, you may lessen the tediousness for each other.

Your determined (and favorite) aunt,
Lady Agnes Fitzwilliam

Don't miss Book 2 of the Highbury Variation

From London with Loyalty

September 2021

Amid hard decisions and disappointments, Elizabeth is once more reconciled to being an old maid, and Jane Fairfax to being a governess. But London never quite leads where one expects...

ABOUT THE AUTHOR

CORRIE GARRETT has worked an array of jobs from pet grooming shops and ESL schools, to aerospace research laboratories and highway construction field offices. Now she has the oddest job of all, writing historical romances and science fiction! From the finer points of historical opium to chemical explosives, her google search history probably confuses the government algorithms meant to track us all! She lives and works in Los Angeles, California with her husband and four children.

For more information on books, series, and new releases visit her website at www.corriegarrett.com. Or follow her Facebook page at Corrie Garrett, Author for updates.

Manufactured by Amazon.ca
Bolton, ON